Forever Mine
(A Miranda's Rights Mystery)
Book III

Linsey Lanier

Edited by
Donna Rich

Editing for You

Gilly Wright
www.gillywright.com

ISBN: 1941191142
ISBN-13: 978-1-941191-14-9

FOREVER MINE

The third book in the popular Miranda's Rights Mystery series.

Just a little while longer and I'll have everything I want...

After she left her abusive husband thirteen years ago, Miranda Steele became a fighter. Over the years, she picked up martial arts and street fighting tactics, and now that she works for the Parker Investigative Agency, she can handle a weapon.

But the battle with her inner demons? Not so easy.

Ace investigator Wade Parker feels more love for the feisty, impossible woman than ever. With her irascible spirit, her strength of will, her need to defend the defenseless and avenge the innocent, he knows they are kindred spirits. And when he takes her to Chicago, he hopes he can at last help her find her stolen daughter.

But in the town of her birth, Miranda must face her horrendous past. An experience that forces her to make one of the most momentous decisions of her life.

And now dead bodies start popping up again. With all the turmoil, can the feisty new detective stop an arrogant creep who just discovered how much he enjoys murdering women?

Or will she become his next victim?

THE MIRANDA'S RIGHTS MYSTERY SERIES

Someone Else's Daughter
Delicious Torment
Forever Mine
Fire Dancer
Thin Ice

THE MIRANDA AND PARKER MYSTERY SERIES

All Eyes on Me
Heart Wounds
Clowns and Cowboys
The Watcher
Zero Dark Chocolate
Trial by Fire
Smoke Screen
The Boy
Snakebit
Mind Bender
Roses from My Killer
The Stolen Girl
Vanishing Act
Predator
Retribution
Most Likely to Die
(more to come)

MAGGIE DELANEY POLICE THRILLER SERIES

Chicago Cop
Good Cop Bad Cop

OTHER BOOKS BY LINSEY LANIER

Steal My Heart

THE PRASALA ROMANCES

The Crown Prince's Heart
The King's Love Song
The Count's Baby

For more information visit www.linseylanier.com

CHAPTER ONE

He stared down at the body.

The dark hair flowing to her shoulders. The perfect makeup. Those dark eyes, wide open in sheer terror. And the gaping hole in her chest.

What had he done?

His breath was ragged with fear and confusion and excitement. His heart pounded in his ears. His gaze moved to the tool in his hand. His fingers were covered with blood.

But it wasn't his fault. It wasn't.

She'd deserved it, the stupid bimbo. If she only would have done what he'd told her. She'd made him so angry. It was all her fault.

And yet, she was beautiful in death. He could have loved her. Instead, he'd destroyed her.

As the insane rage he'd felt a moment ago began to quell, in its place came an intense feeling of power.

His eyes drifted to the bloody wound again. Life and death was in his hands, wasn't it? The idea made him feel like a god.

Then reality set in.

Someone would find her soon. If they connected him to the act, he'd be in trouble. He'd better clean up this mess. How?

He looked down at the things scattered across the apartment floor. Tools. Buckets. Plastic wrap. Construction equipment.

He smiled to himself. That was how.

No one would ever find her. He was too smart to be caught. Too smart for all of them. All it would take was a little effort, and everything would be fine.

Yes. He knew exactly what to do with her.

He bent down and got to work.

CHAPTER TWO

Miranda Steele stood in the vestibule of Holy Spirit Catholic Church on Northside Drive in Buckhead, Georgia, twisting the old-fashioned Art Deco diamond ring on her finger.

She could get through this.

Just six hours and it would all be over. She'd be on her way out of town—headed toward her last hope to find her daughter.

But the muted strains of Handel coming from the organ made her stomach churn, and her wiry hair was so weighted with gel, it felt like a wad of cotton candy under the veil she'd been forced to wear.

Her palms sweating, she peeked through the open door.

The afternoon sun streamed through the stained glass images of apostles and saints, casting a surreal light over the hundred or so out-of-town guests, who were shifting excitedly in their pews.

Miranda scratched at the stiff taffeta of her dark blue halter dress. She must be allergic to weddings. She'd sure as heck avoided them ever since her disastrous marriage to an abusive psychopath ended thirteen years ago.

The music switched to "I'll Be There." The old Michael Jackson song sounded kind of odd on a pipe organ. Miranda gazed down the silk-rose-and-ribbon-lined aisle and caught sight of Parker standing at the end of it.

Her mouth watered and went dry at the same time.

In his fancy tuxedo, so similar to the one he wore the night they met, he stood tall and muscular, wearing that famous, confident Wade Parker smile, a wisp of salt-and-pepper hair falling sexily over his forehead. He might be born to wealth and status, but at his core he was a shrewd, calculating private investigator who had put away killers and who bore scars on his body from street fights.

He was also the desire of every woman in Atlanta. His innate sexuality was so raw and primitive, it was all Miranda could do not to rush down the aisle and tear that tuxedo off him.

2

Their gazes locked for a moment and her heart swelled. As always, his gray eyes were full of tenderness, compassion, love. No human being had ever cared about her like Wade Russell Parker the Third did.

So why couldn't she commit to him?

There was a touch on her arm. "Are you ready?"

Miranda spun around, her mouth open.

Her good buddy Joan Fanuzzi stood beside her all in coral satin, looking like a fashion model. Well, as close to it as the saucy, diminutive road crew worker could look.

Fanuzzi wasn't a beauty queen. She had a longish nose, an oblong face and a gap between her teeth she often displayed in a big grin—unless she was pissed. Right now that face warmed Miranda's heart.

Today, a band of crystals encircled her waist and matched the band in her dark hair. A demure veil topped off the look.

Miranda let out a breath and smiled. "You make one gorgeous bride, Fanuzzi."

"Thanks, Murray." Blushing, her friend nodded toward the bathroom. "Jan's almost ready. My sister's always been a slowpoke." The bouquet in her hand shivered. "I can't believe I'm marrying my childhood sweetheart. I'm so nervous."

"Me, too." Miranda scratched at her belly.

Fanuzzi grabbed her hand. "Don't do that. You'll snag the fabric."

"Sorry." She snorted. "I don't know why I've got hives. I'm not the one in the wedding gown."

Fanuzzi wagged her brows. "Maybe soon it'll be you and Mr. Hot Stuff."

Mr. Hot Stuff being Parker. Miranda opened her mouth but decided now wasn't the time to argue over her own marital status. She gave Fanuzzi a punch on the arm. "What are you saying? You've got your own Mr. Hot Stuff."

"Yeah, I do," she said as she wiggled her fingers at the man standing beside Parker.

Miranda shook her head. It was kind of funny to see her boss next to her two best buds and fellow IITs—Investigators in Training—at the Parker Agency. Tall, lanky Curt Holloway had lost his usual suspicious air. And Becker, the groom, his short, nervous sidekick with his big dark eyes and Groucho Marx nose, had cleaned up pretty nice in a tux. He also looked like a little boy who'd just seen Santa Claus under the Christmas tree—and it was only July.

Fanuzzi and Becker made a cute couple.

"I'm so glad you brought us together," Fanuzzi whispered in her ear.

"Don't mention it."

Miranda glanced over at the Ladies Room door. Still no sign of Jan. "So where are you going on your honeymoon?"

"Disney World. We're taking the kids."

She could imagine Becker and Fanuzzi's three kids giving Mickey a hard time. "Sounds like a blast."

"Guess you and Parker will have to keep Atlanta safe while my honey's gone."

"Guess so, except—"

"What?"

Miranda stiffened. She didn't want to talk about her plans with Parker. "We're going out of town for a few days."

"Really? You didn't tell me that." She sucked in a breath. "You two aren't going to elope, are you?"

Miranda scowled. "Of course not. It's no big deal. Just a trip back home." She winced at the whopper she'd just told. It was a very big deal. Possibly, the biggest deal of her life.

Three weekends ago, in a hotel in Helen, Georgia, her ace investigator boss had given her his best plan to find Amy, the daughter who'd been stolen from Miranda thirteen years ago. They were leaving tonight to follow up on it.

"That sounds nice." Fanuzzi looked disappointed there wouldn't be another wedding. "How long since you've been back?"

"Back home?" Miranda shrugged. "A while."

"Really? How long?"

Uncomfortable, Miranda shifted her weight. How could this woman twist so much personal information out of her? "Long time. Over a decade, really."

"Wow. You must be so excited after all those years."

"Yeah." Like celebrating the thirteenth anniversary of your decapitation. "Oh, here's Jan." Saved by the bridesmaid.

Fanuzzi's sister emerged from the john, dressed in a tall, slim-cut version of the same dark blue outfit Miranda had on.

"Sorry I took so long." Jan whispered with excitement.

Fanuzzi squeezed her hand. "I'm not gonna fuss at you today." All smiles, she gave the organist a nod and the airy tones switched to the Beatles song, "In My Life." She sucked in her breath. "That's our cue."

Miranda froze.

"Go on," her friend hissed through her teeth.

But she couldn't move. The idea of sashaying down the aisle of a church turned her into a block of ice.

"Murray? You okay?"

With all the will power she had, Miranda shook herself. No way was she going to ruin her friend's wedding. "I'm fine. Just fine and dandy."

Slowly she pivoted on her high heel. She could do it. One foot in front of the other. Easy as pie. Her lips quivering in a smile, she started down the aisle.

CHAPTER THREE

"So how'd you like Fanuzzi and Becker's big fat Catholic wedding?"

Parker stretched his legs out before him, which wasn't easy at his height, even in the first class seat of the MD-80 that had just lifted off from Hartsfield Airport. He had changed into a dark blue traveling suit—dressing down for Parker—while she was in jeans and a breezy blouse.

"I rather enjoyed myself. I'm not allergic to weddings like some people are." He gave her a half-grin, sexy laugh lines forming at the corners of his Magnum gray eyes. His aristocratic Southern accent echoed with warm summer breezes scented with magnolia blossoms and mint juleps on the veranda. His pricey cologne smelled of old money.

Allergic. Funny he should use that word. He had to have noticed her deer-in-the-headlights march down the aisle in the church. Nothing got past Parker. And he knew her aversion to commitment personally.

She'd walked out on him twice.

She cleared her throat and twisted the diamond-and-sapphire ring on her finger. Parker's mother's ring. The one he had given her a few weeks ago, saying she could put her own interpretation on it, sneaky devil. She knew his real plan. He wanted permanence, vows—marriage. He intended to wait patiently for her until she wanted it, too. Or at least believed in it enough to say, "I do."

"I had a good time, too," she insisted. Once she'd gotten over her initial case of shellshock. "The bride's family can really get down." Doing the Locomotion with Fanuzzi's Italian relatives at the reception had been a blast and had taken her mind off her troubles for a while.

"The ceremony was lovely as well. Very tasteful."

"It was nice."

"The vows were…interesting." There was a playful note in his voice, its low timbre making her think of a Southern riverboat gambler.

Miranda smiled. Fanuzzi had left the vows up to the priest to please her traditional mother. He'd put in all the "to haves and to holds." Except when they got to that part, Becker, in his nervous Brooklyn accent, had stuttered, "to have and to have." Three times. The crowd was in giggles before he finally got it right.

"I'm happy for the both of them."

"Me, too."

"I'm sure they'll have a long and happy life together." He punched the word "long" as he leaned a little closer.

"Man, it's hot in here." She reached up to adjust the air vent and turned away from Parker's penetrating gaze to peer out the window at the twinkling lights below.

Atlanta. The city had been her residence only since April, but it felt more like home than any place she'd ever been. That had been Parker's doing.

A long and happy life together. For Fanuzzi and Becker, sure. She wished them all the best. But Miranda didn't believe "long and happy" was in the cards for her.

"I'd think someone with your pull could have gotten us on a flight that wasn't the redeye. The hearing's not until Monday." Parker could afford a private plane, but he never liked to flaunt his wealth.

Parker scrutinized her a moment, deciding whether to let her veer off the subject he was using to distract her from the purpose of this trip. He studied her thick, dark hair, more wild than ever after her vigorous scrubbing to get out all the gel she'd worn earlier. He took in the angles of her profile, which was much lovelier than she realized.

Never in his life had he known such a woman. With her stubborn tenacity, her nose for trouble, her uncanny ability to get herself into the thick of danger, she'd put him through the gamut of emotions from terror to despair. And yet, he couldn't stop loving her. Couldn't stop admiring that irascible spirit, that strength of will, that need to defend the defenseless, to avenge the innocent. They were kindred spirits, and the undeniable bond between them grew stronger every day.

She would finish her training as an investigator in a few weeks, and then...he would have something he'd wanted all his life without knowing it. A partner.

On her last assignment, he had been overbearing, overprotective of her, and it had almost cost him everything, including his own life. As her boss, he'd promised to be less sheltering of her, to give her some freedom. But he suspected he'd be struggling to keep that promise for the rest of his life. Especially now.

She turned to look at him, her deep blue eyes with their spiky black lashes mesmerizing him as always. He saw yearning in them. And pain. He gave in to her need to talk about what lay before her.

"I thought it would give us time for some additional research." He took her hand in his, turned the ring to its proper place and kissed her palm. "That is, if you're up to it."

Miranda shivered as a warm flutter rippled up her arm and over her heart at the touch of Parker's exquisitely skilled lips. "What kind of research?"

"We don't have a lot of proof about the cause of your mother's death."

She exhaled, wishing they had more evidence. This was her last shot. They were playing Parker's last card to find the child her ex-husband took from her thirteen years ago.

She closed her eyes as a shudder went through her.

Even after all this time, she could still see the tiny baby smiling up at her from her crib. Still hear her cry. Still see the distinctive dark mark on her neck. Still feel the panic that had ripped through her the morning she'd found her gone. Her bastard ex-husband, Leon Groth, had taken Amy and given her up for adoption. He might have killed her, for all she knew. He was a murderer, after all. But at the time, Miranda had believed him. She'd searched for her daughter for thirteen years.

And never found a trace of her.

After joining her search back in May, and after putting out dozens of feelers that had led nowhere, Parker was convinced the best way to find Amy was to get a judge to open her adoption records. But the Illinois laws were tight. The only way to do that was to prove she might have inherited a life threatening disease.

"You're certain your mother died of a heart attack?" Beside her, his voice was a gentle murmur. Parker had charmed, cajoled, and bribed every clerk in Chicago's Cook County, but no one could even locate Hilda Steele's death certificate.

Miranda turned back to him, squeezed his hand for comfort. "My mother was only forty-two when she died, so it couldn't have been from natural causes. I remember the neighbor calling me. That's what she said. 'Your mother had a heart attack.'" It was sixteen years ago. She had been married to Leon a little over three years at the time. When she got the news, he'd comforted her by slapping her around and yelling at her for being so listless.

Parker sighed aloud. "We do have the letter from your aunt."

Hilda Steele had had one older sister named Lu, who lived in Minneapolis. The last time Miranda saw her was at the funeral. Her aunt had never liked her, but she'd forced herself to look the woman up, write to her, and ask if she could verify what caused her mother's death. Aunt Lu had replied with a terse letter saying her own daughter should know she died of a heart attack. She refused to testify in court, claiming health issues.

But there was more. "I remember everyone talking at the funeral, saying what a shame it was because she was so young. I know people mentioned a heart attack."

"Yes," Parker murmured thoughtfully.

"It's got to be enough."

"If only we had some conclusive documentation. A specific diagnosis of her condition from a doctor."

"Where are we going to get that?" The Steele's family doctor had passed away five years ago. They'd found no record of heart problems at the hospital where her mother worked.

Parker's face took on a pensive look. "It's a long shot."

"This whole thing's a long shot." She'd never had anything but long shots.

"Why don't we try your mother's house?"

She frowned. "I have no idea who's living in it now."

"But you know the address."

"Of course."

"It's a peculiar behavior, but sometimes when people move into a house, they hold onto the former resident's belongings. My father has seen that." Parker's father was one of Atlanta's top real estate moguls.

"You mean some folks are natural pack rats, even when it comes to other people's stuff?"

"Exactly. Someone might have tucked away her medical records."

She thought a moment, then shook her head. "That won't work."

"Why not?"

"Because after my mother died, Leon went and got all her things and stuffed them in our attic. I'm surprised he didn't burn it all. He'd been hoping to find money."

Parker was silent a long moment. "Well, then…"

Miranda gasped.

Slowly, she turned her head and glared at him. "You want me to go back…*there*?" Back to the house where she'd lived with Leon? Where she'd suffered so many years of agony and humiliation? The house where she'd last cuddled Amy in her arms? The house Leon had kicked her out of?

Swiftly, Parker clasped both her hands in his, kissed her knuckles, which were turning a little white. "Oh, my darling. No, not if you can't handle it."

In Parker's firm grip, her fingers trembled.

A stewardess appeared at the front of the plane, rolling a metal beverage cart down the aisle to serve the passengers.

Miranda inhaled a gulp of air. "I think I need a drink."

CHAPTER FOUR

Miranda sighed as she sank back into the sudsy warm water of the sunken tub and against Parker's muscular, wet chest.

After landing at O'Hare International and taking a taxi into the city, Parker had fed her a too-lavish meal of Irish Salmon with Lobster Mashed Potatoes at a late night steakhouse, while he dined on a prime cut sirloin. Then he'd checked them into a luxury hotel off Michigan Avenue.

Typical behavior for the suave investigator. He liked to spoil her. Besides the tub, the suite included a small kitchenette, a sitting area with a marble fireplace, and a bed almost as big as the one in the Parker mansion.

"You know," she said, sipping from the flute of Dom Pérignon that had become Parker's signature prelude to a night of glorious lovemaking, "I think this tub is a little smaller than the one we use at home."

She felt his smile against her cheek. "Do you?"

They'd been living together in the big house for over a month now—if you didn't count the second time she'd left him. She put her nose in the air and put on a snobby tone. "I think I'm going to have to call the manager and complain."

She felt him chuckle. "But in a smaller tub, you won't be able to escape so easily." He ran his hands down her wet arms, making her shiver, despite the temperature of the water. It had taken her a long time to let Parker get close.

But tonight, she needed escape of another kind. She took another swallow of wine and set the glass down on a tray. "You know, you might be the one who wants to escape tonight."

"Oh? What do you intend to do with me?" He leaned in and brushed his lips against the nape of her neck. Little ripples of sensation trickled down her spine. Oh, that felt good.

But she broke away and turned to face him, sending an undercurrent through the water. She gazed into those solemn gray eyes, so full of understanding and wisdom. She knew he was distracting her with everything he had from the idea of going back to her old home.

She decided to let him. "Hmm. I'm going to have to think about that."

"Hmm," he echoed.

She studied his mouth a long moment. His lips, so skillful and delicious. Then she bent her head to kiss him and gave his lower lip a quick little bite and drew away.

His face lit up.

Grinning, she swooped in and gave him another little bite.

"So you're going to tease me, are you?"

She laughed low. "Why not?"

His eyes flashed with passion. "We'll see about that."

"Yes, we will." She dove in for another bite, but before she could reach his lips, his hands grabbed at her. Giggling like a schoolgirl, she slid away, the soapsuds making her slippery.

There really wasn't a lot of room for swimming in the tub. She turned around in time to see Parker charging right for her. "Uh oh."

With one swift move, he trapped her against the other end of the bath and braced his muscular arms on either side of her, hemming her in.

He grinned wickedly. "Now we'll see who teases whom," he murmured in his sexy, low, Southern drawl.

She could have fought him, but she was already quivering with anticipation.

A gleam in his eye, he gazed at her lips, the way she had at his. The gleam grew evil and her stomach shuddered.

Slowly, he bent his head and lay his mouth over hers in a kiss filled with more raw sensuality than he'd ever given her before. She sucked in air, fighting for breath as his mouth fairly devoured her. His tongue teased her lips open, thrust inside her, raking over the roof of her mouth.

She gasped a muted cry of pleasure and went as wet as the water surrounding them. She let him linger for a long moment. Then panting, she broke free of his authoritative mouth. "That's not fair, Parker," she warned.

"Who said we were playing fair?" He let go of the tub and ran his fingers up her sides, making her dizzy with sensation.

"You devil."

He laughed. "I told you, you couldn't escape."

"Oh, yeah?"

She made a move to get around him, but he simply blocked her with a strong arm and took her breast in the other hand. "Not so fast."

Her body went weak as he rolled his thumb over her flesh. "No fair," she whispered in a hoarse voice.

"So you keep saying." He angled himself between her legs and gently slid inside her.

"Oh," she moaned. She was a goner now.

He began to thrust and unbearable pleasure surged through her. "Give up?"

"Never."

He thrust harder. Her body coiled around him like a greedy boa constrictor. She wanted to beg him not to stop, but that would be too humiliating. And then his lips were on hers again, even more fiery. They moved over her mouth, fanning the blaze burning below her navel. His tongue thrust inside her, matching the strokes of his body.

He thrust faster.

Water splashed onto the tile around the tub. Her whole being throbbed and writhed with delicious, titillating sensation. It built and built to unbearable pressure, until release erupted so hard, she thought her pulsating could cause a tidal wave in China. The tremors seemed to go on forever. Then her body relaxed in utter satisfaction. Parker had won.

But she'd never admit that to him.

Parker watched her spasm with delight. His heart overflowed with love for this marvelous woman. Learning to make love to her, what aroused her, what tempted her, what drove her insane, had been a sheer delight over the past weeks.

He intended it as a prelude for a lifetime together.

Resting her head on the tile at the edge of the tub, she groaned loudly. She opened her lovely blue eyes, looking up at him groggily through her thick, black lashes. Tenderly he kissed her forehead. "Time for bed?"

"I think so."

She let him pull her out of the tub and dry her off with a thick towel, a favorite occupation of his, and they strolled into the bedroom, arms around each other.

She climbed onto the large mattress and as soon as Parker was settled next to her, turned the light off. She'd had a long day and hadn't realized how tired she was until just now.

Parker slipped a comforting arm around her, stroked her cheek to soothe her.

The man was a psychic. She knew he had wanted their lovemaking to chase away her fears, but the sight of the hotel room brought them all back. She leaned her head against his shoulder, trying to forget why they were here. Her stubborn nerves got the best of her. She had a decision to make.

So she made it. Right then. No sense being a baby about it. "I'm going to take you up on your idea."

He stopped stroking her face. "The one we talked about on the plane?"

She nodded. "I'm going back to my old house tomorrow."

"Are you sure, Miranda?" Worry riddled his voice.

She was quiet a moment. "What choice do I have? You said we need all the evidence we can get."

His chest moved against her as he inhaled. "But at what expense?"

"I've already paid over and over for the things Leon did to me. What's a few more bucks?"

"It might undo the weeks of therapy you've been through." He had finally gotten her to see a shrink. A good one. Dr. Valerie Wingate was helping, and she didn't want to start all over again.

But Parker was right. She had to find more evidence about her mother's death, or the judge could deny her petition to open Amy's adoption records.

She held up her hands. "I'll have to just suck it up and deal with it. Besides, if I do find something we can use in that house, it would be a kind of poetic justice."

He took her chin in his hand, admiration in his eyes. "I love you, Miranda Steele. I love your strength, your resiliency, your determination. I'd do anything to ease your pain."

"I know that, Parker."

"But I'm afraid this time, I've only given you more of it."

She scoffed. "Don't be silly. None of this is your fault. No one's ever helped me like you have." He'd given her a job she'd fallen in love with. He'd given her personal training. He'd given her love. He'd given her a life.

His smile was sad. "Are you finally starting to see that?"

"Maybe I am." And with that declaration, she laid her head on his chest again, closed her eyes, and fell asleep.

She lay crumpled in a heap on the floor, holding her arms over her head. But they did little to shield her from the blows. The strikes crashed down against her shoulders and sides, sharp and stinging and relentless. He was using a coat hanger this time.

"You. Stupid. Bitch." He punctuated each word with a lash. "Why didn't you iron my shirt? What am I going to wear to the station?"

"I'm sorry. I forgot. I'll do it now." She tried to get up.

He shoved her back down. "You'll do it *now*? It's too late to do it now."

The blows came harder. Faster. They hurt so badly. He was going to break a rib.

"Stop," she cried out in pain.

Then somehow, she saw herself scramble across the carpet and crawl to the edge of the staircase.

"Run," she whispered to herself.

She did. She forced her body to clamber up the steps. Just as her foot hit the top stair, she heard a baby cry. "Amy."

"She's gone, Miranda. You'll never find her again." His strong hands snatched the tail of her robe, and she stumbled back.

No.

Her heart hammered in her chest. She'd never seen him this mad. He was going to kill her.

Slowly, she turned around. Her breath coming in snatches, she took in his greasy black hair, his black eyes glaring at her with pure hatred.

All at once, her body changed. She grew strong, muscular. Her mind became filled with years of the karate moves she'd studied, the judo, the dirty fighting tricks she'd learned in bars.

She pushed him off her. He slipped down.

"Go away, Leon." Her voice was strong and commanding now.

12

"How dare you speak to me that way?" He started up the stairs again.

She waited. Just as he got close, she thrust out a leg and kicked him hard in the chest. He rolled to the bottom. But as soon as he hit the floor, he bounced, reversed course, and rolled back up again, like a plastic ball in some maniacal mechanical game.

She gasped as his hands reached for her, caught her by the arms.

She grabbed his throat with both hands. They tumbled back down stairs, head over feet. Over and over each other, until they landed on the living room floor with a heavy thud.

Without even stopping to catch their breaths, they thrashed around the carpet, arms and legs flailing. She got him in the ribs. On the side of his head. In the groin. Then they rolled again, and she was on top of him.

Now. She'd stop him now. Stop him for good.

She hauled her fist back and with all her might, she thrust at him, throwing the hardest punch she ever had in her life. Something caught her wrist like a vice.

Miranda's eyes shot open. "Oh, my God."

Parker lay beside her, holding her arm in a death grip. Her fist was only an inch from his alarmed face.

"At last," he breathed.

"What?"

"You woke up."

She blinked at him and trembled, her heart still pounding against her sides. "I tried to hit you."

"You didn't." He let her arm go and put his around her, drawing her close.

Her mind cleared. She was in the hotel. She glanced at the clock. It was early morning. She'd been dreaming about Leon. About a vicious battle with him. And she'd almost smashed Parker's handsome jaw. Good thing he had sterling reflexes.

A shudder went through her. "What if you hadn't woken up in time to stop me?"

He raised a brow. "I couldn't sleep with you thrashing about like a wrestling alligator."

She ran a hand over her face. She couldn't believe what she'd almost done to him. "Oh, Parker."

"I've faced worse before. I think I can handle it." He pressed her close to him.

She laid her cheek against his chest, kissed it, amazed at his patience with her. "God, I wish…" She didn't want to say aloud that she wished she were more normal.

He stroked her hair, her face, kissed her forehead with a determined pressure. "Oh, my darling. If only I could change your past. If only I could take away your pain."

That would be nice. She sniffled against his bare skin. Her cheeks were wet. How embarrassing. Beat up your lover in bed and then break down in tears.

"Just keep up your black belt." She pushed away from him and got up, heading for the bathroom. "Be back in a minute."

She hoped Parker didn't see her slip her cell off the nightstand.

She closed the door behind her, slid down to the floor, her whole body trembling. She hadn't had a bad dream in weeks. It was the idea of going back to that house that had triggered it, she knew. In her mind, Leon was still there, waiting for her. After all, hadn't he stalked her for years?

Parker might want to help, but only one thing could truly ease her fears right now. She steadied her phone and dialed the number to Brandywine-Summit Memorial Hospital in Atlanta.

"Third floor," a voice answered after the second ring.

Miranda looked at the time. Five-thirty. Almost shift change. "I'm wondering if you can tell me the condition of a patient?"

"I'm sorry, ma'am. We can't give out that information to anyone but close family members."

"I don't need details. Just his general condition. I'm his sister." The lie had worked before. "I was there to visit him a few weeks ago. I don't live in state."

There was a pause as the staff member spoke to someone in a murmur. Hopefully asking permission of a lenient supervisor. "Who's the patient?"

Miranda suppressed a sigh of relief. "Leon Groth. Could you hurry please? I'm on my way to work." Parker would figure out what she was up to if she stayed in here too long.

She heard computer keys and hoped the woman wasn't checking out her identity. After a moment, she spoke again. "I'm sorry ma'am, there's no change in that patient's condition."

"He's still in a coma?"

"Yes."

"And the doctors have no idea when he'll come out of it?"

"No, the doctors can't say. I'm so sorry, ma'am."

"Thank you for your help." She clicked off and let out a long slow breath as her shoulders began to relax. At least Leon Groth wasn't going to bother her while she was awake.

CHAPTER FIVE

When Miranda returned to the room, she found Parker dressed and at the desk with the laptop he'd brought along. She could smell coffee brewing.

"Charles and Nancy Wang are the current residents," he told her as she came to peek over his shoulder. He'd done a reverse search on the address of her old house, which she hadn't given him.

"How'd you know where I used to live?"

"I did run a background check on you before you were hired, if you recall."

"Right." And went farther back than any employer she'd ever applied with before. The sneaky sleuth had been checking her out and had discovered not only all the construction jobs she'd had across the country, but her marriage to Leon as well.

"I have the number. Would you like to call them?"

"To ask if I can look in their house?"

"It might be better to prepare them first."

Nerves prickling her spine, she considered it a moment, then shook her head. "I'll just take my chances when we get there."

"Are you sure, Miranda?"

She didn't want to talk about it anymore. She strolled to the desk and picked up a brochure. "Hey, the hotel has a gym. Let's go work out."

Parker shook his head at her, but he was too concerned over her emotional state to argue.

They changed into sweats and hit the exercise room.

For forty-five minutes, they pumped iron and did the treadmill thing, then showered and went down to the hotel's fancy-schmancy restaurant for a breakfast of Eggs Florentine, Belgian Waffles, and just-roasted espresso.

Parker apologized that the place didn't serve a plate of raw serrano peppers to go with her eggs. He was trying to make her smile, but she wasn't much in the mood for it.

After paying the bill, he rented a car. They got inside, headed down Wacker Drive to the Eisenhower and continued on toward the West suburbs.

Traffic was light and by the time they turned onto Austin Boulevard near the L station in Oak Park twenty minutes later, Miranda's stomach was in a Gordian knot. She wondered if she was going to lose those fancy eggs she'd eaten for breakfast.

They drove past a park Miranda recognized and rows of apartments and office buildings that seemed familiar. She began to gnaw on her thumbnail. When they turned onto Jackson, she was almost down to the quick. She was glad Parker was using the GPS. Right now, she couldn't speak to tell him directions. She was also glad he had it on mute.

He reached across the seat and clasped her hand. "I want to say it will be all right, but I'm not sure that's true."

"I'll be fine." She wasn't convinced, either.

At last Parker pulled alongside the curb behind a little Volkswagen. She closed her eyes.

"We're here," he said gently.

She nodded. "I know." She forced her eyes open and made herself turn. Her heart pounding, she studied the house.

It looked smaller than she remembered, but it was still a friendly little building. No one would have suspected the violence that had gone on inside its walls, not even the neighbors. At least not the ones she'd had back then.

Someone had painted the place a welcoming yellow. The yard was cut and green, the hedges neatly trimmed. Salmon-colored geraniums grew along the cement porch.

She stared at the steps. The very steps Leon had pushed her down the day he threw her out. The day he took Amy from her. She rubbed her arms, still feeling the cold of that day.

Broken dreams, broken promises, broken bones.

Her body, at least, had healed. And she was here now to set part of that ugly past straight.

Ire rose inside her. "You won't beat me down this time, you son of a bitch," she muttered and got out of the car.

Parker was right behind her, radiating compassion and concern, as she made her way up the walk. She climbed those wretched concrete steps, forcing herself to think only about getting her hands on her mother's medical records. She stepped onto the porch, not letting herself hesitate, and rang the bell.

Fidgeting, she waited for an answer.

After a minute, a well-dressed Asian woman opened the door. Nancy Wang was very pretty, her black hair cut in a neat shoulder length style. She had on nice earrings, a demure necklace, and a light blue business suit. Overdressed for Sunday, Miranda thought.

"Can I help you?"

She should've taken Parker up on his idea to call ahead. Too bad she hadn't come up with what she was going to say yet. Telling the stranger she was with the Census Bureau wouldn't get her what she wanted, so she tried honesty.

"Hello. My name is Miranda Steele, and this is my boss, Wade Parker. We're with the Parker Investigative Agency."

The woman looked confused. "Has there been some sort of crime committed?"

If you counted what happened thirteen years ago. "No, ma'am. We're investigating a personal matter."

"Personal?"

"The truth is…gosh, I feel so silly." She laid the back of her hand against her temple.

Nancy Wang tilted her head and frowned.

"The truth is, ma'am, I used to live here with my husband. Well, he's my ex-husband now."

The woman blinked in surprise. "In this house?"

"Yes. It was quite a long time ago. But…" She bit her lip, trying to look sad and helpless, then burst into a soliloquy. "You see, my mother gave me a ring when I was little girl. It was too small to wear as an adult, so I put it away. I was looking for it last week and couldn't find it anywhere. Then I thought back all those years and remembered my ex put it in a box with some of my mother's things after she passed away."

She could feel Parker's sidelong glance. Okay, the "truth" was getting a little muddy.

The homeowner looked at Miranda like she had just come from the looney bin. "And?"

"I really do feel silly. I just thought it might still be here." She gave an awkward laugh, then smiled sweetly.

Nancy Wang just stared at her.

Parker reached into his pocket for his wallet. "This is my identification, ma'am. I'm President of the Parker Investigative Agency in Atlanta." He displayed his PI license.

"You two are from Atlanta?" She was getting more suspicious by the second.

Miranda patted Parker on the shoulder. "I work for him there. At the Agency. We're in Chicago for a consultation with a client, so I asked my nice boss to humor me."

She heard Parker inhale deeply.

"The local police don't know me, but you can verify who I am by calling Lieutenant Hosea Erskine of the Atlanta Police Department."

Nancy Wang considered the offer a moment, then nodded. "I think I'll do that. Wait here." She closed the door and turned the deadbolt with a click.

"I don't blame her for being cautious," Miranda said. "We must look like a couple of lunatics."

Parker lifted a brow. "A ring?"

Guess she had rings on her mind lately. She shrugged. "Erskine knows we're here?"

"I told him we were flying to Chicago on a personal matter."

Since Atlanta wasn't so safe when Parker wasn't around. Miranda hugged herself and began to pace across the concrete.

"I wish there were an easier way to do this." Parker's voice was full of tenderness.

"I can handle it," she snapped. And was sorry for her tone.

Parker simply put his hands in his pockets, remaining his understanding self about her mood. She watched him study the house, the eaves, the windowpanes. She saw his jaw tense. He was probably wishing he had sent Leon Groth to meet his maker when he had the chance.

After about ten minutes, the door opened again. This time Nancy Wang was all smiles. "I had a nice chat with your Lieutenant Erskine. It seems we have a mutual friend. Noreen Tan."

Parker's smile was broad and genuine. "Detective Tan is my Chief Assistant. She's one of my best people."

"So the Lieutenant said. Please, come in."

Who would have thought hard-ass Detective Tan would be the key to the woman's heart? She opened the door, and Miranda stepped through it with Parker just behind.

"I roomed with Noreen in college for half a semester before I transferred to U of I."

"At Penn State?"

"Yes."

"Noreen had an excellent record there."

"I was always jealous of her grades."

Parker and Nancy chatted away, but Miranda was frozen, staring at the living room.

Gone was the shabby, secondhand furniture, the ratty old brown carpet that had been so hard to clean. In their place were gleaming hardwood floors, sleek couches and chairs, and salmon colored walls dotted with tasteful art and family photos.

She couldn't help stepping over to peep into the kitchen. It too had shiny hardwood floors and new stainless steel appliances. Gone was the rickety old stove she had to cook on. And the linoleum she used to clean her own blood off of.

"Can I get you something to drink, Ms. Steele?"

Miranda shook her head. "No thanks. If you don't mind, I'd just like to look for my, uh, ring."

"Of course. Let's see." She put a finger to her chin. "I think Charles found some boxes in the attic when we moved in. I believe he left them up there. He didn't want to throw away other people's things." She laughed, shaking her head. "He can be such a pack rat at times."

Miranda's heart skipped a beat. She shot Parker a knowing look. The sly devil had been right.

"It's right up here," Nancy said, leading them upstairs. "But, of course, you already know that."

"Yes." Miranda stiffened at the bottom step remembering her dream last night. *It was just a nightmare*, she told herself sternly. Besides, the staircase had also been redone in hardwood. The place didn't even look like the same house anymore.

At the top of the stairs, Nancy led them down the hall. It took all Miranda had to pass the room that had been Amy's nursery.

She must have turned a little pale, but Nancy didn't notice. She proceeded to the end of the hall and tugged on an overhead drawstring. The attic stairs yawned open before them with a creak. Their hostess opened a drawer in a little cabinet against the wall and handed Parker a flashlight. "You might need this. Just let me know when you're finished."

Parker took the light with a nod. "Thank you. We'll try not to be long."

"Take your time. Charles got called into work today. I was going into the office myself, but I don't really need to. I'll just be downstairs."

"Thank you," Miranda echoed Parker in a whisper.

Parker nodded. "You've been very gracious."

"Anything for friends of Noreen."

Friends. Right. But Miranda had other things to think about right now than the surliness of her drill sergeant instructor. Taking a deep breath, she started up the stairs.

It was dark and warm in the attic. As Parker found a light switch, Miranda stepped onto the creaky plywood floor and squinted as she scanned the area.

She didn't see much. Some crates and boxes against one wall that were too neatly labeled to be her mother's or Leon's handwriting.

"Over there, I think." Parker shined the flashlight in the corner, where several more boxes were stacked.

Miranda blinked, her eyes adjusting to the light. She took a step in the direction of Parker's beam. Could that be what she thought it was?

Quickly she crossed the floor, its boards moaning beneath her feet. Beside the boxes sat a trunk made of wood.

Her throat constricted.

"That was my mother's hope chest."

She bent to brush off the layer of dust on top of it, then gingerly raised the lid.

Parker was at her side the next moment. "What's in there?"

She wiped her hands on her jeans, squatted down to pick up a bit of lacy material. "Looks like napkins and a table cloth." Beside them, something had been carefully rolled in newspapers. She pulled a corner of the paper back and saw crystal. "I think it is my mother's trousseau. I've never seen it before. I was never allowed to look inside this box."

She laid the linens on the floor beside her, and gently placed the glassware on top of it. She dug further. "Old costume jewelry." She pulled out an old necklace and some earrings that couldn't have cost very much. "I never saw my mother wear jewelry. Not even costume jewelry."

She opened a small box. There was a star on a ribbon. "Some kind of medal?"

Parker leaned down to get a better look. "I think that's from Vietnam."

Shivers tripped across her skin. Had it been her father's? She didn't know he'd fought in Vietnam. And then she saw the photographs.

"Oh."

She glanced up at Parker. His face was full of concern. "You want me to look at the rest?"

She shook her head, then sucked in her breath. "Oh, my God."

"What?"

Gently, she set the box down and picked up the old photos. Pictures of the three of them when she was little girl. She leafed through them. Birthday parties. Christmases. Easters.

One was in an eight-by-ten frame. She sat back on her heels and held the frame in her hand.

Herself as a little girl. Her hair just as wiry as it was now. A happy smile on her face. She was wearing a frilly dress and holding a big lollipop. Behind her, stood her parents. Her mother in a plain, old-style house dress, tall and thin, a full head taller than her father. That stern look in her narrowed eyes. She looked like the woman with the pitchfork in American Gothic.

And there, with his hand resting lovingly on his daughter's shoulder, was Edward Steele.

Her father.

He was dressed in a luau shirt and shorts, his paunch bulging a bit from the shirt.

He was just as she remembered him. Rosy cheeks, curly black hair, bulbous nose, and that infectious smile. And there, on the side of his neck was a small dark mark. The same one she'd seen on her baby's neck.

Her throat went dry as the attic's dust as she ran her hand over the dirty frame. "He left us when I was five, I think."

"Yes, I know."

Parker watched grief spread over her face and his heart broke anew for her. He'd had some terrible battles with his own father growing up, but at least he had been there for him. He couldn't even imagine what it would be like to be abandoned as a child. And apparently her mother had abandoned her emotionally, as well, driving her into the arms of Leon Groth. No wonder Miranda Steele had so much trouble with commitment.

Miranda's voice was a hoarse whisper. "My mother never talked to me about him. She didn't talk much about anything. She was pretty strict." She swiped at a tear wetting her cheek. "I loved him. And I hated him for leaving us."

Parker bent down and put his hand on her shoulder. "Why don't you let me finish here?"

She shook her head and wiped both her hands under her eyes. "I'm okay. Really." She set the photo down on the floor and started again. There had to be some clue to her mother's heart condition in here.

She peered into the box. Beneath another lacy napkin were some papers. Bundles of letters and cards. "These look like personal documents."

Handful by handful, Parker took them from her, spread them out on the floor. They sifted through them. There were canceled checks, old bills, bank statements. "Here's something." He drew a yellowed bundle out from under the mess.

Miranda looked through it quickly. It was a stack of medical receipts. "I see something for," she sounded out the word, "Chlor-o-thi-a-zide."

"It's a diuretic that can be used for high blood pressure."

"Well, that's something. But I don't see anything else."

Parker began stacking the papers, attempting to sort them. "Let's keep looking."

She reached into the box one more time. Near the bottom lay a large manila envelope. She pulled it out and held it a moment, studying its brown stains and creases. Then she undid the string clasp and peeked inside. There was a thin sheet of paper. Her heart almost stopped as she read the words printed at the top of it.

State of Illinois. Division of Vital Statistics.

"Bingo."

"Let me see."

Her heart beating hard, carefully, she slid the paper out of the envelope. She let out a long, slow breath. "Here it is. My mother's death certificate. Leon must've stuffed it in there."

"What does it state as the cause of death?"

She held it up and they read it together. As Miranda tried to decipher scratchy writing, her heart sank back down to the plywood floor. Confusion riddled her mind. "'Subdural hematoma'?" She'd watched enough CSI to know what that meant. "A brain injury?"

"There's more." Parker pointed to the lines.

She read the rest aloud. "'Heart failure.' 'Fracture of the cervical vertebrae.' What does it mean?"

Parker's face was grim and hard as granite. "It sounds like she fell and broke her neck."

"That can't be right."

"Miranda, is there something you're not remembering about your mother's death?" Parker was in full investigator mode now.

She stood up, her mind racing. She ran a hand through her thick hair. Think.

The funeral. Her aunt's letter. Her mother never showed any sign of illness, except in her attitude toward life. "It didn't make sense for her to have a heart attack. I remember thinking that at the time."

"And what else?"

She put her head between her hands and forced her thoughts back to her mother's house, the grim life she lived there. She saw herself as a little girl on the porch playing with a paper doll the neighbor across the street had given her.

She remembered the creak of the screen door and the sound of her mother's hard-soled shoes stomping toward her. Her mother had snatched the doll out of her hand, tore up the bits of paper that were her clothes, and stuffed them in her pocket. "Foolishness," she'd grunted. Then she'd turned and gone back inside. Miranda had put her head in her lap and sobbed into her old, secondhand dress. That was when the same neighbor saw her and invited her over for milk and cookies.

Her head shot up. "Mrs. Gavinski."

"What?"

"Why didn't I think of her before? Mrs. Gavinski. The neighbor who called to tell me about my mother when she died. Maybe she's still in the neighborhood." She started across the floor.

"Where are you going?"

"I've got to find Mrs. Gavinski." She spun around." Take me to my mother's house, Parker."

CHAPTER SIX

Her old neighborhood was only about five blocks away, but it seemed to take an eternity to get there.

At last, Miranda spotted the church on the corner that she used to pass on her way to school. Parker made the turn, and she sucked in her breath. It was bright and sunny, but the elms lining the street cast a flickering shadow overhead.

Slowly, they drove past the rows and rows of two-story bungalows, all different, but looking alike at the same time. White with dark green trim, beige with brown trim, red with light green trim, pink with black trim. The muscles in the back of her neck tensed.

There it was.

Three lots down stood her mother's house. Plain and dirty white, just as she remembered it. It looked small, like Leon's house had. But she barely noticed for the memories washing over her. Not memories of parties and playtimes, but of drudgery and work. Of so many hours of loneliness.

Gritting her teeth, she suppressed the past and folded her arms tightly around her as Parker pulled the car along the curb across the street, this time behind a tan SUV.

Before he had turned off the engine, she was out of the rental and halfway up the walk.

Parker shot up the path behind her and was at her side in an instant. "We should check out the address first, Miranda. Your neighbor might not even be alive. She might have moved."

"And she might be right there." Miranda waved her hand at the cheery green home with the white awnings.

She knew he wasn't so concerned about the logistics as what this late morning trek down memory lane was doing to her psyche. She didn't care. She had to find out what happened to her mother.

She bolted up the stoop and rang the bell without even waiting to catch her breath. She heard the sharp yip of a dog. And a television.

After what seemed like an eternity, the door finally opened a crack. "Yes?"

Miranda laid eyes on a small woman dressed in a pink quilted housecoat she had thrown over a blue plaid blouse and khaki culottes. Her back was bowed with osteoporosis, and her white hair was done in that short, curly, old lady style. The face seemed like it had aged a hundred years, but sure enough, it was Mrs. Gavinski.

Miranda blinked back sudden tears. "Hi, Mrs. G. Do you remember me?"

The woman raised her snowy brows and narrowed her eyes at Miranda. She stared at her through a thick pair bifocals. "Excuse me? I'm sorry. I already take the Trib." She stepped aside to close the door.

"Mrs. G, don't you remember me? I'm the kid from across the street." She pointed over her shoulder.

Mrs. Gavinski's gaze wandered to her mother's old house across the street. "Little Markie Newman lives in that house. He's such a sweet boy. He comes over for milk and cookies after school sometimes."

"You used to give me milk and cookies. Don't you remember? I'm Miranda Steele."

Once more the woman examined Miranda. Her eyes focused for a moment, then drifted across the street, as if she were lost in faraway thoughts. Then she blinked and her head shot up. "Miranda? Miranda Steele? How could you think I'd forget you? Why, you're all grown up. I thought I'd never see you again after your mother passed."

Miranda closed her eyes and let out a slow breath of relief. "Yes, that's what I want to talk to you about, Mrs. G. My mother."

"Well, come in. Come in." She beckoned with a friendly hand.

"I have a friend with me."

Mrs. G raised her head and spotted Parker, seeing him for the first time. "Oh."

Parker extended a hand. "I'm so pleased to meet you, Mrs. Gavinski."

Mrs. G took it gingerly, with the expression of a mousy teen who'd been asked to prom by the quarterback. She winked at Miranda. "Is this your husband?"

Miranda cleared her throat. "He's my boss. He's helping me, uh, on a case."

"I see. Come in, both of you, please."

She led them into a dark paneled living room crowded with an overstuffed couch, a rocking chair, and a big recliner. Doilies that looked hand crocheted were scattered everywhere. On a big screen TV against the wall, Henry Fonda and Katharine Hepburn were frozen in a demure kiss—a scene from *On Golden Pond*.

"Let me turn that off." Mrs. Gavinski reached for the remote and the screen went black. "Please make yourselves at home."

Miranda took a seat on the couch close to the recliner. Parker settled in beside her.

The smell of coffee drifted in from the kitchen, accompanied by the sound of nails tapping on the linoleum. Suddenly a small creature bounded into the room like it was on fire.

"Yip, yip, yip, yip."

Miranda barely had time to recognize the thing as a Chihuahua when the high-energy ball of muscle and short hair jumped into her lap. She caught it under the ribs before it swiped her face with its long tongue. Out of the corner of her eye, she watched Parker chuckle as she struggled with the wriggling mass.

"Now, ChiChi," Mrs. G shrieked. "Where are your manners? Behave yourself."

Miranda managed to set the little dog down on the floor.

"Go lie down," Mrs. G commanded.

His big brown eyes full of remorse, ChiChi hung his head, trudged over to a little doggie bed in front of the television, turned around three times, and plopped down in with a sigh. Miranda had to smile.

"He isn't used to visitors."

"That's all right, Mrs. G. I—"

"Oh, let me get us some coffee."

"Don't go to any trouble," Miranda said.

But the woman ignored her and waddled into the kitchen. ChiChi thumped his tail but remained in the doggie bed.

Miranda caught Parker's eye while they waited. She could tell he didn't think they were going to get anywhere. Avoiding his gaze, she turned her head and studied a needlepoint pillow on the rocking chair that read "World's Greatest Great Grandma." ChiChi scrutinized her with his sad eyes.

"Here we are." Mrs. G padded back into the room carrying a tray. "Some nice black coffee from the local shop on the corner and some of my favorite sugar cookies. Do you remember how you used to like those, Miranda?" She set everything down on the small coffee table.

"Yeah, I do." She remembered the smell of cookies baking in this house. It always made her mouth water. Today the cookies were store-bought, but they still warmed her heart with memory.

Mrs. G served them both, then took a seat in the recliner. "So what have you been doing with yourself all these years, Miranda?"

Her favorite question. "Oh, I've been around. I got a job that required me to travel a lot."

"I see."

"I ended up in Atlanta and went to work for Wade Parker here. He's president of an investigative agency."

"Oh, how impressive." Mrs. G's eyes sparkled with interest. She was just as bowled over by Parker's charm and good looks as any female. "Do you solve many murders?" She asked him.

Parker gave her a half grin. "A few."

Miranda took a bite of her cookie so she wouldn't have to add to that.

Mrs. G's brow wrinkled. "So if you work in Atlanta, why is it that you're here in Chicago?"

Miranda took a deep breath and set her cup down on the coffee table. Might as well be straightforward. "I'm looking into my mother's death, Mrs. G. I'm hoping you could help me."

"Oh my. Your mother's death? What can I do for you, dear?"

"Well, I've just come into possession of her death certificate. And I...I don't really understand what it says."

Parker set his cup down beside Miranda's. "The document seems to indicate there might have been foul play."

"Foul play?"

"There might have been some injury to Mrs. Steele." Parker's voice was tender but firm.

Mrs. G rubbed her forehead. "Let me see. Hilda had a lovely funeral, as I recall. It was so tragic for her to pass at such a young age. She was only in her early forties." She leaned forward, reached across the arm of the recliner and took Miranda's hand in hers. "I was glad you were already married and had someone to take care of you." She frowned. "What happened to your husband?"

Miranda shifted on the couch's cushion and tried not to pull her hand away. "It didn't work out."

"Oh, I'm sorry." She shook her head. "That seems to happen a lot these days."

"Yes." The woman had been more of a mother to her than her own, but she had to keep her on track. She squeezed her hand and spoke as gently as she could. "Mrs. G, the death certificate says my mother broke her neck. What do you know about that?"

Mrs. G looked stunned for a moment. She pulled her hand away and Miranda's whole body tensed.

The woman rocked back and forth in the chair, looking very pensive, but she didn't say anything.

Miranda tried again. "Mrs. G, you were the one who called me. You were the one who told me my mother had a heart attack."

Slowly, Mrs. G nodded. "Yes, that's true. I did tell you that. It was some nasty business."

Miranda swallowed hard. "Nasty business?"

She stopped rocking and raised her head, looking like a child who'd just gotten caught lying about her report card. "We thought it best to just tell everyone that she had a heart attack. She did have heart failure from the accident."

"Accident?"

"Yes. You see, she was at work at the hospital. She was working a double shift."

"She used to work them a lot."

"Yes. I hated the way she'd leave you alone."

Miranda was touched, but sometimes fending for herself had been better than being with her grouchy mother.

"But this was later. After she became a nurse. She worked so hard to get her certificate."

"It took her years." And was one of the reasons she'd been around less and less when Miranda was a teen, though she didn't begrudge her mother her career. "Go on."

"She had medicines to deliver to patients. She was late. She was supposed take the elevator, but she was late with her rounds. That's what one of the other nurses said. So she took a shortcut and went down the stairwell. She must've been very tired, or she would've seen the sponge."

Miranda swallowed. "Sponge?"

Mrs. G nodded. "One of the cleaning staff had dropped a wet sponge on the steps. Hilda didn't see it in time. She stepped on it, slipped and fell down the stairs onto that cold, hard concrete. A whole flight down." Mrs. G closed her eyes and shuddered. "She broke her neck and died instantly. But the doctor who declared her dead mentioned heart failure." She gave Miranda a heartbreaking look. "Oh, honey." She sank back in the recliner.

Miranda sat as stiff as her mother's starched nursing uniform. She felt as if the floor was moving beneath her, ready to open up and swallow her whole. This couldn't be happening. She heard herself murmur, "So it wasn't really a heart attack."

"Not directly. But the hospital thought it would be best to tell everyone that. They didn't want problems."

Parker's eyes flashed. His face was stony with anger. "They didn't want the liability, you mean. It was a cover-up."

Miranda drew in a breath, trying to make sense of this new information. "But she was on high blood pressure medicine."

Mrs. G frowned again, then nodded. "Oh, yes. I remember Hilda told me about that. It was just a minor condition."

"So she didn't have any health issues, any heart problems, anything else that you knew of?"

"Oh, no. Hilda was healthy as a horse. That's why what happened was so tragic. It was just a freak accident. I'm so sorry, dear. So sorry. We were just trying to make things easier for everyone. Especially you, dear. I probably should have…"

Miranda shot forward and grasped her hand once more. "It's all right. You did exactly the right thing, Mrs. G."

CHAPTER SEVEN

"We should investigate the hospital. This is a case of negligence."

"A sixteen-year-old case. What good would that do?" Miranda sat on the end of the big hotel bed staring at the muted TV. The gyrating bodies in the late-night Zumba infomercial were a blur.

She was numb.

She could barely remember the meditative stroll through Millennium Park she and Parker had taken that afternoon. Or the fancy Italian dinner he'd used to try to cheer her up. She didn't know why he bothered, why he thought that would work. He was just as upset as she was.

Now he sat at the computer, trying to play the blood pressure medicine angle. They both knew he wouldn't get anywhere. His anger over the situation was driving him. But she was just deflated.

Healthy as a horse. She must've known deep down her mother didn't have a heart condition. She should've known this idea of his wouldn't work. She'd let her mind get clouded with wishful thinking.

Parker was wonderful to petition the court and bring her here, but finding Amy had never been in the cards for her.

She half-groaned a sigh. "We should go home and skip the hearing tomorrow."

"Don't give up, Miranda. We can at least talk to the judge." She could feel the determination in his voice.

She lay back on the bed. "If you say so." She didn't have the energy to argue with him.

"Oh, my darling." He rose and came to the bed, lay down beside her and stroked her hair.

She watched the concern in his deep gray eyes as he studied her. He was so handsome. Her heart filled with feelings for him. She reached up to touch his cheek. "You're so good to me. What did I ever do to deserve you?"

"I might be able to give you many things. But I can't give you the one thing you want most." She'd rarely heard him sound so discouraged.

"At least I've got someone to share my frustration with. I've never had that before."

He smiled a weary smile and then bent to kiss her lips. "Why don't you get some sleep? You need to be rested tomorrow."

So she could be alert when the judge told her he was denying her petition? She didn't dare say that aloud. "And what are you going to do?"

He didn't answer right away. She narrowed an eye at him.

"I just want to finish up here." He got to his feet and returned to the computer. If there was anything to discover, Wade Russell Parker the Third would find it. But she knew there would be nothing.

She reached for the remote, turned off the TV, and snuggled under the sheets.

With the Monday midday traffic the next day, the two-mile drive from the hotel to the Richard J. Daley Center took longer than going out to the suburbs had the day before.

They had to park a block away. It took them several minutes to traverse the busy sidewalk, then make their way across the noisy street. As they crossed the wide plaza, city pigeons took flight at their footsteps and flew up to circle the rusty old Picasso that stood in the middle of the expanse of concrete.

Miranda recalled a fifth grade field trip where the teacher pointed out the odd looking sculpture. Everyone tried to guess what the thing was. One classmate said a griffin. Another said an angel. Her best friend at the time said it was a sheep dog.

Miranda said it was a big goose with the measles.

Her memory fast-forwarded as she stared up at the tall, dark building, her mood going from gloomy to high anxiety. She'd petitioned the Cook County courts once before, and it had ended up in disaster.

"Let's get this over with," she said as they reached the busy entrance. "As they say, here goes nothing." She slipped inside the revolving doors before she could hear Parker's reply.

They made their way down a long, crowded hall, went through Security, and headed to the elevator bank. They took one to the seventeenth floor.

Twenty minutes later, the clerk had called her name, and she and Parker were standing before the polished bench in the paneled courtroom, waiting for Judge Felix Rozeki to finish shuffling through his papers.

The judge was a kindly looking old gentleman with white hair and round cheeks. He kind of reminded Miranda of the dude in the *Wizard of Oz*. As he perused the documents before him, his brow was riddled with concern. Not a good sign.

"Everything seems to be in order," he said with a speculative note.

It should be. Parker had enlisted the aid of Antonio Estavez, his surrogate son, one of the best criminal defense attorneys in Atlanta. Antonio, in turn, had handpicked a member of his law firm to draw up the petition and double-checked the work himself. But even all that effort couldn't produce facts out of thin air.

"So your mother passed away due to a heart condition, Ms. Steele?"

Miranda flushed crimson, feeling more demoralized than ever. "Uh, there's been a new development on that, Your Honor."

"Your Honor," Parker interrupted. "I have some additional evidence concerning Ms. Steele's case."

Miranda glared at him. Why was he making this more painful than it was? "We have to tell the truth, Parker," she muttered to him under her breath.

Parker drew in air and gave her a stiff, all-business look. "Miranda, let me handle this, please."

"You don't have anything," she hissed through gritted teeth. It was *her* case. They were going pro se—fancy lawyer talk for do-it-yourself—because it was the most sympathetic approach. Parker was there as an advisor, a pseudo-counselor, because of his experience and knowledge of the law. She didn't want to draw out the agony any longer than necessary.

Judge Rozeki cleared his throat. "You two don't seem to be on the same page."

Parker gave him a polished smile. "I apologize, Your Honor."

Miranda took a step closer to the bench. "Your Honor, I don't want to waste your time."

Parker moved up to stand just a little ahead of her. "Your Honor, I have a few things to present for your consideration."

"Parker," she warned him. What could he possibly have?

The judge closed the file with a slap. "Why don't we discuss this further in my chambers?" He rose and exited through a side door.

The clerk gestured to them. Now Parker had done it. Miranda had a good mind to walk out. Instead, she followed the clerk through the door with a grunt, Parker right behind her. He led them down a narrow paneled hall and into a small paneled office lined with bookcases.

Judge Rozeki took a seat behind an oversized, ornate desk and gestured to two leather chairs in front of it.

Suppressing a huff, Miranda took the one on the left and watched Parker settle into the other, irritation on his face, which he turned into a slick smile as soon as the judge addressed him.

"What do you have for me, Mr. Parker?"

"Your Honor, I've discovered Ms. Steele's mother was under doctor's care for high blood pressure. I have prescriptions for chlorothiazide and records of doctors visits for three years prior to her demise." He reached into his briefcase, handed the judge another folder.

Judge Rozeki took it from him and looked it over.

Miranda stared at Parker. Had he dug all that up last night?

He gave her a satisfied grin.

The judge turned to Miranda. "Do you have your mother's death certificate?"

The flicker of hope Parker had just ignited in her died out as her heart slid to the floor with a thud. She ran a hand through her hair. "That's what I was about to say, Your Honor. We just discovered yesterday—"

"Here's a copy of the death certificate, Your Honor." Parker leaned forward with another paper and placed it on the desk.

The judge picked up the paper, studied it, frowning. "This indicates she died from an accident. Sounds like she broke her neck."

Miranda opened her mouth.

Parker spoke before she could. "Yes, but it also states 'heart failure' is one of the causes of death. Hilda Steele might not have died from that accident if her heart had been in better shape."

Did Parker really think that angle would fly?

The judge sat back, rubbed his chin for a long moment. "High blood pressure is a common ailment. Chlorothiazide," he squinted at the papers, "especially this low dosage, doesn't indicate anything severe or life-threatening. Do you have any evidence of something like angina or congestive heart disease?"

Parker sat back, his shoulders fighting the urge to slump. "No, Your Honor. I don't."

The judge's face lined with sympathy. "Do you have any other close relative who might have a life-threatening, hereditary illness? Your father perhaps?"

"I don't know my father," Miranda replied. "There's no one else."

"I see." The judge stared down at the papers for several long moments, then shook his head. "I'm so sorry, Ms. Steele. I wish there were something I could do. I just don't see enough here to give me a valid reason to open your daughter's adoption records."

At least he knew how to get to the point.

"Your Honor," Parker said. "As we stated in the petition, there is something else. Miranda's ex-husband. He gave the child up for adoption without her consent."

The judge frowned with suspicion. "How did he manage that?"

"He took the three-week-old infant out of the house one morning when Ms. Steele was asleep."

"He gave away his own daughter? After she'd been in the house for three weeks?"

Gritting her teeth, Miranda hugged herself tightly. She really didn't want to bring this up. "It wasn't his daughter," she murmured.

"No?" The judge sat back. "Whose child was it?" The real question being, *were you cheating on him?* His gaze drifted to Parker.

Miranda focused on the pipe collection on the judge's bookshelf. "I was raped."

The judge paused a moment, as if he didn't know what to say. "Did you press charges, Ms. Steele? Do you know who the perpetrator was?"

She'd always wondered if a pipe tasted as nasty as a cigarette. "No, it was cold outside. He wore a ski mask."

"Did you report it?"

She dug her nails into her arms. The pipes were displayed attractively in an acrylic rack. Various shapes of shiny reddish wood, with straight or curved mouthpieces. No, she didn't think she'd take up pipe smoking. "Leon, my ex-husband, didn't want me to."

"It was a case of spousal abuse," Parker said flatly. Might as well put all her cards on the table.

She dared to look back at the judge and watched him shake his white head slowly from side to side. "I'm so very sorry, Ms. Steele. But without—"

"Evidence. Yes, I understand, Your Honor."

"You understand I can't open your daughter's records without it. The adoptive parents would want to file charges if I did that. It would be worse for you that way."

And he'd risk losing his judgeship. She couldn't ask him to do that. She couldn't blame him for being careful. He had to uphold the law, after all. She got to her feet. "Thank you for your time, Your Honor. I appreciate your listening." She held out her hand.

The judge shook it warmly.

"You do have the option of waiting until your daughter turns twenty-one," he added. "The Confidential Intermediary program can help you then. Especially if she's initiated a search for you."

"Thanks," Miranda said again.

Still in his chair, Parker cleared his throat, his irritation back. "Your Honor. Leon Groth falsified Ms Steele's name on the adoption papers."

The judge sat back down. "Is that true?"

Miranda wanted to groan out loud. "He'd have to. I certainly didn't sign them."

"With your permission, Your Honor, I request that a sample of Ms. Steele's handwriting be compared to the adoption record."

Miranda felt the tears stinging her eyes. Didn't Parker know how good Leon was when he wanted to be? "That won't work."

"Why not?"

"Because they already did that when I petitioned the court before."

The judge scowled. "You petitioned before? Why don't I have a record of that?"

Miranda shrugged. "It was almost thirteen years ago."

"But," Parker said in a voice that betrayed his impatience. "They didn't use a forgery expert of my choosing."

Miranda shuddered, tears burning her eyes. "Parker, please. I can't do this."

CHAPTER EIGHT

Miranda lay sprawled across the bed in the hotel room, her face buried in the pillow.

Parker sat in an armchair nearby, reminding her of Dr. Wingate during one of her therapy sessions. Except that he was riffling through the newspaper, pretending to read it.

"I wish you would let me hire a handwriting expert," he said, breaking the long brooding silence that had hung in the room since they'd returned to it.

She turned her head away. "You will, no matter what I say."

He didn't answer.

"What good would it do, Parker?" she said without looking at him. "Do you think your expert would find some curlicue or dot over the *i* that would suddenly prove what Leon did?"

She heard the paper rustle behind her. "Why not? It's been what? Eleven years? Technology has vastly improved."

She closed her eyes. "It might be my signature, for all I know. Leon had me sign papers once in awhile. Without reading them, not that he'd let me. If I'd been an heiress, he could have swindled me good. I was so stupid." She gave the pillow a punch and shoved her face into it again.

"You were frightened. And rightly so."

"I was weak. I couldn't stand up to him. Not back then." It had taken years of martial arts training and brawling in bars before she could do that.

"All the more reason to bring in a handwriting expert."

"The judge didn't seem to think newer technology would matter. He clearly stated there had to be more evidence than just the handwriting." She leaned up on her elbows to look Parker in the eye. "It was in your classes that I learned handwriting analysis isn't definitive. That's why it's not admissible in court."

His face grew weary. "It could lead to other evidence."

"There is no other evidence." She took a deep breath. "I just can't go through this again, Parker. I can't hear another judge tell me 'no.'"

Parker held her gaze for a long moment. "I'm sorry it went so badly today."

33

A lot of people were telling her they were sorry lately. But she found comfort in his soothing tone. A defense against the despair crouching at the edges of her heart, ready to pounce. She forced herself to smile at him. "At least I hired the best."

"I don't feel like the best right now."

He was the best. And even he couldn't find her daughter. She twisted the diamond-and-sapphire ring on her finger. Maybe it was time for a change. She should be sobbing into the pillow, into Parker's shoulder, but she couldn't. She couldn't cry any more when it came to Amy.

Maybe she'd spent her allotment of tears. Just now, she felt herself slipping into that cold, dead numbness she'd felt after Leon attacked her when he'd found her in Atlanta. She rolled over on her back and touched the scars on her chest. The knife wounds the monster had given her over two months ago had healed now, but the marks would always be there. Just like the ones on the inside would always be there.

She let herself snicker out loud. "At least I'm not going to blow up the courthouse john this time. Not at the moment, anyway." She put her head down and closed her eyes. "On the other hand…"

Parker's paper rustled again as he turned the page. "I don't have the pull in Chicago that I have in Atlanta, if you're thinking about getting yourself arrested."

"A girl can dream." But no, she didn't want that. What she needed was a good murder to solve. Maybe she should put in a call to her buddy Officer Chambers at the Atlanta PD and see if anything was shaking.

Parker folded the paper and put it in his lap. "I'd like you to think about what the judge said concerning other relatives."

She opened one eye to scowl at him. "You mean my aunt in Minnesota?"

"You know whom I mean."

Yeah, she knew "whom" he meant.

"Your father," he said when she didn't respond. "We can try to locate him."

She opened the other eye and smirked. "Yeah. That would be a walk in the park."

"No more difficult than looking for Amy."

She rolled over on her back again with a frustrated groan. "And if we could find him, what do I say? 'Hi, Dad. Long time no see. By the way, you have any life threatening diseases? Oh, you do? Well, just give me some documentation, and I'll be on my way. See ya.' No, thanks."

She watched him take an irritated breath and pick up his paper once more.

Parker studied the woman lying before him, the curves and muscles of the body he knew so well. Every sinew of those muscles, every lean fiber had been wrought in the fire of her indignation over what Leon Groth had done to her. He loved her determination, her resilience in the face of horrors he couldn't even imagine. If only he could help her. He'd never felt so useless in his life. He didn't like the feeling one bit.

Miranda saw something in the paper catch Parker's eye.

"I want to take you out tonight," he said.

They went out every night. "I don't feel like celebrating, Parker."

His mouth went tight at her remark. "I didn't mean it that way."

She ran her hands over her face. "I was thinking of ordering room service and going to bed early. We've got a plane to catch tomorrow."

"Humor me." There was the hint of a twinkle in his eye.

Oh, God. She knew what could happen when Parker wanted her to humor him. She raised herself on one elbow and rested her head on her fist. "What did you have in mind? Is there a sumo wrestling match at Soldier Field?"

"A little classier than that. But I want to surprise you."

Parker and his surprises. He was always so thoughtful, so careful of her feelings. She didn't think this surprise would help much. She uttered a whiny groan. "I really don't feel like it."

"It might cheer you up a bit."

He'd keep it up until he won. She didn't have the energy to fight with him, so she caved. "Okay. Sure. Whatever you say." Her groan turning guttural, she forced her body up. "But if I'm not cheered up, don't say I didn't warn you." She plodded to the bathroom to shower and get dressed.

CHAPTER NINE

Parker wore a charcoal suit that looked like it cost a pretty penny, a crisp white shirt, and gray silk tie, and she was in the ruby dinner dress he'd packed for her. It was low-cut, had a row of sexy diagonal ruffles at the hem, and included a silky matching shawl Miranda didn't exactly know what to do with.

While in general she hated getting dressed up, she was starting to get a kick out the way Parker's eyes always lit up at the sight of her in a party dress.

They ate dinner at a crowded Rush Street spot, then headed for Parker's "surprise," which turned out to be a fancy piano bar called *La Chic* that served swanky drinks and chips with serrano-laced salsa. Okay, those were pretty good.

The low lights and polished red wood of the bar and tables furnished a lush atmosphere that was a match for Parker's apparel and taste. She was more used to dives.

They sat in a secluded corner, with a good view of the piano, which was empty.

Miranda tied her silky shawl around her waist, scooped up some salsa with her chip and shoved it into her mouth. It was fresh, juicy, and had a real kick. She had to fight not to flinch.

"The piano player must be taking a break," she said with her mouth full.

"The entertainment will be here momentarily." Parker sipped his Gentleman Jack and gave her that sneaky look of his.

Okay. Her curiosity was roused. "So what's the surprise? Has to be more than this salsa." She took another bite of a sauce-laden chip.

"Are you enjoying that?"

"It's pretty good."

"Is it hot enough?"

"Just right. Have some." She pushed the fancy saucer toward him.

"I'll pass tonight."

"Chicken?" She chuckled, recalling the informal contest they'd had shortly after she met him.

He smiled wryly. "I'm simply not in the mood."

"I see. Already proved your manhood, huh?"

His lips turned up in a sexy half-grin. "I think I've found other ways of doing that since I first ate hot peppers with you."

Yes, he had. She took a sip of her pear martini, which was pretty good, too. And almost empty. She wasn't that big of a drinker, but tonight she was thinking about getting good and sloshed.

Parker had just ordered her a refill when the sound of tinkling piano keys caressed her ears. Then came the soft, sultry notes of a sensuous feminine voice singing "Blue Moon."

Miranda's eyes opened wide. "I know that voice." She turned toward the piano and saw the blond vision of loveliness dressed in a black sequined gown, as classy as the night she'd first met her. "It's Coco!"

Parker sipped his drink smugly. "It is, indeed."

"She's the surprise?"

"She is, indeed."

You sly dog, Miranda thought. The sight of Cora Beth Hinsley, a.k.a. Coco, did cheer her up.

She listened quietly as Coco played, not wanting to throw her off her rhythm, and remembered the last time she'd heard her play. Coco had been none too thrilled to see her at the time. But that was before she and Parker had rescued the girl from her abusive jackass of a husband, Dexter Hinsley. A cheating, philandering, wife-beating textbook salesman in Atlanta.

Coco sang through a mix of oldies. She did "Saving All My Love for You," "Stormy Weather," and a soulful version of "Lady Sings the Blues." Miranda sensed she was expressing her pain through her art, but her voice was stronger, her playing more competent. She didn't seem to be the timid girlie girl any longer. Getting away from Hinsley had been just what she'd needed. But Miranda wondered how she'd gotten to Chicago.

At the end of the set, Coco launched into a medley of Streisand songs while Parker tipped the waitress to deliver a message to the singer.

"...in...the...wo...rld." Coco held out the note as she thundered out the finale on the keyboard, her black sequins shimmering, her face full of emotion.

Man, she was good.

As soon as she ended, the crowd burst into applause.

She reached for the microphone and half whispered into it. "Thanks, everyone. I'll be back in ten," She rose and headed for the back. The waitress met her along the wall.

Miranda watched as she spoke and gestured toward their table.

Coco turned her head. Her eyes went wide. Miranda had to smile watching the girl's hands shoot to her face as she wriggled her slim body like she'd just won the lottery.

She rushed over to the table. Well, as fast as she could shimmy in that long, slinky dress. "Oh my gosh. Miranda," she giggled. "Mr. Parker. I'm just so thrilled to see you both." The girl might be a little less fragile, but she was still bursting with Jessica-Simpson-like femininity.

Parker got to his feet, held out his hand. "It's good to see you again, Cora Beth."

"Oh, please don't call me that. I'm Coco now."

"Coco, then. It's very good to see you." They shook hands warmly.

Coco turned to Miranda. She couldn't just sit there. She rose, but that might've been a mistake.

As soon as she did, Coco threw her arms around her. "Oh, Miranda. I thought I'd never see you again. I wanted to say thank you for helping me."

Miranda patted the girl's arms gingerly. "You did write me a letter." She'd gotten the five-page tome a few weeks after Coco left Atlanta.

"But I wanted to say it in person."

Miranda waved a hand and wrapped her silky shawl around her, since it had come untied, using the gesture to escape the embrace. "Don't worry about it. Why don't you have a seat? Can you talk a little bit?"

"Sure, I've got a few minutes."

Parker held out the chair for her and they all sat back down.

"Would you like a drink, Coco?" Parker asked.

She shook her head. "I've got a soda at the piano. I get all the drinks I want for free." Her big blue eyes glistened. Her hair was shorter and fell to her chin in soft, feminine curls that caught the light, giving her face an angelic glow.

"You're looking very well, I must say." Parker had just the right note of charm in his voice.

"Thanks. I'm a lot better than last time you saw me." Coco looked like she was swooning a bit. Parker had that effect on women.

Miranda took a sip of her martini. "I thought you were in Iowa."

"I was for a while. I was in pretty bad shape when I left your place. Well, you know how I was. So I went and stayed with my Aunt Irene in Doon." She laughed. "Doon, Iowa. Population five hundred and thirty-three."

"Sounds like a hopping place."

She shrugged. "It was pretty boring for a while. But it gave me a chance to think things over. I even went to counseling."

"Exactly what you needed," Parker said.

"He's right. So what made you leave?"

"Well, like I said, I was in pretty bad shape. I cried a lot, even with the counseling. Didn't sleep very well. Didn't eat very much. Aunt Irene was worried about me. She's a terrific cook, but I just didn't have an appetite."

Miranda nodded. She knew the emotions all too well.

"Then suddenly one day, it hit me. I thought, what am I sitting around here moping for? This is my chance to work on my career. There aren't any decent nightspots in Doon. Kansas City was the most logical place to go. So just in case Dexter found out I had left, I decided to go to Chicago instead. Pretty smart, huh?"

"Yeah, pretty smart." Miranda took another swallow of her martini. "Dexter? He hasn't been in contact with you, has he?"

"My mother told him I'd gone to Aunt Irene's for a little while."

Miranda nearly choked on the vodka. "Why did she do that?"

Coco waved a delicate hand, her nails sparkling with pink glitter. "He just weaseled it out of her. You know how he can put on the charm when he wants to."

Yeah, she knew. She and Parker followed the sleaze ball across Georgia, while he put on the charm with a number of middle school teachers. The man had a lot of miles on him. She had to be straight with her. "That wasn't a good idea."

"Miranda is right, Coco," Parker said sternly.

Coco looked like a schoolgirl who'd been caught talking to her neighbor in class. "It wasn't that bad. It gave us a chance to talk."

Miranda's shoulder muscles tensed. "Talk?"

"It was okay. He called me and said he wants me to get on with my life, and he's sorry it didn't work out. He agreed to a divorce. He signed the papers and everything."

Miranda just stared at her. That didn't sound like the Dexter Hinsley she knew.

"I had to send them to Los Angeles. He's out there now. He's staying with his brother and working at a car wash on Wilshire Boulevard. It's called *Sudsies*. Isn't that cute? He said something about trying to get a part in the movies. He always did want to do something special. He's so creative."

Creative with the ways he used to smack her around. Coco sounded like she was still in love with the jerk. Typical for an abused woman. They always go back.

Miranda hadn't. But she would never have left Leon if he hadn't kicked her out. And taken Amy away. She'd fought with her feelings for the monster for years.

She took a sip of her martini. The way Coco could make guys swoon, she didn't need a jerk like that. She could attract high-class men, like successful defense attorneys. Miranda thought of the hormones she'd aroused in Parker's surrogate son when he'd heard her play at the Policeman's Ball.

"So what's your last name now?" she asked.

She shook her head. "Oh, I haven't changed it yet."

"You haven't? What if old Dexter boy decides that means you still belong to him?"

Coco waved a hand. "Oh, he wouldn't do that. Really, he seems happy out there in LA. Everything's fine."

First she says she goes to Chicago so he can't follow her, then she talks to him on the phone like he's an old pal and thinks everything's fine? She opened her mouth to protest, but Coco changed the subject.

"So how about you two?" Coco glanced at the ring on Miranda's finger. "Are you serious? I didn't realize you were together until…well, that night."

None of them wanted to talk about that night.

Miranda shoved her hand with the ring finger under her arm. "We're just taking things one step at a time for now."

Coco looked disappointed. "I see." She glanced at the jeweled bracelet on her arm that held a watch. "Well, I'd better get back. The manager can be a stickler about breaks." She got to her feet.

Parker took her hand again. "It was very nice seeing you again, Coco."

Miranda was worried. "If there's anything we can do, you know how to get in touch with us, don't you?"

A shadow crossed Coco's face. It was a look that had as much fear as sadness, to Miranda's way of thinking. "I don't want to say goodbye so soon," Coco said. "Say, I get off in about an hour. Why don't you both come over to my place afterward?"

"What you think, Miranda?" Parker left the ball in her court.

"Oh, I almost forgot," Coco giggled. "I haven't even been home. I've been out of town and just got back a few hours ago. I came straight here." She regarded Parker with wide eyes for a moment, then started to talk a mile a minute. "We're getting the whole place redone. Zelda's boyfriend is doing the work for free. He's in construction and he wanted to surprise her."

"Zelda?" Miranda managed to interject.

"My roommate. She's been staying with him for a few days. She's not coming back 'til tomorrow. But our place is supposed to be ready tonight. I'd really love for you both to see it." She bounced up and down on her toes.

Miranda could never resist the girl's pleas. "Okay, but we can't stay too late. Parker and I have a plane to catch tomorrow."

Coco's eyes glistened. "Super."

CHAPTER TEN

It was around one a.m. when Coco finished her last set. After she changed into jeans and a frilly fashion blouse, Miranda and Parker followed her in the rental car to a seven-story apartment complex off Division. The parking lot was crowded with residents' cars, but after a while they found a spot and got out.

Parker offered to carry Coco's suitcase. She thanked him and chattered away as they strolled to the front door.

Coco used her key card to open it and led them through. "Zelda insists that I'm a ballad singer. She likes the Billie Holiday thing. But I've been working up some more current stuff. You know, Mariah Carey, Britney Spears? Sort of a new image. Know what I mean?"

Miranda opened her mouth to answer, but Coco pressed the elevator button and kept talking. "The crowds at *La Chic* seemed to like the new stuff, too. I was starting to get a following." She pouted her lips, her blue eyes flashing. "I can't believe that Ralph. I take a little side trip, and he bumps me to Mondays and Tuesdays. All for a job I didn't get."

"Where was the job?" Parker said as the elevator doors opened and they all stepped in. Miranda was amazed he had gotten a word in.

"I'm in five-oh-seven." Coco punched another button. "Indianapolis. There's a really hot piano bar there. They wanted a house singer for five days a week, but the audition was this Friday night, so I had to miss my gig at *La Chic*. I told Ralph I'd only be gone one weekend. I don't see what the big deal was."

Miranda watched the floor numbers tick off. "Long drive to Indianapolis."

"Three hours."

She wondered why Coco had stayed through Monday, but it was none of her business.

Coco waved her hand. "So anyway, I told Zelda I was going out of town and she said, 'why don't we get Jake to fix up our apartment while you're gone?' She was going to stay at Jake's a few days to work with a client in the area. She's an actress, but she does interior design on the side when the acting jobs are scarce. She's always trying to fix up our place."

41

The elevator doors opened on the fifth floor and Miranda followed Coco down the hall.

"I take it Jake is your roommate's boyfriend?" It was second nature for Parker to pump people for information and make it sound like conversation.

Coco shrugged. "On-again, off-again. He buys houses and fixes them up and then sells them. He's a real ambitious type. A little possessive, too, if you ask me. He's got an ego. Even owns his own company. Jake Jeffries Enterprises. Here I am."

Miranda read the number. Five-zero-seven. Must be the place.

Coco got out her key, jiggled it in the door and stepped inside. She switched on the light and gave a little squeal as she moved toward the living room. "Oh, Jake put in the divider and it's nice and deep the way we wanted it. C'mon in here."

Miranda followed her into the larger room. The walls were bare, prepped for painting, the couch and chairs and tables had been shoved aside and covered with plastic. A large canvas drop cloth was spread on the floor. Several large buckets sat in the middle of the room.

Beside them was a good-sized toolbox. More tools lay on the floor beside it. An awful lot of them. Jake must have brought in a crew.

The room was warmish. Miranda watched Coco step over to adjust a thermostat on the wall, and wrinkled her nose as an odd smell hit her. Bleach and something…rotten. Maybe a worker left a sandwich lying around.

"Looks like Jake didn't finish," Coco said.

"Yeah." This scene brought back memories of her construction worker days. Except for…that odor in the air overpowering the scene.

Coco grimaced. "Oh, gosh. What's that smell?"

There was an annoying buzzing sound coming from somewhere, and the nauseating scent seemed to be getting worse. Miranda held a hand over her mouth. "Did your toilet back up?"

"I—I don't know." Coco scurried down the hall to check. "Everything seems okay in here."

The scent was like old tuna and very rotten bananas. "How about the fridge?"

"Miranda," Parker murmured at her side. He handed her a handkerchief.

She took it to cover her face and studied his look. He recognized that smell. Now so did she. Coco headed for the kitchen.

"Never mind the fridge," Miranda told her. "Don't touch anything."

But the girl pivoted and scampered over to the sliding doors of the balcony to open them a crack. "I'm so embarrassed. I don't know what Jake was thinking. I'm so sorry."

"It's okay." Trying to sound calm, Miranda waved a bug away from her face. Bug?

Parker touched her arm and silently pointed at the divider.

It wasn't just any bug. It was a fly. And it was partying with his extended family on the new wall. That's where the buzzing sound was coming from. Chill bumps prickled her arms. She wanted to suck in air, but thought better of it.

"What's wrong, Miranda?" Coco's voice trembled.

In her party dress, Miranda strolled closer to the wall and studied it. Sloppy drywall job. There was blistering, and she could see the tape through the paint. She tapped on the surface. Stud. She moved little to the right, tapped again. She repeated the process a few times, covering about a foot. All solid. That wasn't right.

She ambled over to where the tools lay on the floor. There seemed to be at least two of everything, enough for a team of workers. "Since you just had that installed, it can't be a load bearing wall, right?"

"I'm not sure what you mean."

"Never mind." She looked down at the pile and considered the Sawzall. "The standard way would be to make two vertical cuts. But I don't think we have time for that." She picked up the heavy sledgehammer.

"What are you going to do with that?" Coco sounded alarmed.

Parker stepped to the girl's side. "Stay calm, Coco."

"What is she doing?"

Miranda moved to the new divider, got a good grip on the hammer's handle and swung. Thwack. The wall trembled.

Coco screamed. "What are you doing that for? Are you crazy?"

"Let me help you, Miranda."

"I know what I'm doing, Parker. This is my area of expertise." She gave the wall another whack. It shuddered again. "C'mon, you son of a bitch."

"Stop it," Coco cried. "Mr. Parker, stop her. She's going to wake the neighbors."

Ignoring her, Parker went to the toolbox and picked up a smaller sledgehammer. He joined Miranda and gave the wall a hard smack. That time, the whole building seemed to shake.

Not to be outdone, Miranda swung her hammer again. Boom. At last, the drywall cracked.

Parker took another swing. The crack started to split.

Coco went berserk. "Have you both gone stark raving mad?"

"Stay back, Coco." Miranda hit the wall again. This time it splintered like an eggshell.

"My landlord's going to kill me."

"I think your landlord's the least of your worries." Miranda put down the sledgehammer and picked up a pry bar.

"He'll evict me."

"We'll speak to the landlord," Parker said firmly as he found a crowbar.

"Please tell me why you're doing this."

Miranda didn't want to say. "Why don't you go back into the bedroom until we finish."

They both began hacking at the cracks in the wall with their tools, picking out the chunks of plaster one by one until at last they made a hole.

"It's over here," Parker said. "Don't reach inside."

"I wasn't going to." Miranda hooked the blade of the pry onto the drywall's edge and yanked.

It came loose, spewing more plaster onto the floor.

A little more prying, and at last the drywall and boards yielded. A form tumbled out headfirst, yawning out the gaping hole.

The face was covered with plastic, duct tape had been wrapped around the neck, the dark hair was matted against the skull. But the eyes and mouth were wide open, frozen in that last moment of terror. And in the middle of the chest, was a bright red blood stain.

Coco ran forward, pressed her hands to her cheeks, and stared down at the lifeless body. "No," she gasped.

The flies settled on the plastic making the already distorted face even more gruesome. She had been pretty once.

Miranda couldn't hear their buzzing anymore. All she could hear was Parker dialing 911.

And Coco's bloodcurdling scream as she burst into tears. "Oh, God. Oh, God! This can't be happening. It's impossible. How can that be *Zelda?*"

CHAPTER ELEVEN

Miranda stood on Coco's balcony watching the blue police lights flicker in the parking lot below. She finally knew what to do with her wrap as she hugged it close around her neck and shoulders.

Another dead body. The third one she'd found in three months. Trouble sure knew where to find her, no matter where she went. On the other hand, she had wished for a murder case to solve. Like they say, be careful what you wish for.

Parker stood behind her, wearing the same sad look he'd worn all evening. Only now it was more intense.

"This isn't your fault." The man was a psychic.

She thought of the frozen look of fear on the dead girl's face. Her blood began to boil. "Who would do that to a young woman?" Or to anybody?

"And why?" Parker's tone echoed her anger.

"Good question."

He rubbed his chin. "We know too little about Coco's roommate to even venture a guess."

But that wouldn't stop him, if he wanted the answer. It certainly wouldn't stop Miranda. They had that in common. "We could try to find out."

"The police wouldn't like that."

Miranda turned and peered through the glass doors at the masked police officers marking off the crime scene, examining the body, the area. Detective Robert Kadera, a young, narrow-eyed hotshot, in Miranda's opinion, had Coco outside in the hall and was questioning her alone.

When his crew had finished processing the balcony, he'd ushered Parker and Miranda onto it—after taking their IDs with a suspicious scowl and handing them to another officer to check out. At least he'd let them get some air.

Big of him.

Since her marriage to Leon, she'd never cared for cops, but she'd begun to respect them after going to work for Parker. On the other hand, there were always cops who were jerks.

"Poor Coco," she moaned out loud. "She was just turning her life around. And now this. What can we do for her, Parker?"

"That depends on what the police have to say." His deep gray eyes were full of sorrow.

"That's all *you* have to say about it?"

His sexy dark brows drew together. "We're not licensed in this state, you know."

"Yeah, and we don't have a client yet."

He knew that wouldn't stop her and this time, she had a feeling it wouldn't stop him either.

The crime scene officers had finished taking the preliminary photos. She watched them remove the body from the wall, lay her on the floor for the ME. "My guess is the killer stabbed her with something handy from the toolbox. A screwdriver or an awl, maybe."

"I would concur."

What else would produce that eerie look of frozen horror? "Can you kill somebody that way?"

Parker nodded. "It's been done."

She shivered. "I saw a couple screwdrivers in the toolbox." She watched one of the techs pick up a hammer and spray it with Luminol. "But I didn't see any blood. I'd say the killer took it with him."

"Excellent deduction. That would be my conclusion as well."

"Sure would be nice to find the murder weapon."

"Indeed."

She looked up and saw movement down the little hall that led to the front door. Coco appeared, her hands covering her face. Detective Kadera followed behind her, wearing an angry grimace and carrying their IDs.

He stepped in front of Coco, his mouth moving, his finger in her face. Coco burst into tears.

Miranda reached for the door handle and shoved it open. "Hey, buddy."

"Miranda." Parker's low warning in her ears couldn't hold back her ire.

She strode into the living room, ignoring the nauseating odor. "There is such a thing as police brutality, you know."

The detective spun around, narrowed his already narrow black eyes at her. "We're taking your friend here in for questioning."

Now she really wanted to punch him. "Why? She's a victim."

He gave her a cold, none-of-your-damn-business glare.

Miranda felt Parker's hands on her shoulders. "If you don't mind, Detective," he said. "We'll come along, too."

The detective handed their IDs back to Parker with a smirk. "Suit yourselves."

The tall brick police station on Larrabee was about as warm and welcoming as a jail cell. What did she expect from a place that processed drug dealers, pimps, and murderers?

Miranda paced back and forth over the dingy floor of the small corner waiting area where Detective Kadera had reluctantly stashed them. She marched from the artificial potted plant to the water cooler, to the row of hard black metal chairs, back to the plant. The clicking of keyboards and muffled voices rose over dividers across the hall that made up the cubes belonging to Homicide.

Reaching the water cooler again, she cursed the blasted high heels that were killing her feet. At her sides, her fingers seemed to open and close on their own. "What the hell are they doing with her in there?"

Parker shook his head, meeting her gaze. His eyes said the situation was not good. She already knew that.

"We've got to do something, Parker."

"There's nothing we can do right now."

She brushed back her hair. "I say the boyfriend looks good."

"Jake Jeffries?"

She gave him a nod. "He's a builder, isn't he? He was responsible for that wall."

"Or his crew was."

Which broadened the suspect list. She rubbed her arms. "Yeah, it looks like there were enough tools for a crew." But why would a crew stuff the body in the wall? Why would they kill the tenant they were doing the job for? "And Zelda was supposed to be staying with Jeffries."

"So how did she end up back at her apartment?"

"In the wall." Good question.

A door opened down the hall. Miranda heard shuffling, but no one came out to the waiting room to update them. Why would they? It wasn't like they were family.

With a hard look, Parker got to his feet. "Let's go talk to someone."

"Good idea."

He strode down the short hallway and into the cube area. "Who's in charge here?"

In reply, a balding head rose over one of the partitions. "Can I help you?"

"We're friends of Cora Beth Hinsley," Parker said in a half-professional, half-commanding tone. "The woman you brought in for questioning," he glanced at the clock on the wall, "almost two hours ago."

The man stepped around the divider and folded his arms. His thinning hair was short and curly. He was small and skinny for a cop and wore a blue button-down shirt and slacks that looked like they were a size too big. He ran a hand over his receding hairline. "What about her?"

Miranda read the nametag on the skinny man's cube. *Sgt. Thomas Demarco.* "Can you tell us when she'll be released, Sergeant?"

"I can tell you she's being questioned."

She inhaled, forcing down her temper. "We already know that."

Demarco eyed her and Parker up and down. "What do you two have to do with the Zelda Fleming matter?"

Parker took a step toward the man, stopping short of extending his hand. "We're friends of Cora Beth. And we've already been cleared by Detective Kadera."

The sergeant smirked. "Detective Kadera's a little green."

Miranda studied his dark hair, which was speckled with gray, and the wizened look he wore. This guy had some years on Kadera. Probably was his boss. "We want to speak to her, Sergeant. We're her friends."

"We want to help," Parker added.

"Mm-hmm."

"Sergeant," Parker said brusquely. "There are other people who could have been involved in this incident. Ms. Fleming's boyfriend, for example, Jake Jeffries. Ms. Hinsley could hardly lift the body and plaster her into a wall."

Demarco reached for a toothpick holder on a neighboring desk. He selected one and stuck it in his mouth. "No, but she could have helped the guy who did it."

"Are you looking into the boyfriend?"

Demarco gnawed his toothpick. "We know how to do our business, Mr. Parker."

The frustration was more than Miranda could bear. "Coco couldn't be involved in this. She's been out of town." She could hear Parker clear his throat beside her. Not smart to put all your cards on the table.

Demarco's toothpick traveled back and forth in his mouth while his eyes follow the same pattern. At last he spoke. "There's no record Coco or Cora Beth Hinsley was at the hotel in Indiana where she claimed to stay."

"What?" Miranda looked at Parker.

His face registered disbelief.

"I'm sorry. You'll have to wait until Detective Ka—"

Another door opened a few feet away and speak of the devil, Kadera stepped out into the hall. He scowled at Miranda and Parker with suspicion. "You two still here?"

Parker turned to him, his patience wearing thin. "We'd like to speak to Ms. Hinsley, if we may."

"This is a police investigation. You guys may be hotshot private dicks in your territory, but up here in Chi-Town, you'd better butt out."

Demarco took the toothpick out of his mouth and studied it. "You get anything, Kadera?"

Kadera shook his head.

"Let them talk to her. Maybe they can."

"Sergeant?" Kadera looked like a kid who'd just broken his favorite toy truck.

"You heard me, Detective. Let Mr. Parker and Ms. Steele talk to the lady."

48

"Thank you, Sergeant," Miranda said in as sweet a voice as she could muster, which was probably on the level of a sour gumball.

"Just remember, we'll be watching you." Demarco gestured toward the room. Miranda knew he meant the two-way mirror and probably a closed-circuit camera or two.

Right now, she'd take what she could get.

"Thank you," Parker said with dignity.

Miranda was amazed. Only a man so classy could dig up that level of refinement in a situation like this.

Inside the room, Coco looked like she'd aged ten years. There were dark circles under her eyes, her makeup was smeared, her pretty blond hair was disheveled, her clothes were wrinkled. Sitting at the small table, she had her arms wrapped around her and was shivering like she had the flu.

"Oh, Coco. I'm so sorry."

The girl reached across the table for her hands as Miranda sat down. "It's all right. I'm going to be all right." She didn't sound like she would.

"Why do they think you're involved in this?"

She shook her head. "I don't know. I barely knew Jake."

"Tell us about Jake, Coco." Parker's voice was as smooth and steady as a mother's lullaby.

She turned to him, bewilderment in her big blue eyes. "What do you want to know?"

"You said Zelda's relationship with Jeffries was on-again, off-again?" Miranda asked.

Coco let Miranda's hands go, took a wadded-up tissue from her lap and swiped at her nose. "Yeah. Zelda couldn't make up her mind about him. I overheard him tell her she was fickle once. He was a little obsessive. I thought she might have been trying to let him down nicely. I think she might've been a little afraid of him."

Miranda tensed. "Did he have a temper?"

Coco nodded. "She told me she was at one of his houses once, doing some preliminary work for the interior. One of the guys on the crew cut a board too short. You know? Wasting it? Jake just flew into a rage. Started cussing out the guy in front of all his coworkers."

That wasn't unusual for construction bosses in Miranda's experience. In her case, she'd usually cussed back and lost the job.

Coco pulled at her hair. "I think I made a mistake, Miranda."

"What mistake?"

She bit her lip. "I told the police I thought Jake was good-looking. And that Zelda was probably attracted to him because he had money. I guess I shouldn't have said that. Now they think I might've been attracted to him, too. They think I stabbed her so I could have him." She put her hands over her face. "How could they think that of me? It's so sick. I'd never do such a thing."

"We know, Coco."

Parker took the chair at the end of the table and sat down. "Is there anyone else you can think of who might want to do this? Did Zelda have any enemies? Any other boyfriends?"

Coco frowned. "She was a pretty girl. Guys liked her. But it seemed like Jake didn't want her to date anyone else."

Parker gave Miranda a knowing glance. It was a familiar pattern.

"How did she meet Jake?" Miranda asked.

Coco thought a moment. "She advertised in the Trib. That's how she got her side jobs as an interior decorator."

"Did she check him out?"

"I don't know. I've only been her roommate about a month. I really didn't know her very well."

Miranda wanted to bang her head against the cinderblock wall. "He could be a serial killer for all we know."

Coco gasped. Her hands shot defensively to her throat. "Oh, my God. Could I be next?"

Wrong thing to say. Miranda winced at the scowl Parker gave her. But they couldn't be sure Coco wasn't on Jeffries' list. If he had a list. If they had the right suspect.

Parker inhaled slowly. Miranda tensed, guessing what he was about to say. "Coco, the police can't find a record of the hotel where you stayed in Indianapolis."

Slowly Coco turned her head toward him, her wide, blue, makeup-smeared eyes full of shock. "They can't?"

"Detective Kadera didn't mention that to you?" His voice was low, steady.

She looked away. "Yeah, he mentioned it." She shrugged. "Maybe I got the name of the place wrong."

Miranda's stomach sank. She looked at Parker. He had as weary an expression on his face as the one he'd worn when they left the court building that afternoon. Some policemen could be pretty pigheaded, especially when the facts contradicted themselves, and they didn't want to take time to sort through them. They could book the poor girl on murder one.

"I think you might need a lawyer, Coco," Parker said solemnly. "I'm going to call someone. He's one of the best criminal defense attorneys in Atlanta."

Coco's eyes widened.

"He's not licensed in Illinois, but he can recommend someone here who's good. He has connections."

"Who—who is he?" Coco shifted back and forth in her seat, still wearing that frightened, wide-eyed look.

"Antonio Estavez. He's my son. Adopted, more or less."

Miranda called Estavez Parker's surrogate son. He had taken the Hispanic gangbanger off the streets when the kid was sixteen, raised him, set him on the straight and narrow. And Estavez had grown into a successful lawyer, defending people who'd gotten themselves into trouble.

"You don't have to do that, Mr. Parker."

"You're going to need a strong defense, Coco."

"But you don't have to call anyone."

"I want to, Coco. I want to help."

"But you don't have to."

Miranda reached across the table and grabbed the girl's trembling hand again. "Let us help you, Coco. Why don't you want Parker to call Estavez?"

Parker put his hands on the table, leaned toward her. "Coco, is there something you're not telling us?"

Coco pulled her hand away. Guiltily, she looked at Parker, then at Miranda. "I've already called him."

Miranda frowned. "Who?"

"Who did you call?" Parker echoed, his voice wary.

"Your son, Mr. Parker. Antonio Estavez."

CHAPTER TWELVE

Miranda slid into the rental and waited for Parker to come around to the driver side. Her head was spinning. "Coco and Estavez have been seeing each other on the sly?" He must've been the one who put her divorce papers together.

"Apparently so." Parker took out his cell phone and began pressing keys. He pressed the speaker button and laid it on the seat divider as it rang. He put the car in gear and began to drive.

Finally, someone picked up. "Señor Parker?" It was Estavez.

"Good morning, Antonio. I wouldn't have called at this hour, but I have reason to believe you'd be up."

"You've spoken to Coco."

Parker kept his eyes on the road. "Yes. Miranda and I just left the police station. They're keeping her overnight."

There was a string of Spanish that sounded like cussing to Miranda. "I'll be on the next flight to Chicago."

Parker's jaw tensed as the rental rattled over a covered bridge. "It seems as if you've been doing a lot of flying to the North lately."

Estavez' irritated breath fluttered through the speaker. "Yes. I was with Coco this weekend in Indianapolis. I watched her audition for a job."

And probably a little more than that, Miranda suspected.

"You're a grown man, Antonio. I'm not going to tell you what to do. But have you considered the wisdom of this relationship?"

There was silence for a long moment, as if Estavez was trying to control his Latin temper. "That's correct, Señor Parker. With all due respect, you will not tell me what to do. Coco called me when she was in Iowa with her aunt. She asked for my help. We talked. In fact, we spent many hours on the phone. But this was the first time I've seen her since she left Atlanta. I have nothing to hide."

But his voice betrayed an attraction that was hotter than a steaming plate of tamales.

Parker was silent as he made a left turn onto Lake Street and cruised under the L tracks. "You do have the receipts to prove you were both in Indianapolis this weekend?"

"Yes, of course. I am bringing them with me and will show them to the detective on the case."

"Then I'll see you when you get in." He gave him the information for the hotel and hung up.

Miranda shrugged. "At least that takes care of Coco's alibi."

Parker came to a stop at a red light. "It should be enough to release her from custody."

She turned around to face him and raised a brow. "'The wisdom of this relationship'?"

He glanced at her, a little surprised. "Do you think this is good for either of them?"

She folded her arms. "Were you warning him how tough it is to be involved with a woman who's been married to an abuser?"

He fixed her with a hard gaze. "Don't compare this to us, Miranda. You had no feelings except repulsion and hatred for Leon Groth when we met."

She pursed her lips. Sensitive area. For both of them. Though she had to admit she wasn't convinced Coco was over Dexter. Parker had surmised that, too. But dragging that up now wouldn't help. "I don't want to talk about Leon. What do we do now? I suppose you're going to say we have to go back to the hotel and sleep on this. But I can't do that. I certainly can't leave Chicago tomorrow with Coco in jail, even if Estavez is here to take care of her."

He studied her smugly and she thought she saw sudden pleasure in his eyes. The light turned and he eased through the empty intersection.

"God knows what the police might hang on Coco," she continued. "She's innocent. We ought to look into the boyfriend ourselves."

"I'm crushed, Miranda. You truly underestimate me."

"What do you mean?"

He nodded toward the phone. "Switch over to the map."

She'd wondered where he'd been heading. It sure wasn't toward the hotel. She pressed a button on the cell. And saw a map with a cute little balloon pointing out a location in Elmwood Park. "What's this?"

Parker glanced at her, his heart swelling with feeling. How fascinating it was to see that dogged tenacity of hers come to life. That sacrificial spirit that would not stop until the innocent were free and the guilty punished. How refreshing to be distracted from his concern over Antonio.

"What do you suppose it is?" he asked with the tone of a mentor.

She almost didn't dare to say it. "Jake Jeffries' home address?"

"Exactly. It was in an address book on the desk in Coco's apartment. I looked it up on my phone while we were waiting at the station."

You sly dog, you, Miranda thought, grinning. "Can't wait 'til we get there."

They took the Congress Expressway to the Eisenhower back out toward the West and Elmwood Park. Their destination was just north of where they'd been yesterday. The surprises just kept coming.

After about a twenty-minute drive, Parker pulled up to a two-story stucco building on North 77th.

Jeffrey's house was a large, two-story stucco with a driveway and garage near the back. Miranda didn't see any cars in the drive. Streetlights shone dimly on the front yard as well as the neighbors'. Everything seemed quiet.

"Shall we take a look around?"

"Would be a wasted trip if we didn't." She reached for the door handle, not waiting for Parker to do his Southern gentleman thing and come around to open it for her.

She headed up the drive to the narrow walkway, then up the steps that led to the front door. There was a bell. She was about to ring it when, stepping up behind her, Parker bypassed it and knocked.

She was too excited to scowl at him as they waited for Jeffries to answer.

A minute passed. There wasn't a sound from inside. Miranda stepped back down the steps and squinted at the upstairs windows. No light came on. No dog barked. No cat meowed.

She climbed the stairs again and this time, rang the bell. "Maybe he didn't hear you," she said smugly when Parker lifted a brow.

After another minute, the result was the same.

"What do we do now?" Miranda ran her hand through her hair and stared at the deserted street. Everything was still. Even the crickets chirped quietly. A lot different from the mouthy cicadas back in Atlanta.

In the shadows, Parker's face was lined with intensity. She could see the wheels in his head turning. He studied the surroundings. One neighbor on the side. One across the street. One on the other side. Not a soul out.

"Only one thing to do. Stand right there." He gestured to a spot.

She did and realized her body was shielding him from any prying eyes he hadn't spotted. He reached into his pocket and drew out a small leather pouch. He opened it, and she realized it was a manicure set. He lifted a small nail file. "This ought to do." He studied the door. "No deadbolt. Not very secure for a builder."

Miranda's mouth dropped open. "They didn't take that stuff from you on the plane?"

"I wouldn't bring this on a plane. I took a little trip to one of the shops in the hotel while you were sleeping the other day. You never know when tools like these might come in handy."

She grinned. "Parker, I didn't know you were such a scoundrel."

He gave her a wicked half-smile. "There are a few things you still don't know about me. I hope you're not disappointed."

"Heck, no."

He steadied the nail file. From his coat pocket, he drew out one of his monogrammed handkerchiefs and carefully placed it over the doorknob. "What's this?"

The door swung open without any tinkering.

Looked like Jake Jeffries of Jake Jeffries Enterprises had flown the coop. "Something made Jeffries leave without locking the door," she said.

"Let's see if we can find out what that was." Still holding the handkerchief on the knob, Parker pushed the door all the way open.

Miranda took a step forward.

Parker blocked her with his arm. "Let me go first."

CHAPTER THIRTEEN

"Jeffries?" Miranda called out as she stepped into the dark foyer.

Parker hesitated in front of her. "Jake Jeffries. Are you there?"

There was no answer.

He was being his overprotective self, Miranda thought with irritation. But this wasn't the time to start an argument.

She heard his hand slide along the wall, feeling for a light switch and blinked when he turned it on.

They moved to the end of the short passageway where an overhead light illuminated a wide living room done in browns and sepia tones. It was crowded with an overstuffed leather couch and chairs and chic walnut end tables. Throw rug on the floor. Fireplace along one wall. Clean and tidy as a showroom, but there were no photos. The walls were bare. No pictures or decorations of any kind. Like the owner had just moved in.

No sign of Jeffries or even that he'd been here recently.

She made her way across the hardwood floor that looked newly installed.

Parker ticked off the rooms. "Dining room. Den. Kitchen."

Miranda peeked through an open door and saw a bright red couch across from a TV that took up the whole wall. "Playroom in here." Cubs and Bear banners lined the opposite wall, and trophies decked a narrow bookshelf.

Typical bachelor pad décor, but it didn't look like it had been used much, either.

She stepped inside and scrutinized the shelves. No screwdriver or awl lying around. Using her shawl to shield her hand, she went through some of the drawers. Nothing. She lifted the couches, even peeked into a trashcan. Not even an empty beer can.

While Parker finished with the living room, she went to the kitchen and went through all the drawers and cabinets. Plenty of knives and cooking utensils, but no screwdriver.

"There's a desk in here." Parker stepped into a smaller room across the way.

Miranda trekked over to it. "He must have used this as his office." A flatscreen monitor sat on a lacquered desk that was covered with papers. Office equipment was crowded on a stand in a corner.

Parker went through the drawers. "Looks like he has a landline." Shielding his finger with his handkerchief, he pressed a button on the phone.

"You have no messages," the mechanical voice informed him.

"There's nothing in here," Miranda said.

"Hmm. What's this?" Parker moved some papers on the desk and pointed to a notepad.

"What are you thinking?"

"This trick doesn't always work, but let's see if it yields any secrets this time." Still using the handkerchief, he opened a drawer and fumbled until he found a sharpened pencil. Gingerly, he took a piece of paper off the printer and held it over the notepad. He ran the pencil back and forth quickly for a minute or two, until the edge of the lead had shadowed an area about two inches square. Then he held it up to the light.

Miranda squinted at it. "Is that an address?"

"Looks like it. This could be where we'll find Jeffries."

"Let's go."

"We should check upstairs first."

Miranda swallowed. Parker's words were like a hard punch in the gut. She lowered her voice. "You think Jeffries might be up there?"

"We won't know until we look."

Nodding, she pivoted slowly and forced her feet across the living room and down the hall to the staircase. As she climbed the steps, something felt like a breath on the back of her neck. It made her hair stand on end. She spun around.

Parker was two steps below her. He frowned, concerned. "What is it?"

She'd felt this sensation before. When Leon was following her. It had been sort of a premonition then. But she shook her head. "Nothing." Taking a deep breath, she continued to the landing.

A few feet down the hall, she found a bathroom. "I'll check in here," she said as Parker whisked past her. Covering her hand with her shawl again, she switched on a light and studied the counter. Just a bar of soap and a washrag laid out on the fancy blue marble. She opened the medicine cabinet. Toothbrush still there. Paste. A comb. Didn't look like Jeffries had gone on a trip. Or at least he hadn't packed for it.

She stepped back into the hall and saw Parker standing before a door.

Automatically, her insides twisted in revulsion, her writhing stomach telling her there was something very wrong, even before he turned to her with agony on his face.

"I'm not sure you want to look in here."

"What is it?" She hurried down the hall to where he stood and peered into the room. Her hand went to her mouth. "Oh, my God. Not another one."

"Don't go in there, Miranda."

She didn't intend to. Her mind reeled as she stared at the scene. Parker's voice sounded like it was underwater as he took out his cell and dialed the Larrabee station for the second time that night.

She wanted to look away, but she'd had too much training not to take in the furniture that was so neat and perfectly matched, it looked like a store display—except for the olive green sheets and accent pillows tossed carelessly on the leather-and-black-lacquered bed.

And except for the body.

On the floor, a woman lay sprawled at the foot of the bed, her mouth open in a soundless scream. Her blond head faced them, her wide-open eyes—blue eyes—stared at them upside down, as if she were calling for help, like in some bizarre horror movie. Blood oozed from a gash in her forehead onto the tan and green rug. A silver alarm clock lay upside down on the hardwood floor, a foot or so away. Its display was blank. There was a red splotch along its sharp edge.

She didn't have a stitch of clothes on. This stranger had died naked and vulnerable and completely helpless.

Miranda pressed the edge of her shawl against her mouth, commanding herself not to gag. "She looks like Coco," she whispered.

CHAPTER FOURTEEN

"What is it with you two and dead bodies?" Sergeant Demarco stood in the bedroom doorway of Jake Jeffries' house beside Parker and Miranda, shaking his head in disgust at the scene.

Inside the room, Detective Kadera eyed the deceased woman as again, his team gathered evidence. "Yeah, we ought to hire them as sniffers for the K-9 unit."

Miranda resisted the urge to raise her middle finger at the cop. "Some of us gumshoes just have good instincts, Detective," she sneered.

Ignoring her comment, Kadera opened the pink sequined wallet he held between his Latex-covered fingers. "The vic looks to be in her early twenties. Driver's license says twenty-six. Name's Glenda North." He pulled out another card. "Apparently she was employed by the 'Too Sweet' escort service. Call girl. Jeffries liked the women."

"MO's different," Demarco said. "This one strangulation?"

Kadera squatted and squinted at the victim's neck without touching it. "Looks like it. But there's also that gash on the forehead."

An officer snapped photos of the silver alarm clock on the floor, then gently slipped it into a plastic bag.

"We'll know more when the ME gets here." Demarco turned to Parker and lowered his voice. "There is that little matter of breaking and entering, Mr. Parker?"

Parker raised his hands. "As I explained when you arrived, Sergeant, the door was open."

"Uh huh." He didn't look like he bought it.

"Look, Sergeant." Miranda shot her thumb toward Parker. "My boss here is head of the finest investigative agency in the Southeast. He's not stupid enough to lie to police about something like B and E." At least, she'd never seen him do it. And this time, he didn't have to.

Parker gave her a look that said he'd like to handle this. Okay. She'd can it for now. But only for Coco's sake.

Demarco folded his arms and narrowed an eye at Parker. "So you want me to believe Jeffries killed that woman and ran out, leaving the door open?"

Parker gave the sergeant that confident look only he could produce. "Perhaps Jeffries can tell you himself."

"What do you mean?"

"I'd like to show you something downstairs."

Demarco scowled. "This better be good, Mr. Parker."

"It is."

Resisting the urge to give the cop another piece of her mind, Miranda followed Parker and the Sergeant back down the stairs and across the living room to Jeffries' office space.

"I found this pad of paper in here." Parker pointed to the desk.

"Yeah, so?"

Miranda's heart did a little flip as Parker, with his characteristic confident air, drew out the page he'd shadowed. "I did a rubbing impression on the pad. It seems to be an address Jeffries took down recently. He might be there now. If we're not too late."

Demarco's face registered surprise. He was impressed. He ought to be.

He snatched the paper out of Parker's hand and headed out of the office. "Kadera," he shouted as he reached the stairs. "Take care of things here. I need to take a little drive."

"Yes, sir." Kadera called down in an annoyed tone.

We need to beat him there, Miranda thought. But Parker had already caught up to the skinny man at the front door. "Sergeant, my colleague and I would like to ride along, if we may."

Demarco turned and ran a hand over his receding hairline. "That's not standard procedure."

"I'd say this case calls for more than standard procedure."

The cop exhaled wearily. It had been a long night and would only get longer. Miranda could see the wall of division between cop and civilian cracking. Any help was welcome at this point.

"Since you're cooperating, and you've clearly come to our assistance tonight, I'll make an exception. C'mon."

Scooting through the door—the one Jeffries had left open—Miranda had to admit that at times, Parker's charm could work miracles.

The address Parker lifted was in nearby River Forest, so Miranda took the backseat and let Parker schmooze with the sergeant up front for the two-mile drive. She was used to riding in the back of squad cars.

"We got a hold of one of Jeffries' crewmembers," Demarco said as he headed down North Halstead, past the deserted strip malls and bars. "Actually it was just a buddy who does work for him on the side. Name's Oleski. He claims Zelda Fleming was supposed to stay with Jeffries over the weekend. She stayed one night, then changed her mind and went back to the apartment late Saturday. Jeffries got angry about it and followed her there."

"That fits with what Coco told us about him."

Demarco made a turn onto North Avenue. "Jeffries argued with Ms. Fleming and left the apartment, or so Oleski surmised after Jeffries called him on his cell Sunday morning and told him not to show up to finish the work on the apartment until he could settle her down."

Settle her down. Miranda clenched her fists. She'd like to settle Jeffries down.

"That explains why the tools were left there," Parker observed.

"Oleski tried to come back for his tools, but the door was locked and nobody answered. Said he was pissed. Was even more pissed when I told him he couldn't get the tools back until we finished processing them."

Demarco made another turn, and they wound their way through the neighborhood streets. After a few minutes, he pulled up to a large, gray brick building with green striped awnings.

They got out of the car and walked up to the front door, passing decorative wrought iron light fixtures that lit up the front yard.

Demarco pounded on it the way only cops can. "Jake Jeffries? Chicago Police."

No answer.

Demarco blew out a frustrated breath and tried again. "Jeffries? We need to speak with you about an incident tonight."

"Shall I try my B and E skills?" Parker said wryly.

Demarco gave him a sour look. "We're not even sure Jeffries is here. This could be a wild goose chase."

Parker studied the door. "I think a good lawyer could argue exigent circumstances."

"And I think I'd have my ass in a sling if I went in there without a warrant."

Cops had no imagination at all. Disgusted, Miranda turned and strolled across the small lawn, making her way to the side of the house where a tall redwood gate barricaded the backyard. Lights were on in the area.

"Hey," she called to Demarco in a whisper. "He might be back here."

The cop shook his head, but after a moment, both he and Parker were at her side.

"We can't go in there," Demarco warned.

Miranda stepped forward and gave the gate a push. It opened. She turned to Parker. "Isn't this the party we were invited to?"

"I believe it is."

Quickly, she moved through the opening with Parker right behind her. She heard Demarco cuss under his breath.

"Like I said before, we gumshoes have good instincts." Miranda came to a stop in front of an outdoor patio set. Three padded wrought iron chairs were arranged around a glass table. Atop the table, sat a single bottle of bourbon. Within reaching distance of the bottle, a man lay stretched out on a chaise lounge.

Parker positioned himself in front of the man. "Jake Jeffries? We'd like a word with you."

Demarco cussed again and marched across the lawn giving Parker and Miranda an I'm-in-charge-here glare. "Sir, are you Jake Jeffries?"

The man didn't answer. He didn't move, but Miranda could tell he was breathing. That was a relief. She didn't think she could face a third body tonight.

The man was dressed in a yellow polo shirt with a crocodile logo on the chest and dark chinos. Even in the dim light, Miranda could tell Jeffries was painfully good-looking, with a head of thick, glossy black hair, a movie star profile, and a hunky, bodybuilder physique. The kind of guy who thought he was God's gift.

"Wake up, Jeffries," Demarco demanded.

At last, the body stirred. Slowly he lifted his hands and rubbed them over his face. "What?"

"Are you Jake Jeffries." This time it was more of a statement than a question.

Without getting up, he squinted at him. "Yeah, who are you?"

"Sergeant Demarco of the Chicago Police Department." Demarco flashed a badge. "I have a few questions for you."

"Police?" Jeffries sat up and shook himself. Then he raised a hand to his brow. "Oh, my head. Where's that guy?"

"What guy?" Miranda asked.

He waved vaguely across the table. "There was a guy."

"Mr. Jeffries," said the sergeant. "What are you doing here?"

"Huh? What?"

"Why did you come here tonight?"

Jeffries squinted at Demarco, one eye closed. He did look like he had a hangover from hell. Celebrating after his last kill? "This is one of my properties. I got a call. Someone wanted to see it, so I met him here."

"Who?"

"I—I don't remember his name. Uh, he gave me his card." He patted his pants. "Where did I put it?"

"How are you involved with Glenda North?"

Jeffries pressed his hands against his temples, looking like he might throw up. "I made a deal with that guy for this property I have for sale. We had a drink to seal it." He peered at the table. "Where are the shot glasses?"

"How are you involved with Glenda North, Jeffries?" Parker repeated for the man's convenience.

"Oh, my head. Who?"

Demarco rocked on the balls of his feet, betraying his annoyance. "Glenda North," Demarco repeated. "The young woman who was killed at your residence in Elmwood Park tonight."

That woke him up. "What?"

"Did you hire Glenda North for her professional services tonight?"

"What are you talking about? I don't know any Glenda North."

Demarco straightened his shoulders. "Mr. Jeffries, I'd like you to come down to the station with me to discuss the matter. And what you know about the death of Zelda Fleming."

Jeffries dropped his hands and glared up at the sergeant, his eyes wild. "Zelda? What are you talking about? I haven't seen her since Friday."

"That appears to be the time of her demise."

"Demise?" He shook his head. "There's no demise. Zelda is fine. I just told you I saw her a few days ago."

"Her body was found in her apartment earlier tonight."

Jeffries shot to his feet, then wobbled a little. "What is this? Some kind of sick joke?"

Demarco took a step back and his hand slipped toward his holster. "It's no joke, Mr. Jeffries. My people were called to Ms. Fleming's apartment tonight after her body was discovered."

"Body? Zelda? That can't be. You're lying." Jeffries looked like he was about to hit Demarco.

The sergeant forced himself into the standard protocol. "I'm sorry for your loss, Mr. Jeffries, but your girlfriend is dead."

Jeffries plopped back down on the chaise. "Zelda's dead? Oh, my God." His eyes grew wild for a moment, then filled with tears. Then his expression changed. He must have seen the trouble he was in. "I didn't have anything to do with it."

Right away, Demarco jumped on the suspect's vulnerability. "How are you involved with Cora Beth Hinsley, Mr. Jeffries?"

"Cora Beth?"

"She goes by the name Coco."

"Oh, Coco. She's Zelda's roommate. Don't tell me she's dead, too."

"You know she's not dead. We suspect she was your accomplice."

Jeffries face blushed with anger. "Are you crazy? Coco probably killed Zelda. I don't think they got along."

Miranda showed her teeth. "Shouldn't say things you can't prove, buddy."

Parker touched her arm. She glared at him but bit her tongue.

"How are you involved with Glenda North, Mr. Jeffries?" Demarco repeated.

"I told you. I don't know any Glenda North. I got a call about six this evening, and I came straight here to meet the guy who was interested in buying this property. I showed him the house. He brought a bottle of bourbon." He pointed to the one on the table. "We made a verbal agreement. He wanted to drink to it." He rubbed his eyes again and blinked hard. "He must have put something in that drink."

Miranda inhaled. This could take all night, and Jeffries hadn't said anything that would clear Coco. Biting back her impatience, she let her gaze roam across the patio to the row of neatly trimmed hedges dividing the yard from the neighbor's. Jeffries must pay a lot to keep the place so tidy.

Wait a minute. What was that? She blinked hard. If she wasn't dreaming, there was something shiny at the root of one of those bushes. They couldn't be that lucky, could they?

She glanced at Parker. He had seen it, too.

She sidled across the patio and onto the yard. "I think there's something over here you might be interested in, Sergeant."

"What?" he snapped.

She bent down beside the bush and saw Parker move in beside Jeffries in case he tried to run.

"Don't touch anything," Demarco warned as he came closer to get a better view.

"Wasn't going to." Miranda peered through the leaves. Sure enough, tangled in the roots lay a twelve-inch Phillips screwdriver.

Demarco trudged to the edge of the patio and squinted at the bush. After a minute, he gave a low whistle and ran his hand over his head. "I'm sorry, Mr. Jeffries. I'm going to have to take you in." He reached for his cell and punched it to dial the local cops. "This is Sergeant Demarco of District Eighteen. I'm requesting assistance at…"

Miranda held her breath as she listened to the sergeant rattle off the address. She hoped to God Coco hadn't touched that screwdriver.

Coco. Her heart grew heavy as her hopes for the girl went up in smoke. Even if they booked Jeffries on murder one tonight, the cops wouldn't let her go. There still wasn't enough to get her off the hook.

Estavez and his hotel receipts were their only hope.

CHAPTER FIFTEEN

Miranda wanted to go back to Larrabee station, but Parker insisted on taking her to the hotel instead. After they watched the cops haul Jeffries away and were driven back to Elmwood Park, there was nothing more they could do tonight and she was dead tired, he claimed.

She argued that she was too agitated to be tired, but when they reached the room and she crossed the carpet, stripped off her clothes, and plopped onto the bed, she was asleep before her head hit the luxury pillow.

The next thing she knew, it was morning, and there was a loud knocking on the door. Rubbing her eyes, she glared at the digits on the nightstand. Ten o'clock.

"I'll get it." She shot up, threw a robe around her and made it across the room before Parker was on his feet.

She flung open the door and was greeted by a handsome face and that delicious Latin accent. "Good morning, Ms. Steele."

Estavez.

With his long, slick, jet-black hair pulled back in a ponytail, his jet-black suit, his button-down shirt and silk tie, his bronze skin and confident air, he looked like an Aztec god freelancing as a GQ model. Well, he had been Parker-raised.

"About time you got here." She was about to drag him into the hotel room when she caught sight of the weary-looking, bewildered figure beside him and gasped. "Coco. They let you out?"

"Oh, Miranda," Coco blubbered and threw her arms around her neck. "This has been such a horrible, horrible night."

Gingerly, Miranda patted the girl's back, offering what comfort she could and hoping she wouldn't break into serious sobs. "It's morning now." She pulled out of her boa-like embrace. "C'mon inside. We don't need to talk about this in the hall."

She ushered them inside and turned to catch Parker tying the waist of a classic gray-and-navy silk robe. She took in his tussled hair, his sexy, muscular frame, his five o'clock shadow. She could all but sniff that pricey cologne mixed with his natural scent. Her mouth watered. As glad as she was to see Estavez and Coco, for an instant, she wished she could be alone with Parker so she could tear that robe off him.

He locked eyes with her and looked like he was thinking the same thing. Rain check, she decided, as Parker moved to Estavez and the two men exchanged a masculine embrace.

"Antonio."

"Papa."

Miranda was touched. She'd never heard Estavez use such an endearing term with Parker before.

"Excellent work, Antonio." Parker extended a hand to Coco. "I'm so sorry for the ordeal you've been through, Coco."

"Me too." Coco gave his hand a quick pump. She was wearing the same T-shirt and jeans they'd seen her in last. She didn't look good at all.

"I'll order us all some breakfast," Parker said, ushering their guests into the sitting area.

Having a suite could come in handy, Miranda thought as she watched the pair settle into the chocolate-colored chairs beside the marble fireplace.

"No, thanks. I can't eat." Coco rubbed her arms and stared out the window, looking as if she didn't even see the magnificent city skyline.

"I don't care for anything, either." Estavez eyed Coco like a hawk.

"Miranda?"

She shook her head.

"Well, I for one, need coffee." Parker strolled to the credenza and pressed the button on the fancy brewing machine. After a moment, the mouth-watering aroma of fresh java filled the room.

Miranda settled herself on the silk padded window seat across from her two guests and eyed the tricky lawyer. "How'd you get Coco out so fast?" Of course, he'd done the same for her a few months ago. The man was good.

"It wasn't easy," Estavez said. "The leads on the case, Sergeant Demarco and Detective Kadera, had gone home by the time I arrived at the police station. The officer I spoke to was not very cooperative. I had to threaten to sue the Department for incompetence before I got him to take a statement from me."

Parker set four china cups on the little table and began to pour. "Good bluff."

Estavez dumped two creamers and three sugar packets into a cup, then handed it to Coco before reaching for one that was black. "It was no bluff."

Miranda grinned at the attorney with admiration and took the cup of dark liquid Parker offered her. She blew on it before taking a much-needed gulp. "So just like you told Parker on the phone, when the officer saw your hotel receipts, they realized they didn't have a case against Coco. Right?"

The room went silent.

Estavez gave Miranda a steady gaze while Coco stirred her coffee until it turned a shade of light brown. Oops. The lawyer hadn't known Parker had had him on speakerphone last night. But Parker would have told her that part.

After an uncomfortable pause, Estavez nodded. "That, and the fact that Jeffries' builder remembered Coco was out of town this weekend."

"Oleski?"

"Yes. He called again while I was there to ask about his tools and mentioned it. When I pointed out to the officer that he now had no evidence to hold my client," he reached across the small round end table between their chairs and squeezed Coco's hand, "he said she could go."

"But he told her not to leave town, right?"

Coco frowned. "Nobody said that."

"I don't think she has to stay here," Estavez said. "They booked Jeffries on two counts of murder, thanks to your work last night. The facts are rather incriminating."

Parker took a seat beside Miranda at the window. "Unless forensics results turn up something different."

"They won't."

"The guy's guilty as sin," Miranda concurred.

Parker gave her one of those warning looks. Okay, she shouldn't jump to conclusions. Be patient, stay objective, innocent until proven guilty and all that. She knew the rules, but how innocent could a guy with a dead hooker in his bedroom be?

She didn't want Coco taking the rap for what some guy with an oversized ego had done. She looked at her friend and dared to ask the sixty-four thousand dollar question. "What are you going to do now?"

Coco stared at her, her big blue eyes wide. "I don't know. I can't go home, of course. There were reporters outside when we left the station. I guess I'm on the news." She winced.

Miranda glanced over at the TV, glad she hadn't turned it on.

Estavez hadn't released Coco's hand. He laced his fingers through hers. "Have you considered my suggestion?"

Miranda felt Parker tense beside her. "What suggestion is that?"

"I'd like Coco to come back to Atlanta with me."

"What about your job at *La Chic*?" Miranda asked.

Coco shrugged. "When Ralph heard about me getting arrested, he fired me. He left a message on my cell. Couldn't even talk to me in person."

"The cold bastard."

"I hated working for him, anyway. He was cheap."

"So there's nothing keeping you here." Reluctantly, Estavez released Coco's hand and reached for his coffee.

There was nothing keeping any of them here, Miranda realized. The job was done. She and Parker could go home, too. That gave her an idea. "You could stay with us." She looked at Parker. "That would be okay, right?"

"Of course. You're always welcome, Coco."

Coco's eyes went wide. "You're living together? Oh, I don't want to impose."

Parker smiled warmly. "We're living in my father's estate, though he's moved out. It's hardly an imposition in such a large house."

Estavez looked like he'd been hoping Coco would move in with him. Miranda didn't think the girl was ready for that. Especially now. She knew Parker wouldn't be doing backflips over that idea. But they could keep an eye on her in Atlanta.

"We've already missed our flight," Parker pointed out looking at his watch.

Estavez set down his cup. "Then we can book one together. How does that sound?" The lawyer was full of helpful suggestions this morning.

Coco looked bewildered. "I don't know. What about poor Zelda? Her family?"

"The police have already notified them," Estavez told her gently. "They will ship her remains back to Minneapolis after the investigation is concluded."

"I don't have any of my things. I don't have anything to wear."

"You could wear some of mine," Miranda offered.

Tenderly, Estavez smiled at Coco. "We can get you some clothes before we leave. There are plenty of shops here in the city."

Coco eyed him with caution, as if she was wondering if he wanted to pay for her clothes. Miranda knew that awkward feeling.

Parker cleared his throat. "We can take care of any practical issues as they arise. If you want to go back to Atlanta, Coco, we'll help you get there." Ever the generous one. But this time Miranda was in total agreement. What if the cops couldn't hold Jeffries? Coco didn't need to be in Chi-Town by herself.

Coco shrugged and swiped a hand under one eye. "Can I really leave? I don't want to get into any more trouble with the police."

Estavez' voice was steady and soothing. "We'll keep tabs on the case. If they want you to testify, we can return."

Miranda noted the "we."

Coco looked at Estavez. Then at Parker. Then at Miranda. "Okay. If you're sure it's all right."

Miranda got up and patted her arm, wondering where that motherly gesture had come from. "Of course, we're sure."

Parker rose with unusual stiffness. "I'll make the reservations, then." He turned and proceeded to the nightstand to get his cell.

Miranda studied the couple before her. They looked pretty cozy. What was wrong with that? They deserved some happiness.

Besides, this case was closed. They'd just helped put away an insane killer who'd stuffed a woman in a wall to hide his crime, then, just for kicks, murdered a hooker. She should be relieved, right?

But as she rose and headed for the closet to start packing and look for something for Coco to wear, she couldn't shake the feeling that something about this didn't seem right.

CHAPTER SIXTEEN

Parker re-booked their flight for early afternoon.

Enough time to eat, take Coco shopping, and get hold of Demarco to give him the address to ship the girl's belongings. The sergeant's words revealed he didn't like that she was leaving town, but he appreciated Parker's assurance that he could get in touch with her anytime he needed to.

As Miranda settled into another first class seat on the plane headed back to Atlanta and buckled her belt, the futility of their trip to the Windy City suddenly hit her. Up to this moment, helping Coco and catching a killer had completely taken her mind off her own troubles.

Now Judge Rozeki's words came back to her like cold water in her face.

There was nothing he could do for her. Her only option was to wait until Amy turned twenty-one. Eight years from now. She braced herself for the familiar despair to wash over her, to take hold of her gut and twist it into a hangman's knot. She waited for the cold numbness to creep over her. But just now, she didn't feel either desolation or deadness.

Instead, she felt a kind of peace. She'd done all she could to find Amy. It was time to let go.

She looked over at Parker sitting beside her with his eyes closed, his head leaning against the headrest, his hands clasped elegantly in his lap. He was tired, but he was also avoiding the sight of the couple across the aisle. Estavez and Coco were absorbed in each other.

The lawyer had changed into a polo shirt and Chinos while Coco was sporting pink jeans and a matching sequined blouse that she'd picked out on their quick shopping spree.

Parker had dressed in one of his dark blue suits, a dark blue shirt and a stunning tie. He always dressed up but never looked overdressed. As if he could turn occasions to the style he desired them to be. Everything about him was stunning and elegant. He was sharp and kind and wonderful. The best teacher she'd ever had.

She twisted the diamond-and-sapphire ring around her finger.

Doing investigative work with Parker had been the most fulfilling experience she'd ever had in her life. She loved the work, the chase, the putting the pieces together, the thrill of stopping killers. The longer she had this job, the more she wanted to do it.

That's what her life would be like with Parker, wouldn't it? They would solve cases together, just like this one. She'd keep learning from him, growing. It would be great. Oh, she wanted that life. Suddenly she understood just how much. She turned the ring around to its proper place, a knot of nerves tighter than a prizefighter's fist in her stomach.

Nothing lasts forever. Nothing ever did. But maybe that didn't matter. Maybe it was time. Time to take the plunge. Time to put away the past and take a chance on the future.

She turned to Parker and swallowed hard.

Sensing her in that telepathic way of his, he opened his eyes. "What is it?"

"Hi," she breathed.

His lips turned up. "Hello."

"Interesting trip, wasn't it?"

His smile turned to a frown of sympathy. "Miranda, I'm so sorry—"

She held up a hand. "I don't want to talk about...." She sighed. "Funny how things turn out so differently from what you expect."

"Life has a way of throwing curves at us."

"Yeah, it does." She looked down at her ring, her heart beating way too fast. "Remember when you gave me this?" She held up her hand.

"Of course."

"You said I could put my own interpretation on it."

"Yes, I did." Caution riddled his tone.

She shifted in her seat. "Could that interpretation maybe *change* from time to time?"

He scowled, probably thinking she wanted to break up again. "What do you mean?"

She took a deep breath. God, this was harder than she thought it would be. "I mean if you meant what I thought you meant when you gave it to me..."

"Yes, Miranda?"

She scratched her head, then twisted the ring around a full three hundred and sixty degrees. "If that's what you meant, I, uh, I guess I'd like to take you up on that deal." There. She'd said it. She grinned at him, feeling silly.

"And which deal would that be?"

She narrowed an eye at him. So he was going to make this difficult, was he? "You know, the thing Fanuzzi and Becker just did?"

She watched shock flicker across his handsome face. Stoically, he tried to hide it with an indifferent look. "And what thing is that?"

She rolled her eyes. "You know perfectly well what thing. The marriage thing."

"Marriage thing?"

The plane jerked as it started to taxi, and the pilot gave them a short greeting, saying the weather was fine and the flight should be uneventful.

She grunted through her teeth. Why was Parker being purposely obtuse? "You know. Getting dressed up? Going down an aisle? Saying some vows?"

His elegant dark brow rose in disbelief. "Are you saying you want to get married?"

Now he got it. Duh. "Yeah. Don't you?" Her heart began to hammer. He still wanted to, didn't he? Or did she just make a colossal fool out of herself?

Parker studied the flame in Miranda's eyes, unable to believe he'd just heard the words he'd wanted to hear for so long.

When he first met Miranda Steele, she'd distinctly told him she did not need a man. When he asked her to move in with him, she told him it could never work for them and walked out his door. She would have left town for good, if a child's life hadn't hung in the balance. Not so many weeks ago, she walked out on him a second time. It was only his promise not to be so overbearing that made her consider staying.

He had fully suspected the ticking time bomb to explode again sooner or later, and she'd walk out a third time. Perhaps the last time.

Instead, *this?*

"Are you sure, Miranda?"

Those deep blue eyes flashed for just an instant. Then she lifted a shoulder. "Sure, I'm sure."

She wasn't. He could see it in the worry lines tracing her lovely brow. In her viselike grip on the arm of her seat. The wise thing, the mature thing would be to tell her to wait until she was ready.

But the Miranda Steele he knew would never be ready. He might never get this opportunity again, and he was tired of waiting. He loved her and he wanted her for his own.

Slowly, he wrested her hand from the armrest, lifted it to his lips, and kissed her fingers. "Yes, Miranda Steele. I'll marry you."

Miranda couldn't explain the girlish gasp of relief that filled her throat. Or the tears that suddenly burned in her eyes. Parker still wanted her. She grinned giddily at him. "That's great. Really great." Her voice broke and she felt like a doofus.

The plane made a turn onto the runway where it would take off and stopped. The pilot announced there would be a short delay. She wiped a hand under her eyes. "Glad that's settled."

Parker reached into his pocket and handed her his monogrammed handkerchief.

She took it and swiped at her face. Wait. This couldn't be that easy. "Now what?"

"The customary procedure is to set a date and plan a wedding."

"A wedding." She wadded the hanky into a tight ball, feeling itchy. She was sure she'd have a good case of hives by the time they reached Atlanta.

"What sort of wedding would you like, Mrs. Parker?"

Miranda inhaled so hard she sounded like a rusty gate. "I don't know about the name thing."

"Very well. Would you like to be Mrs. Steele-Parker?"

"Hyphenated?" Why had her voice gone up two octaves?

"Or would you like to remain Ms. Steele?"

She handed the hanky back to him and rubbed her hands on her slacks. "Hell, I don't know, Parker. I'll have to think about it."

"All right. What kind of wedding, then?"

"What kind?"

"It would be difficult to plan without knowing what kind."

Her mind raced. She and Leon had gone to the justice of the peace. With all her baggage, going to a judge would suit her just fine. But Parker? A man of his stature? He deserved better than that. He'd been married before. Judging from the fancy social affairs he attended, he'd no doubt had a fancy, very public wedding the first time. The idea of that made her queasy.

But Parker would love it. A big, glamorous shindig, with all the trappings and all the wedding bells and wedding whistles. And all the Atlanta upper crust in tow, dressed to the nines.

She loved him. She could admit that now. She was brimming with love for him. So she'd compromise. No, she'd do better than that. She'd give him just what he wanted. "I think I want a big church wedding," she told him with satisfaction. He'd never let her do it just for him.

He blinked in surprise. "You do?"

"Yeah. Leon and I just went to the justice of the peace. I don't want to do it that way."

"You don't want a small, intimate wedding?" He knew her too well.

"Heck, no. All girls dream about a big fancy wedding. I don't see why I shouldn't have one."

He lifted a sexy brow. "But we're talking about Miranda Steele."

"Yeah, Miranda Steele. I was a little girl once. I just thought it would be nice. But if you don't want to go to the expense…" She put her nose in the air and sniffed.

"You know that isn't my point."

She shrugged, trying to look wounded. Coco could do this a lot better. "So I'm weird. So shoot me."

He chuckled with a knowing grin. "Very well. A big church wedding it shall be."

She blew out a breath, relieved she'd pulled that off.

Until Parker asked, "And the date?"

Uh oh. "The date?" What was wrong with her voice? There must be helium in the air of this plane.

"The day this big fancy wedding will take place?"

Take place. Just like Fanuzzi and Becker's wedding had *taken place.* She saw herself strolling down the aisle of a huge, gaudy cathedral in a huge, gaudy dress, being gawked at by a huge number of Parker's upscale friends. She suddenly felt like she had sand in her mouth. Oh, God.

She grabbed the armrest and fought the urge to reach for the barf bag.

No. She would not back out. She would go through with this. The big, fancy wedding would *take place*. The last thing in the world she'd do was let Parker down on this one. But it would have to be soon—very soon—or her nerves wouldn't hold out. "Three weeks," she blurted out before she could stop herself.

His brows shot up. "Three weeks?"

"Yeah. You know, the number after two and before four?" She held up her fingers, echoing his sarcasm.

"A large wedding can take six months to put together."

"So? I can do it."

"Really?"

"Just watch me." She sat back with a satisfied smirk. Even though she suspected Parker's x-ray vision could see the butterflies laying eggs in her stomach.

At last, the aircraft started down the runway, but the sick pressure in her gut wasn't from the acceleration. She turned her head and gazed out the window as the ground angled away below her. Soon they'd be high in the air, gliding their way back home. It was really her home now.

The city of her birth came into view below in miniature. All that had happened there would be a distant memory after awhile. Even her memories of Amy. It was time to make a new life. She would do it. She would start fresh. She would plan a big wedding and marry Wade Parker.

Even if it didn't last, even if she ended up regretting it for the rest of her life, just now, it felt right.

The plane was like a majestic eagle, winging its way across the bright blue sky.

He stood on the airport observation deck, staring out the glass. Watching until, at last, the aircraft disappeared into the wispy clouds. It wasn't until he could see it no more that he felt the stab of desperate loss.

The same agony he'd felt when he'd come home to an empty house so many weeks ago.

He'd wept for days then. Like a helpless child. How could she leave him? How could she hurt him like that?

What was he going to do without his Cora Beth?

After his arrest, he'd lost his job. Soon he' would have lost the house, his possessions…everything. So he'd put the house up for sale and went out to LA to stay with his older brother.

Derek had become a stuntman in the movies and tried to get him into it, but he wasn't interested. Instead, he got a low-paying job in a car wash with the ridiculous name of Sudsies. It was far beneath him, but it gave him time to think. To regroup. To plan. He began to write poetry.

Visiting his brother on the set of a cheap Kung Fu knockoff rekindled his interest in the martial arts. Daddy had insisted both of his boys take lessons when they were young. He found a sensei and started training again.

That fit nicely with the plan forming in his head and would give him the skills he'd need to face the likes of Wade Parker.

Parker.

His dick hadn't functioned the same since that bastard had worked him over. He'd never been so humiliated in his life. No one ever humiliated him without living to regret it. And that stupid bitch Miranda Steele, thinking she was so smart, so slick, filling Cora Beth's head full of drivel about independence and freedom and doing what you want.

Cora Beth.

His dear, lovely Cora Beth. How he longed for her pretty face. Her smooth hands against his flesh. Her sweet mouth against his belly. After a month in LA, he knew he had to get her back. He called his mother-in-law and charmed Cora Beth's whereabouts out of her. Like all women, the biddy was gullible and easy to manipulate.

Then he called Cora Beth in Iowa. He'd played it low key, used his wiles to lower her defenses. He thought she was coming around, until she told him she wanted a divorce. Her words stung like angry hornets. He wanted to put his fist through the phone and knock some sense into her.

But he'd kept calm. He agreed, told her it was for the best. He pretended not to mind, let her think he didn't care. That alone should have been enough to make her come back to him. But it wasn't.

He waited for her to call and say she'd changed her mind. She didn't.

So he flew out to the stupid little bitch in Iowa to make her see reason. When he called again, she wasn't there. Her aunt said she'd left town and didn't want him to know where she'd gone. He told her he understood and promised he wouldn't bother her. He didn't say he was in Doon.

He'd have to be careful, he knew. In a small town, gossip was always rampant. He colored his hair dark and cut it shorter than he used to wear it. He wore plain, nondescript clothes instead of the flashy things he liked to wear. He'd gained some weight, was more muscular after training with the sensei. He took to donning dark glasses.

He remembered a friend Cora Beth used to talk about when they first married. He looked her up and found she was a real estate agent in Doon. He pretended to be an investor looking for farmland.

It took him a week to get the friend to let her guard down enough to tell him Cora Beth was in Chicago. A few more sweet lies and kisses and she told him where Cora Beth was working as a singer and playing piano.

The news crushed him. She was using those lovely hands of hers for nonsense when they should be serving him, pleasing him. And she'd taken that ridiculous stage name, Coco.

He knew now that she wasn't coming back to him of her own will. He'd have to use force. Daddy always said the man had to show who was boss.

He flew to Chicago on Saturday, but when he got to the bar the friend had told him about, Cora Beth was gone. Again. He looked up her address and went to her apartment. He found her roommate.

He'd poured on the charm and gotten her to let him inside, chitchatted enough to learn she had a boyfriend who bought and sold properties and was fixing her place up.

He hadn't meant to harm her. He'd only wanted to know where Cora Beth was. But when she'd refused to tell him, he couldn't hold back his temper. He asked, demanded, screamed at the bitch to tell him where Cora Beth had gone.

She told him to get the fuck out. She shouldn't have said that. How dare she speak to him like that? He'd flown into a mindless rage. The kind of rage that used to overcome him when he was with Cora Beth.

Stupid bitches. Why couldn't they just do what they were told? Mama always said he deserved what he wanted. Daddy said the man had to show he was boss.

He picked up the first thing his hand found and jabbed it at her. It hit her chest and sunk in deep, straight to the handle.

She gasped, staggered back. The shock, the wordless helplessness in her eyes was like a drug. It was powerful to hold another's life in your hands. Even if it was just a woman's life.

He stabbed her again. Again. Again.

Her body dropped to the floor.

He stood there, staring at it for what seemed like hours. Then he looked down and saw the bloody tool in his hand. A screwdriver from the tool chest on the floor.

Panic set in. He would go to jail for murder now. He ran to the kitchen, cleaned his hands and face at the sink. He found some plastic gloves and a bottle of bleach in the cabinet. He cleaned the floors, the furniture, the wall.

But what could he do with the body?

He looked at the wall the boyfriend was putting up. The drywall was already cut and partially up. He'd done some construction work when he was in high school. Daddy said a man ought to know about such things. All he had to do was nail up the rest, tape, plaster and paint. He got to work.

It took all night. It was almost dawn when he finished. He studied his work, pleased. Someone would find the body in there and call the police. The boyfriend doing the work would be the first suspect. He hoped Cora Beth would be the one to realize her roommate was in that wall. She'd be so upset, she'd be sure to call him for comfort. Who else could she turn to?

But then he began to worry. Was there enough evidence to convict the boyfriend? What if there wasn't? Would the cops start looking for him?

He went to the roommate's desk and riffled through it. There were notes and cards that gave him all the information he needed about the boyfriend. Addresses, cell number. Jeffries was his name. He lived in Elmwood Park. He repeated all the information several times, so he'd remember it, then left it there.

He slipped on the jacket he'd brought with him so no one would see the blood on his clothes. He took off the plastic gloves he'd worn all night and stuffed them in his pocket along with the screwdriver. Making sure he left no footprints, he stole out of the apartment and made his way back to his hotel room. No one saw him.

The next morning, he called Jeffries and told him he wanted to look at one of his properties in River Forest. The idiot told him he couldn't make it until Monday night. He had to agree or he'd look suspicious.

So he waited.

Alone in his hotel room, he was beside himself. What if Jeffries went to talk to the roommate? What if he found the body first? As the hours ticked by, he darkened his hair and the moustache that he'd grown in California with shoe polish. He calmed himself with the pills a doctor in LA had given him for his nerves. He drank whiskey and slept and dreamed of Cora Beth. She'd be back with him soon.

Jeffries didn't go to the apartment. He showed up at the River Forest house at the appointed time, as innocent as a baby. The rest was easy. All he had to do was turn on the charm. He gave him a business card he'd picked up in a restaurant and told him he was the owner. He made a deal for the property and poured him a drink to celebrate. Jeffries was too happy to notice when he slipped some of those pills into the glass of bourbon that he offered the stupid sap.

He'd tossed the screwdriver away in a dumpster near his hotel, along with his bloody clothes. But he'd bought a second screwdriver and hid it in the bushes along Jeffries' lawn.

The idea of the whore had come to him as he'd stood in the backyard watching the boyfriend's eyelids close and his body slump back in the chaise lounge. He'd simply gone back to Jeffries' home in Elmwood Park, broke in and called the escort service saying he was Jeffries.

He ordered a blue-eyed blond, like his Cora Beth.

He'd made her suck him hard first. Might as well get his money's worth. When she finished, he'd turned her around and slipped an arm around her neck. She'd been expecting him to enter her from behind, he supposed. Instead, he'd executed a *hadaka-jime*, the naked strangle he'd practiced with his sensei. But she'd clawed him good, the bitch, and loosened his grip. She'd rushed across the floor to get away.

If she hadn't skidded on the carpet, if he hadn't grabbed the alarm clock in time and bashed it into her empty skull...what might have happened to him?

He'd hurried outside and parked in a neighbor's driveway. He sat there in his rental car for hours, hoping the police would come.

Then, out of the blue, Wade Parker and Miranda Steele showed up.

Out of nowhere.

What a stroke of luck, he'd thought. Fate must be smiling on him. Certainly, his chi was aligned.

After a while, the cops came, too. Then they took off for the River Forest property.

Blood pumping in his ears, he followed them, watched them go into the backyard, laughed when they took Jeffries away in handcuffs.

But he still didn't know where his Cora Beth was. Parker and Steele must know, he realized. Why else were they involved?

He followed them back to some luxury hotel downtown. He parked along the street facing the entrance and watched. Sleep overcame him. He woke up in daylight, just in time to see Parker and Steele getting into a car—with *Cora Beth* beside them. A tall Hispanic man wearing a long ponytail helped her into the backseat, then got in.

Who the hell was that? Blood pounded in his ears, but there was no time to find out. The car pulled into traffic, and he had just enough seconds to start his engine and follow.

He was going on pure adrenaline now. It was time for his nerve pill, but he didn't need it. Killing those bitches had been such a rush. The danger. That flirtation with disaster. It was powerful…addictive. That's what he needed. A rush like that. And soon.

The roar shook the windows as another plane took off. Blinking, he forced his mind back to the present and looked around.

There was a family beside him. A little boy pointing at the aircraft out the window. He managed a smile for them, turned and headed down the concourse. The walkway was crowded with people from all over the world with their exotic clothes and smells. They hurried past him, rolling their luggage or carrying small bags and briefcases, but he barely noticed them.

It had worked. By God, it had worked. He'd heard the news on the radio while following Parker and Steele out to the airport.

Jeffries was in jail. The police thought the builder was a serial killer. They'd lock him away and never be the wiser. He'd fooled them all.

Now it was time for a change of scenery.

At the ticket booth, a young woman grinned at him with broad white teeth. "Can I help you?"

"Ticket to Atlanta."

"That flight leaves in an hour, sir."

"That will be fine." He handed her a credit card and an ID.

"Mr. Thomas Miller?"

"That's me." He'd had no idea that the fake cards he'd bought on the street Sunday night would come in handy so soon.

"Round trip?" she asked.

"One way."

She busied herself and after a moment, handed him a ticket. "Have a nice flight."

Feeling giddy, he turned to find his boarding gate. He hadn't felt so good in weeks. It was all coming together. Soon he would have everything he wanted.

He'd pay Parker and Steele back for what they'd done to him. He knew how to take care of people like that now, didn't he? He'd go after that tall Hispanic asshole, as well. And if he could do what he wanted with them, maybe his balls would finally be back to normal. Then, at last, he'd have Cora Beth in his arms again.

No woman would ever get the best of him. He would take back what was his. Soon.

"And then, Cora Beth," he murmured softly to himself. "You'll never escape me again. You will be…forever mine."

CHAPTER SEVENTEEN

Three weeks.

She, Miranda Steele, had promised to marry Wade Russell Parker the Third in three lousy weeks. Had she been out of her freaking mind?

She didn't want to think about it. She shoved it out of her thoughts as they landed at Hartsfield airport that afternoon. She suppressed the idea as they drove home and got Coco settled in. She ignored the nagging feeling in her abdomen as they kicked Estavez out and headed for the master bedroom for a much-needed nap.

When she woke in the early evening, she thought she had jet lag. Then she remembered there was only an hour time difference. Then she remembered what she'd done on the plane—and panic set in.

The door opened and she caught sight of Parker, dressed in a cotton shirt and dress slacks and carrying a tray across the room.

She rubbed her eyes and sat up, sniffing a luscious aroma. "Huh? What's this?"

"Dinner for my fiancée."

The word made her shudder. And lose her appetite.

Parker set the tray on the bed and lifted the silver cover to reveal Steak Diane, parsley potatoes cut like roses, and a serving of casserole that looked like it could add five pounds around the waist with each bite.

"The cook really went to town."

"I think she missed us." He sat on the bed and began to cut the steak for her.

"What about you?"

"I ate while you were finishing your nap." He held out a bite of the succulent steak on a fork.

It smelled delicious. Her mouth watered. Guess she could take a bite, even if it made her feel silly to be fed like a baby. "Hmm," she moaned when the tender meat hit her tongue. "That's wonderful."

"Nothing but the best for my fiancée."

She narrowed an eye at him. "You say that like you're skeptical."

"Not at all. Potato?" He held a piece of the butter-drenched spud out to her.

Inhaling in defeat, she opened her mouth. Delectable. She wanted more. Good thing she was going back to work tomorrow. She'd hit the gym hard.

God, this wasn't fair. When she first met Parker, she warned herself not to get too used to the cushy lifestyle he'd try to foist on her, but she'd had no idea it would be this good.

She took a swallow of the delicious imported coffee he always served. "If you're worried I'll go back on the deal we made on the plane, don't be. Like you, I keep my word."

"That's reassuring." Not sounding reassured, he held out another bite of steak to her.

She opened her mouth again and chewed.

After letting him stuff her till she was bloated, she set the tray aside. It was time to get to work. She slipped out from under the covers.

"Where are you going?"

"I've got some phone calls to make." Time to bite the bullet and get this show on the road. She grabbed her cell off the nightstand, whisked past Parker and his sexy raised brows, and headed out the bedroom door.

She scampered down the hall and found the office Parker had set up with the three computer screens on the three black lacquered desks. She settled into a cozy chair and dialed Fanuzzi's number.

After five rings, a shaky voice answered. "Yeah?"

Miranda sucked in her breath as nerves dancing around on the prime steak in her stomach. Why did she let Parker make her eat so much? "Hi, Fanuzzi."

"Huh? Oh. Hi, Murray." She sounded tired.

"Did I wake you?"

"Not really. It's okay." She yawned.

Miranda felt guilty. "Uh, how's it going?"

"Going? Well, the kids are in the pool now. Though I need to keep an eye on Callie. She threw up on the Dumbo ride today."

Dumbo ride? Oh, crap. Disney World. Fanuzzi was still on her honeymoon. "I'm sorry. I didn't mean to disturb you. I'll call back some other time."

"No, it's all right. Is something the matter?"

Miranda stared at the phone, recalling that Becker wouldn't be back in the office until next Monday. That would be too late. "Uh—"

"What's wrong, Murray?"

"Oh…nothing. Plenty."

"You can tell me. We're friends."

They were friends, weren't they? Miranda took a deep breath and blurted it out. "Parker and I are getting married."

There was a span of dead air space that seemed to last about ten minutes. Then Fanuzzi let out a piercing squeal that could break the sound barrier.

Holding the phone from her ear, Miranda could imagine her friend's lithe little body prancing around in a Snoopy dance of sheer ecstasy.

"That is so cool. I'm so excited for you!"

"Thanks. We, uh, set a date for three weeks."

There was another moment of silence. "*Three weeks?* You guys gonna elope?"

"No, we're not." Miranda twisted her hair around her fingers. She didn't want to admit she set the date so soon because she didn't want to lose her nerve. "So, uh, I could use some help with the arrangements. You available?"

"I think so. You need a caterer for the reception, right?"

She hadn't even thought about a reception, but she guessed that would be necessary. "I need help with everything. The whole enchilada."

"O…kay. And how big is this enchilada gonna be?"

She tapped her fingers on the shiny desk and stared at the screensaver swirling around on the middle panel. "Parker said something about five hundred people?"

Fanuzzi sounded like she'd choked on something. "Honey, I'm only one person."

"So?"

"I can't do the whole thing."

"But you helped me so much with the fancy party I gave a month ago."

"A party of about thirty people. Not a wedding with five hundred guests."

Miranda put her head in her hands. What had she gotten herself into? "What am I going to do, Fanuzzi?"

"I don't know, Murray. Okay, I'll do the food, but you'll have to find someone else to help you with all the rest. Is Parker paying for it? What kind of budget do you have?"

"Budget?"

"You haven't talked to him about it?"

"Uh…"

Fanuzzi gave her a you've-got-to-be-kidding groan. "Sounds like you two need to work out the details. And you'd better get started if you want to be ready in three weeks. You have a lot of decisions to make."

Miranda twisted the ring around her finger as a feeling of dread settled over her. "Are you telling me I can't make a couple of phone calls and be done with it?"

Fanuzzi's laugh rippled through the speaker. "Honey, even small weddings aren't that easy. Maybe you should reconsider that date."

Or the eloping idea. No, Parker wanted a big, fancy wedding, and he was going to get a big, fancy wedding if it killed her. "No way. Where do I start?"

"Talk to Parker. Check out some websites. I'll have some ideas ready when I get back. Sorry I can't start sooner."

"That's okay." Miranda felt guilty enough for bothering Fanuzzi. She wasn't about to ask her to cut it short. "I'll let you get back to your honeymoon."

"Sure. We're having a great time. Dave is so sweet."

That made her smile. "That's good. Have fun."

"Oh, we are." She snickered. "I can't wait to tell Dave the good news."

Miranda's stomach flinched. The "good news" would be all over the office when Becker got back, and everyone would give her grief. Maybe she should fly to Tahiti for the next three weeks.

A childish shriek came through the cell. "Charlie, stop slapping your brother with those Mickey Mouse ears. I gotta go, Murray. Talk to you next week. Bye."

"Bye." She hung up, grabbed a keyboard and Googled *big fancy wedding*. She clicked *checklist* and scanned the information. "Reserve six months to a year for planning." Her heart sank down to the floor.

"Always the independent one."

With a squeal, she spun around and saw Parker standing in the doorway, that sexy wisp of salt-and-pepper hair draped over his forehead.

"Huh?"

"Were you really going to handle a wedding with five hundred guests all on your own?"

"Eavesdropper." She pressed the heel of her hand against her eye. "Oh, Parker. I'm no good with social stuff." She waved at the screen. "And this says it'll take months to plan." Like Parker had said. Why did he have to be right so much of the time?

He came and sat down beside her, gently pulled her hand away from her face and kissed it. "That's why, dear Miranda, I have the perfect person to act as your wedding planner." He turned the ring on her finger around so that it was straight. "*Our* wedding planner."

She brightened. That was right. Parker knew all kinds of people. He had whole armies of social strategists. Folks would drop everything they were doing in a flash to help him plan a party. They could do this shindig up right. "Who is it? Somebody I know?"

"Oh, yes. You know her pretty well."

Miranda frowned. She couldn't think of anybody she knew who could plan parties except Fanuzzi. "Who?"

Parker's lips turned up in a sly grin. "Gen."

Miranda's blood turned to Popsicles in her veins. "*Gen?* You got to be kidding."

"I'm perfectly serious."

"Gen?" she squeaked. Parker's daughter and tight-ass office manager, who everyone called "The General" behind her back? The one who wanted to fire her when she started at the Agency? "She hates my guts. And my liver and gallbladder, too."

Parker sighed. "I will have to tell her that we're getting married, you know."

Why didn't she decide to elope when she had the chance? Her stomach started doing the Boogaloo. "*Gen?*" she said again, this time with a sneer. "She won't plan our wedding. She probably won't even attend it."

"I'm hoping I can convince her otherwise."

Parker's charm could go a long way. But against another Parker? Against Gen? That was a tall order. "She might even sabotage the ceremony. Maybe put a firecracker in my bouquet."

He chuckled darkly with confidence. "If she did that, she'd know there'd be hell to pay. I'll speak to her. If you're all right with that?"

All right with that? Hardly. But she was doing this for Parker and if he wanted Gen to plan the wedding, he'd get Gen. She shrugged her shoulders. "Sure. How bad could it be?"

"It's settled then." He reached for paper and a pen from the desk. "And as to the budget…. This is the amount I'm thinking." He held the pad up for her to see.

Blinking, she gulped at the number. That much? Feeling a little dizzy, she sat back and whistled. "It's going to take me a long time to pay that back out of my salary."

Parker's eyes twinkled. "I'll have to give you a raise then. We'll talk about it after you graduate."

She frowned. "Graduate?"

"You do remember that IIT graduation is in two and a half weeks."

Miranda's mouth gaped open.

"You did figure that into the date you set for the wedding, didn't you?"

She'd forgotten all about it. Well, it was more like suppression. There would be final tests and she hated tests. But she sat up, straightened her blouse. "Uh, of course. Sure." Her head starting to pound, she wondered when this train wreck was going to end.

CHAPTER EIGHTEEN

Graduate in two and a half weeks. Get married in three. She could do it. Piece of cake.

Wedding cake.

Was Fanuzzi doing the cake? Or should she order one from a grocery store? No, Gen would take care of that. Gen. Oh, Lord.

Miranda slid down in her seat. IIT classes at the Agency had always been a snorefest, though she'd absorbed the material pretty well. Since she hadn't slept too well last night, she was hoping to cruise this morning, until their intrepid instructor, Detective Judd—a large man with a dour face and a low, monotone drone—strolled over and put a paper in her hand.

She sat up. "What's this?"

"A list of topics you'll be tested on for the final exam. Eighty percent is required to pass."

Eighty percent? She felt a little sick.

Beside her, her buddy Curt Holloway put a hand over his mouth and whispered, "This test is going to be a bear."

"Yeah. A twelve-foot grizzly." She surveyed the other students.

The Parker Agency training room had the same classy blue-and-silver motif as the rest of the floor. It included several rows of long tables and padded chairs, most of which were empty. Of the twenty IITs who had started together ten weeks ago, twelve had dropped out of the rigorous training or taken other jobs, leaving eight.

Of those still in the classroom, only a handful would remain at the Parker Agency. One of the current survivors was flame-haired Janelle Wesson who used to hang with Cindy Smith—Smith and Wesson—a standard joke among the class. Neither of them liked Miranda, but after Smith left, all that ire seemed to have siphoned into Wesson.

"Becker's going to have a hard time catching up when he gets back from his honeymoon," Holloway hissed.

"We'll study together. You'll both do fine," Miranda hoped, scanning the list.

Record Searches, Interrogation Methods, Fingerprint Methodology. She should do okay with those. Surveillance, Firearm Safety, Evidence Handling. What was this on the bottom? Gun Range Competition? The class had been to the shooting range several times. She could handle a firearm, and everyone had been required to get concealed weapons permits, but a firearm wasn't her defense of choice. And she'd barely squeaked through getting her permit, with Parker's help.

She looked at the last line on the page. Martial Arts Competition. Now that was her thing.

"Questions, Ms. Steele?"

She ran her gaze up the length of Detective Judd's tall, intimidating body, which was topped by a head of thick, wavy gray hair and a long, bulbous nose. Then she tapped the page. "How much does the Martial Arts Competition count?"

"I was just getting to that." Judd put his knobby hands behind his back and paced toward the front of the classroom. "Currently there are four Level One Investigator positions open at the Parker Agency. They will go to the four students who make both eighty percent on the written exam and place first or second in either the Gun Range or the Martial Arts Competition."

It was a little hard to breathe in here. "What happens if you don't make it?"

"Your record will be reviewed, and you may be offered a clerical position."

"Doing searches and background checks?"

"Correct."

The part of the job she despised. Talk about pressure.

She thought she knew the material pretty well, but eighty percent?

Her whole life, she'd never wanted to be anything in particular. She'd had no ambitions when she married Leon. After he threw her out, she'd taken construction jobs to get fit, to prove she could be as strong as a man—with a little brainpower thrown in for leverage. But since her last case at the Agency, she'd known she wanted to be an investigator with every fiber of her being.

What if she didn't make it?

CHAPTER NINETEEN

Alone in his office, Parker studied his computer screen, his jaw tight.

Miranda's aunt had checked out to be, like Hilda Steele, healthy as a horse. That left him only one option.

There were several hundred Edward Steele's across the United States, with residences ranging from Alabama to Wyoming. Amy might turn twenty-one before he found Miranda's father. And yet, he had to try. He'd start with elimination by age.

There was a knock on his door. "Come in," he said, without looking up.

"You left a message you wanted to see me?"

"Yes, I did." Parker gestured to a chair and came around his desk to perch on the edge of it, while Gen seated herself.

Stroking his chin, he studied her dark eyes, her short, platinum hair, which he wished she would let grow back to its natural color. Her suit was military-like, a dark blue cashmere. She wore no jewelry except for the tiny diamond earrings her mother had given her before she passed away.

He was proud of his daughter. He appreciated her professional efficiency. But he knew that inside she could be as vulnerable as a child. Especially when it came to certain topics. He wouldn't hurt her for the world, so he'd have to tread gently. If that were possible.

"Did you want to go over the status of the IITs?"

"Later. I have something personal I want to discuss first."

"Oh?"

He caught the note of caution in her response. "You know that Ms. Steele and I have been seeing each other for some time."

She straightened her skirt with a stiff movement of her hand. "Yes, I know that, Dad."

"And you know that we've been getting rather close."

"Yes. Are you trying to make a point? I've been nicer to her lately."

There was no easy way to do this. "Genevieve, we're getting married."

She stared at him for a moment, then gave a little gasp. With a shudder, she rose and went to the window. For a long moment, she stood in silence, staring out at the downtown Buckhead buildings. Then she put a hand to her mouth and whispered, "No."

He was afraid of that. "She saved my life twice, Gen," he said quietly.

"Judd saved your life once, too. And you wouldn't have been in either of those situations if she hadn't gotten you involved."

Wrong. But Gen didn't know all the tight spots he'd been in. "Nonetheless, I'd like your blessing."

She spun around, her black eyes flashing. "Blessing? Do you understand how awkward this is for me, Daddy?"

"What's awkward about it?"

She lifted her hands. "So now she'll be my stepmother *and* my employee?"

Parker exhaled in sympathy. "Stepmother" was not a term that fit Miranda at all. For Gen, the idea must be exquisitely humiliating. But he had hoped they'd find a way to become friends of some sort. "It won't be as difficult as you think."

She snorted. "Want to make a bet?"

"Gen, I love her."

"Oh, Daddy." She moved back to the chair and put her head at her hands.

Not tears. He didn't want this news to make her cry.

"I just—I wish Mama were still alive." Her voice trembled.

He moved to where she sat, touched her shoulder gently. "I know you do, Gen. I've wanted that too. For three long years. But it's time to move on. For both of us."

She sat quietly for a moment, her shoulders heaving with controlled, silent sobs. She lifted her head, wiped her hands under her eyes, and stared off into the distance as if she were coming to grips with the news.

"What does Antonio have to say about this?"

"I haven't told him yet, but I'm sure he'll be pleased." He was confident of that, but Gen and Antonio were close. She'd probably be on the phone to her adopted brother as soon as she left his office.

Finally, she composed herself with a quick breath. "All right. If you're sure this will really make you happy, I'll learn to put up with it somehow. I must really love you, Dad."

He gave her a sad smile. "I'm glad you do. Because I need your help."

She cocked her head with an apprehensive glare. "With what?"

Again, no easy way to say it. "Planning the wedding."

Her mouth opened. "You're kidding."

"I've never been more serious."

She waved her hands in the air the way she used to when she was a teenager. "There must be a dozen wedding planners in the phone book. I'm sure you know several personally."

He caught her implication and ignored it. "But I want you. And so does Miranda."

Gen rolled her eyes. "Yeah, I'll just bet she begged you to ask me."

He returned to lean against his desk and folded his arms. "As a matter of fact, no. But she's willing to work with you. Perhaps she's simply more mature about the matter."

"Oh, don't you play those psychological tricks on me, Daddy."

He suppressed a chuckle. "I'm sure I don't know what you mean, Gen."

"Stop it. Those games won't work on me." She set her jaw and glared at him. Then, as if reminding herself that any protest was futile, she nodded stiffly. "But since you're the most stubborn man I know, you won't let it drop until I say yes. So I'll save us both the trouble."

"You'll agree to do it?"

"Like I said, I must really love you."

Grinning, he walked over and gave her a peck on the cheek. "As much as I love you and your sweet, gentle spirit."

"Flattery will get you nowhere."

Now he did laugh. "Very well then. And you'll try to get along with Miranda?"

"All right. I'll try." But her teeth were gritted.

"That's a start. So to begin, Miranda wants a big, lavish affair."

Gen smirked. "Of course she does. Now that she's landed one of the richest men in the Southeast."

Parker scowled. "She's wanted a big wedding since she was a little girl. And what did you just promise me?"

"I have my opinion, Dad."

And he wouldn't abide it. "I assure you," he said firmly. "Miranda Steele is no gold digger. If you treat her like one or with any kind of contempt, this won't go well. And I won't be happy."

"Okay, I'll be sweet." She forced a smile.

He decided to accept that for now. "I'd like you to come join us tonight around eight to get started."

Gen's lip curled as she groaned out loud. "Do you mean at Grandpapa's house?"

"You know I'm staying there with Miranda. And I'd appreciate it if you curtail the attitude."

Gen shuddered and looked for a moment like she would pout, then she stiffened her shoulders. "All right, Daddy. Once again, only because I love you."

"That's better."

She grabbed a notepad off the shelf, sat down again and crossed her legs. "So. When do you want this big, lavish soiree to take place?"

Miranda sat at the desk in her cube, buried in information. After lunch, Judd told the class to study for the rest of the day and she'd done just that.

She'd dug out every handout, every book, every bit of the sparse notes she'd taken in class. She'd read through the information, copied it neatly into a notebook, clicked through all the online references and saved them.

She was so deep into Forensics and Evidence Collection, when the phone rang her butt flew three inches off the chair.

Jeez. Her heart pounding, she glanced at the time on her computer. Four o'clock already? She picked up the receiver. "Parker Agency. Steele speaking."

"Good afternoon, Ms. Steele. This is Sergeant Demarco, District Eighteen, Chicago."

Demarco? Why was he calling? "Hi."

"I couldn't get through to Mr. Parker, so I asked to speak to you."

Now what would make Parker hold his calls? Uh oh, he must be talking to Gen. Funny, the ground wasn't quaking. "What can I do for you, Sergeant?"

"Courtesy call on the Fleming case." Miranda shuddered at the memory of Coco's poor roommate when they dug her out of that wall. "Jeffries submitted to blood and DNA testing."

"Okay." She felt the muscles in her shoulders tense. Did Jeffries think he'd get a lighter sentence if he cooperated? She hoped not.

"His lawyer is pushing for test results, so we ran a prelim against skin cells we found under Glenda North's fingernails and the semen found in her stomach."

At the visual those words evoked, Miranda's gut clenched. "Yeah, and?"

She heard Demarco exhale, as if he didn't want to answer. "So far, it doesn't indicate a match."

It took her a minute for the words sink in. "Excuse me? Did you say the DNA wasn't a match?"

"Not yet."

"So what does that mean?"

"Don't know. We're still processing the rest of the evidence. Like I said, that test is a prelim. Just passing along information, Ms. Steele. Oh, and Ms. Hinsley's things have been sent to the address Mr. Parker gave me."

"Thanks."

"I'll let you know when we have further developments."

"Appreciate it." She hung up and pressed her hands to her head, her mind racing. Jake Jeffries' DNA didn't match the semen found in the call girl's stomach? The one found dead in the bedroom of his house?

Maybe Glenda'd had another client that night. Maybe Jeffries had a partner. Or maybe...they had the wrong guy.

But she'd found the murder weapon at Jeffries' property. Unless...someone else put it there. Jeffries claimed he had a visitor that night. Someone interested in that property. Someone who made a deal with him and gave him bourbon to drink. Could Jeffries have been telling the truth?

She thought back to her conversation with Coco at the piano bar.

Dexter had gone out to Los Angeles. He'd been there for weeks. Where did she say he was working? A car wash. What was the name of it? Coco thought it was cute. *Sudsies*. That was it.

She grabbed her keyboard and banged the name into her search engine. There it was. Wilshire Boulevard. She snatched up the phone and dialed the number.

"*Sudsies*. We outshine the rest." The voice didn't sound very shiny.

"Yes. I'd like to speak to the hiring department."

"That's me. I'm the owner." His voice was as gravelly as a New York gangster's.

"Then you're the one I need to speak to, Mr.—"

"Barker. What can I do for you?"

Miranda thought fast. "Mr. Barker, my name is Ms. Smith. I'm with human resources at, uh—" she glanced at her notes on fingerprint analysis. "Fingerhut. We have an application from a Mr. Dexter Hinsley. I'm wondering if you could verify his employment."

"Who?"

"Dexter Hinsley. He claims that he worked for you recently?"

It sounded like his hand went over the receiver as he yelled to someone in the back. Then he returned to the line. "Oh, yeah. That schmuck ran out on me weeks ago."

"Really? How many weeks ago?"

"Had to be at least two. Maybe three." He cut to the chase. "Wouldn't hire him if I was you. Ain't a good worker, know what I mean?"

Her heart began to pound. "Yes, I do. Thank you very much for the information, Mr. Barker." She hung up.

She took a deep breath, trying to calm herself, and looked down at her papers. After all that training, she knew better than to jump to conclusions. The DNA results were just a prelim. They could come back positive later. Dexter's disappearance from his job could just be a coincidence. But if it wasn't...? If the DNA prelim was right...?

Feeling sick, she grabbed a notepad and headed straight for Parker's office.

CHAPTER TWENTY

Bam!

Miranda froze at the end of the aisle and peered down the hall that led to Parker's office. Gen had just slammed the door and was rushing away, puffing like a locomotive on steroids.

That meeting went well. At least the human volcano was headed in the opposite direction.

She tiptoed down to the corner office and knocked.

"It's not open for negotiation," Parker boomed from inside.

She cracked the door and peeked inside. "Gen didn't care for the idea of us getting hitched?"

Parker scowled at her from the window, then waved her inside. "I talked her into that. Barely. It was the three week timeframe that set her off."

"I see. Well if she doesn't want to do it…"

"She'll do it. She just needs time to settle."

Settle. Okay. "Well, that's not why I'm here."

"What's wrong?"

Miranda studied Parker's large corner office. Its floor-to-ceiling windows and glorious view of the city. Its pristine glass furniture. Its familiar blue-and-silver décor. It was here she got her first taste of detective work and discovered an appetite for it as insatiable as the one she had for her boss. It was here she'd walked out on him the first time.

"Demarco called," she said flatly.

"Oh?" Parker didn't move.

She closed the door. "Jeffries submitted to DNA testing."

"That's good."

"The prelim against the contents of Glenda North's stomach came back negative. The sexual contents."

He nodded grimly. "That doesn't sound conclusive."

"It isn't. The police aren't finished processing all the evidence yet."

"And?"

She stood there a minute, digging the toe of her shoe into the plush, blue carpet, letting him read her mind.

"What are you thinking, Miranda?"

"Well, do you remember what Coco said about Dexter?"

"That he gave her the divorce easily."

"Yeah. That didn't click. She also said he was working at a car wash in LA."

"Yes."

"Sudsies on Wilshire Boulevard. I checked on it."

"Oh?"

"He hasn't shown up for work in maybe two or three weeks."

Parker rarely showed anything like alarm, but she could see just a hint of it in the way he set his jaw. He moved to his computer. "We'll put a watch on Coco while she's with us."

"Judd?"

He punched buttons on his computer and studied the screen. He shook his head. "I can't spare him now. The IITs are too close to graduation. I'll put one of my regular men on it." He began to type the order into an email, Miranda assumed.

Nice to have a staff of professional bodyguards at your disposal. "We should check on Coco."

"That's a good idea. I have some things to finish up here, but I'll be home shortly. Why don't you leave now."

Good thing she drove her own car today. "I will. I'll give her a call on the way out and make sure she's okay." She hoped the girl hadn't decided to go out shopping or anything.

"Don't say anything to alarm her."

She nodded and turned to go. "I'll be discreet." Or try to be. "We'll have to say something to her before she spots the guard."

Parker considered that a moment then nodded. "We'll do that tonight. And Miranda."

"What?"

"Take your Beretta."

She grimaced. "I have pepper spray. And as you know, I'm not too shabby in the dojo." She hated carrying her weapon. It was awkward.

"Humor me this time." She knew he always carried a Glock under the seat of any car he drove.

There was no time to argue, so instead she gave him a mock salute. "Aye, aye, boss."

CHAPTER TWENTY-ONE

Everything looked normal at the Parker estate when Miranda pulled into the driveway. For a moment, she sat before the door to the three-car garage, studying the place.

Surrounded by willows and live oaks, the gorgeous ten-bedroom mansion had been in Parker's family for four generations and had been extensively remodeled by Parker's ex-playboy-slash-real-estate-mogul father, whom Miranda affectionately called Mr. P.

The exterior of the massive three-story structure had been redone in natural stone, complete with tall, Grecian columns, porticos, and a sprawling stone balustrade around the front, sturdy enough to deter a Roman army. The interior included rooms that ranged from modern to sensually exotic to something out of an English castle.

But right now what caught Miranda's attention was the lone, dark-haired figure of a girl sitting on the granite steps, almost hidden by the iron filigree railing, a black cat curling around her legs.

Wendy Van Aarle.

Familiar, tender feelings danced across her heart, and her stomach clenched at the thought of the trauma they'd been through together. Four months ago, she'd received a letter from an unknown thirteen-year-old girl and had come to Atlanta hoping to find Amy. She'd found Wendy instead.

She got out of the car and hustled up the steps. "Hello there."

"Oh, hi." The girl sounded glum.

She had her head down, and Miranda could see the highlights that her mother had put in her dark hair had faded. She had on plain sneakers that looked new, jeans with holes in the knees, whether from wear or the latest style, Miranda couldn't tell, and a black T-shirt with a boy band logo.

"What you doing here?"

The girl shrugged. "Inky ran away again. I guess he likes coming over here ever since you gave him that bowl of milk." Wendy lifted her chin.

The dark Goth makeup the girl used to wear was gone, but so was the more recent, light pink lipstick and blush. She wore no makeup at all. Her complexion was pale. And that painful scowl was back.

The last time Miranda had seen Wendy was when her cat had wandered into Parker's backyard and she'd left a bowl of milk to lure her out of hiding. Weeks ago.

"Guess so. I haven't seen you around in a while."

She rolled her eyes. "I've been traveling to Paris with my mother."

"More than once?"

"Three times." She said it like she was talking about having the flu.

"You don't like Paris? It sounds exciting to me."

Wendy made a face. "It's mostly sitting around in the hotel room while my mother goes traipsing around the city taking care of her business. Or she takes me to the lab, and I sit in her office while she goes traipsing around there."

"I thought she was teaching you her business." Iris Van Aarle was the CEO of Iris Rose cosmetics. A very busy and successful lady.

"She was. But I got kinda bored with it."

"You don't want to follow in your mother's footsteps?"

She shrugged. "I don't know. I like figure skating."

The interests of a young teen could change more often than their underwear, or so Miranda had heard. "Well, I need to get inside." Coco was waiting for her after she'd called and pretended to chitchat on the way home.

"Miranda?"

"Yeah?"

"Can I come in for a while?"

Miranda's brows shot up. "You want to come inside?"

"Something came up, and Mom couldn't pick me up from figure skating practice. I asked Brianna's mother to drop me off."

Brianna? "New friend?"

"Kind of." Wendy had trouble making friends.

"I thought I could hang out here until Mom gets home."

Miranda scratched her scalp. She didn't want Wendy to hear what was going on with Coco, but she couldn't leave the kid out here by herself, either. "Sure, but I have someone staying with me."

"I know. The blond lady."

"You saw her?"

"Yeah. When she opened the door to let in that guy. I was over there looking for Inky." She pointed toward the garage.

Miranda's heart stopped. "What guy?"

"The tall guy with the ponytail. You know. My lawyer?"

Miranda squinted across the street and spotted a red Ferrari parked along the curb. Didn't want to block the drive? A few feet behind the sports car sat a nondescript Acura, its green color so pale, it faded into the background like the chariot of a ghost. The bodyguard from the Agency. He must have arrived just before she had.

She let out a sigh of relief.

Estavez had untangled the mess Wendy had gotten herself into a few months ago. Just like he'd done for Miranda. She had that in common with the kid. No doubt Parker wouldn't care for the lawyer dropping by, but she was glad he was here to help keep an eye on Coco.

She dug her key out of her pocket. "Come on in, Wendy."

"What about Inky?"

"Bring her, too. What time's your mother getting home?" Miranda asked as she pushed open the big, fancy front door.

"She said around six."

"Then you can stay for dinner, too."

"Cool."

Miranda found Estavez with Coco in the large living room with its airy, modern leather-and-teakwood décor and big screen TV. His dark cashmere suit told her he'd come from work.

The sultry Latin lawyer shot to his feet as soon as he spotted her. "I am so sorry for my presence, Ms. Steele. I wouldn't disturb you and Señor Parker for the world."

Miranda waved a hand. "Don't worry about it. Sit down."

He remained standing while she turned to Coco, who seemed more rattled than Estavez. She had on a frilly cotton blouse and blue jeans that matched her big, wide eyes.

"How are you?" Miranda said.

Huddled in the corner of the cream-colored sofa, Coco patted her blond curls, adjusted her posture, and slid her bare feet onto the floor. "I'm fine. How should I be?"

"You should be fine." From the blush on Coco's lips, as well as her cheeks, it was obvious some kissy-face had been going on. But Miranda was just glad the lovebirds hadn't found their way to the Taj Mahal bedroom upstairs. Parker would have a cow.

The cat meowed, and Estavez managed one of his blazing white smiles for the youngest guest in the room. "It's good to see you again, Wendy. How are you getting along these days?"

Wendy rubbed her nose and shrugged. "Okay, Mr. Estavez. Thanks for helping me. I never got to tell you."

"It was my pleasure."

Wendy had been in trouble some time ago. Light-years for a kid. For her to remember to thank him now meant she'd learned something from that tragedy. At least Miranda hoped so.

She looked back at Coco, trying to gauge her mood. "Sergeant Demarco called and said he was sending your things. They should be here in a couple days."

Coco brightened. "Wonderful. I'll be so glad to have my own clothes back."

Miranda wanted to tell her about the rest of the call, to ask her exactly when was the last time she'd heard from Dexter, but Parker was right. Not a good idea to send her into hysterics for what could be no reason.

"Meow." The whiny cat struggled in Wendy's arms. Better take care of it.

"Come on, Wendy," Miranda said, crossing to the long hallway. "Let's get Inky something to eat."

She scuttled to the kitchen and got a carton of milk out of the big, stainless steel fridge. She had to dodge the two cooks who were scurrying about, busily preparing something that smelled mouthwateringly delicious.

Parker had extended the staff and their hours, including hiring a head housekeeper named Sarah. A spunky, thirty-something woman with a head of copper-colored curls and a touch of an Irish accent. Miranda found herself liking the woman, although she'd never get used to having servants.

For tonight, it was better than feeding her guests a bag of chips and salsa.

She told the cooks there would be two more for dinner and headed for the dining room, where Sarah was no doubt setting out the Parker china and laying out each piece just so.

Miranda was just showing Wendy one of the downstairs bathrooms where the kid could wash up when she heard the low rumble of men's voices down the hall. Parker was home and he'd found Estavez and Coco.

This should be interesting.

Dinner turned out to be beef bourguignon. Miranda thought it was just fancy pot roast until she tasted the applewood smoked bacon, the organic veggies, the prime cuts of meat, and the expensive Cognac.

Still, the meal was an awkward affair in the muted blue dining room with its Cupid-lined ceiling and statuary of exotic lovebirds. A design spawned by Mr. P's libido when he used to use the house as his own personal love nest. Parker's mother had died when he was a boy, and Mr. P had played the field like a champion until he'd met a red-haired beauty from Ukraine a few months ago. They were married in a small, quiet ceremony two weeks before Fanuzzi and Becker.

Weddings must be contagious right now.

Parker put on a good front, but Miranda could see he was uncomfortable with Estavez sitting there next to Coco, giving her dark, secretive looks during the meal. And with Wendy present, he couldn't talk about Demarco's news or the bodyguard sitting outside in the street. But they'd have to tell Coco some time. Preferably before she noticed the guard.

She was the hostess, so Miranda guessed she ought to be making conversation. She thought of Estavez' sports car. "That's a hot little number you have parked outside."

Coco frowned. "What are you talking about, Miranda?"

Estavez dabbed his lips with his linen napkin. "She means my new Ferrari."

"Oh. It is very nice."

Miranda bet he'd taken her for a ride in it this afternoon. "I was drooling over it. She's got to be a cruiser."

He sat back with a sly grin. "Oh, just five hundred sixty-two horsepower. Three ninety-eight torque. Zero to sixty in under four seconds."

Now who said lawyers weren't modest? "Sweet."

Parker studied her with a funny look as he swirled his wine around in his elegant glass. "I neglected to mention something to you earlier, Miranda."

"Oh?"

He gave her a self-satisfied look. "Gen will be here at eight to start planning."

She put down her fork. Must've eaten too much of the rich roast beef.

Coco looked at Miranda wide-eyed. "What are you planning?"

Parker broke a smile. "May I tell them?"

Miranda took a slug of Merlot. "Sure." No use hiding. No reason to be so polite about it.

"Miranda and I are getting married."

Coco squealed and started bouncing up and down in her seat. "Oh, Miranda, congratulations. You must be so excited."

That wasn't exactly the word for what she felt. "Thanks."

Estavez raised his glass in a toast. "I wish you every happiness, Señor Parker and Ms. Steele." He sure was being gallant. Maybe she should get him to talk to his surrogate sister.

Miranda clinked her glass against his and took another swallow of wine, wondering if she could down the whole bottle before Gen arrived. "Just don't say anything about it being a match made in Heaven or anything like that."

Estavez chuckled. "Ms. Steele, you have moved my romantic soul."

Parker gave her a steady gaze. "Exactly, Antonio. Miranda is such a romantic."

Coco's big blue eyes glistened. "Have you set a date yet?"

"First weekend in August."

"That's so soon."

"Three weeks." Miranda stared at the amber liquid in her glass. She was going through with this, if it killed her.

Okay. To have a big wedding, you need bridesmaids. To have bridesmaids, you need girlfriends. Fanuzzi was the only woman she'd been close to for a long time. If you could call that close. Coco was a distant second. Good enough, she decided.

"Hey, Coco. Wanna be a bridesmaid?"

Coco gasped and waved her delicate hands in the air, her nails sparkling with pink glitter as she pressed them against her chest. "Really? Are you serious?"

"Of course, I'm serious. I don't joke about my wedding." Only about me getting married.

"I'd just love to, Miranda. Thank you for asking."

Parker cracked a wry grin and reached for her hand. "You beat me to it, darling." With his other hand, he raised his glass. "I would like you to be my best man, Antonio."

Estavez returned a solemn nod. "I am honored, Papa." There was that rare term of endearment again.

Since they seemed to be on a roll, she turned to Wendy. "Maybe you could be a flower girl."

Wendy wrinkled her nose and poked at a piece of boiled potato on her plate. "I'm too old for that."

"She could be a junior bridesmaid," Coco offered.

They had junior bridesmaids? "Sure. How about that?"

"Seriously?" Wendy's grimace went to fifty percent. Progress.

"Yeah. Of course, seriously."

The girl lifted a shoulder without looking up, making a figure eight with her fork in the rich gravy. "I'll ask my mother."

Just then the doorbell rang. A moment later, the head housekeeper appeared in the arched doorway. "Mrs. Van Aarle is here, sir," she said to Parker. "I seated her in the foyer."

"Guess that's my cue." Miranda wiped her mouth on her napkin laid it on the table as she rose. "Be right there, Sarah." She turned to Wendy and pointed to her plate. "Finish that or you can't go home." Couldn't have Iris complaining that she didn't feed her daughter.

The girl pursed her lips in a suppressed smile, then opened her mouth and popped the potato into it.

CHAPTER TWENTY-TWO

Miranda stepped across the marble tile floor of the grand hall that served as the Parker mansion's foyer and found her guest perched on the fancy fauteuil chair next to the fancy rosewood credenza, admiring its fancy gold inlay.

She hadn't seen the woman since she'd picked Wendy up from a therapy session several weeks ago. And that was only the back of her head inside a car.

Iris Van Aarle had a short, angular body befitting the ambitious, self-made woman she was. Always fashionable, tonight she was dressed in cream-colored slacks and matching sweater. Light from the chandelier overhead gave her gold earrings and chains an iridescent glow. Her hair was longer than Miranda remembered it. Dark, with tasteful blond highlights. As always, her makeup was exquisite. But what did you expect from the CEO of a cosmetics company?

Iris stood and extended a hand as Miranda approached. "Thanks for taking care of Wendy," she said in her sophisticated voice. "I'm so sorry to impose on you, but I've had such a hectic schedule lately."

"Sure. Anytime." Miranda shook her hand, wondering if that was a touch of phoniness in her tone.

Iris smiled awkwardly. "Any time? Really?"

Knew it. "What do you mean?"

She rubbed the arms of her cashmere top. "Well, Wendy's gotten into this ice-skating kick."

"*Figure* skating, Mother." Wendy shuffled in from the adjoining hallway.

Miranda eyed the girl as she moved to her mother's side, resisting the urge to go back and check if she'd cleaned her plate.

"Very well. Figure skating. Anyway, I'm working on a new campaign, and business has been picking up lately. It's really going to be difficult for me to fetch Wendy every day."

"She goes every day?"

"Well, yes, since it's summer and there's no school."

Wendy had been kicked out of the exclusive academy she'd once attended when she got into trouble. Miranda didn't know if any school would be ready to take her in the fall.

"So, I was wondering..." Iris patted her hair with her hand, making both her rings and her French manicure sparkle. "Could you help me out, Miranda?"

My, aren't we chummy? Miranda ran her tongue over her teeth and studied the woman, not knowing what to say.

It wasn't just that she had a wedding to plan, a graduation coming up, and a possible stalker in the area. It was also that not so long ago, she'd hated Iris Van Aarle for neglecting her daughter while she was cheating on her pro golfer husband with her web designer.

Of course, Shelby Van Aarle had been cheating on Iris with a neighbor at the same time. Her parents' shenanigans had been part of what had sent Wendy over the edge.

"How's Shelby these days?" Miranda asked, as if she were just making small talk. She was getting almost as good as Parker at casually pumping folks for information.

Iris waved a hand in the air. "Oh, he's fine. Right now, he's getting ready for the Open Championship in Lancashire."

Miranda did a mental geography check. "England?"

"Mm-hmm." Iris seemed distracted for a moment. "So what do you think? Mondays through Fridays, Wendy needs a place to stay until I get here around eight. It'll only be for a month or so. Until I get things under control. Or she loses interest."

Beside her mother, Wendy scowled and traced the design in the marble floor with the toe of her sneaker. But the glance she stole at Miranda revealed a glint of hope in her dark eyes.

Miranda melted. "Sure. She can stay here. I'll give her a key so she can let herself in if I'm late. There's usually staff here." And there'd be Coco, probably Estavez, and a bodyguard out front, as well. The kid should be safe.

"That would be wonderful. Thank you so much." Iris looked like she might hug her. Instead, she shook Miranda's hand again with several vigorous pumps.

"No problem."

Iris stroked her daughter's hair, eliciting a grimace from the girl. "Well, I guess we'd better be getting home. Early day tomorrow."

"Sure."

Miranda walked them over to the door and opened it for them. "See you tomorrow, Wendy. I'll have that key ready for you."

"Okay," she muttered, her head still down.

As mother and daughter stepped outside, Miranda thought she saw Wendy break out a surreptitious smile.

Miranda strolled back to the dining room and found it empty except for Sarah, who was clearing away the dishes.

The woman gave her a motherly smile. "Mr. Parker is in the sitting room with your guests, ma'am. He'd like you to join them."

"Thanks." Now which way was the sitting room?

Sarah's green eyes twinkled. "Near the library, ma'am."

"Thanks, again."

Miranda pivoted and went back the way she'd come. She wended her way across the majestic foyer, through an archway, then down a long, brightly lit hall lined with fanciful paintings and long glass tables topped with odd-shaped lamps and delicate statuary that looked like they might break if you breathed too hard.

She'd never get used to living in this place, any more than she'd get used to having servants. She'd only come here to save Parker's heritage. If it didn't last between them, at least he'd still have it.

Nearing the end of the hall, she knew she was getting warmer when she heard piano music floating through the air, along with Coco's distinctive voice. At an open door of walnut that bore a trefoil design, she turned and stepped inside.

The two lovebirds were at an ebony baby grand, picking out a tune, while Parker had settled in on the sofa with an after-dinner coffee.

The high-ceilinged sitting room was done in blues and greens and tans. Painted ivy ran along the borders of the walls, giving the illusion of a garden. Heavy brocade curtains hung from the windows, antique-looking mahogany furniture was scattered about, and tall potted ferns stood in the corners.

Now she remembered the room. She and Parker had served coffee to the Taggarts in here when they came to visit. Most of the chairs weren't too comfortable, but the sofa could be cushy if you arranged the satin pillows just right.

Parker rose as she entered. "I'm glad you're here, Miranda. Is Wendy all right?"

"She's fine. She left with her mother. Uh, she needs a place to stay after figure skating practice during the week. Iris can't pick her up until eight. I said she could come here. Is that okay?"

"Certainly. She's always welcome here." Parker had a fondness for the child, too. But she could see concern in the lines of his solemn gray eyes. Not only for Wendy's situation with her parents, but for the current circumstances.

"Oh, Miranda," Coco squealed from across the room. "Antonio's helping me write a song."

Miranda turned her attention to the couple at the piano. "Yeah?"

"He's a wonderful poet."

Smiling, Estavez looked like he was about to blush. "I've written poetry in my spare time for years. I never thought any of it would see the light of day."

"He's very talented."

"Really?" Miranda was stunned.

With a cocky nod of his head, he slipped his hands into the pockets of his suit. "Contrary to popular opinion, we lawyers do have souls."

Coco ran her hand over the polished finish of the piano. "This is a wonderful instrument. I don't think I've ever played anything so nice. Thank you for letting me practice on it, Mr. Parker."

"Not at all," Parker sat down again, while Miranda settled in beside him on the sofa. He cleared his throat and she felt his body go taut. "There's something I need to tell both of you."

Estavez tensed. "What is it?" He obviously knew Parker's serious tone.

Miranda wanted to bite her lip as Parker uttered the next words. "Sergeant Demarco from Chicago phoned the office today."

"Miranda told me he's sending my things." With a bounce in her step, Coco rose from the piano and moved to one of the uncomfortable chairs on the opposite side of the low, oval table where coffee cups were waiting. Estavez followed, choosing the teal chair with swirling mahogany arms next to her.

"Sent them out today," Miranda confirmed.

"I'm so glad."

Parker continued. "The police have run a preliminary on the DNA found at the second crime scene."

"Oh?"

"Testing it against a sample Jeffries gave. It came back negative. No match."

Estavez leaned forward. "Preliminary tests are inconclusive."

"Yes, but the test hasn't proven he did it, either."

Miranda's turn. "Just to dot our i's and cross our t's, I ran a check on Dexter."

Coco looked perplexed. "Dexter? He's in California."

"I checked on that carwash where you said he worked. He hasn't showed for work in two or three weeks."

Coco stared at her a long moment with an I-can't-believe-you-did-that look. Then she shook her curls, the lines in her pretty brow deepening. "You must be mistaken, Miranda."

"Sudsies? On Wilshire Boulevard? That's it, right?"

"Yes, but—"

"As a precaution, I've got a man stationed outside," Parker said firmly.

"What?"

"Just for the time being."

Coco shot to her feet. "What's that supposed to mean? What are you saying, Miranda?"

"I'm not saying anything. We're just pointing out the facts."

"Facts like there's a 'man' stationed outside watching me?" Coco huffed back to the piano. Instead of sitting down, she just stood there staring at it. She was pissed. Parker had been right about the hysterics.

"It's standard procedure," Parker assured her in his most soothing Southern voice.

She spun around, her blue eyes glistening with tears. "Standard procedure for what?"

"It's simply a precaution while Demarco continues his investigation."

Coco rubbed her arms. "I don't like this."

"*Mi querida.*" Estavez rose and crossed to her. He took her in his arms and drew her close to him. "There, there. It will be all right. Everything will be fine."

Mi querida? They were certainly getting friendly. Miranda stole a glance at Parker. His brows knit together in a strained scowl. He was definitely uncomfortable with this relationship going on right under his nose.

Coco wiped her eyes and took a deep breath. "All right. I'm in your debt, so I can't complain. You're both professionals. You must know what you're doing, even though I don't understand it at all."

Miranda started to relax until Coco uttered her next words. "But I'd really like to get my own place soon. I was even thinking of getting my old job back at the Gecko Club."

"We'll have to talk about that," Miranda said, trying not to grit her teeth.

There was a knock at the door and Sarah appeared in the archway. "Excuse me for interrupting, but Ms. Genevieve Parker is waiting for Ms. Steele in the drawing room."

Miranda looked up at the clock and remembered Parker said Gen was coming over to plan the wedding. It was eight. The witching hour.

Suddenly, she wanted to barf into one of the potted ferns. Instead, she forced herself up as Parker gave her hand a reassuring squeeze.

"Thanks, Sarah. I'll be there in a minute." She laughed awkwardly as she moved to the door. "Sorry to break up this lovely chat, but I have a wedding to plan."

The upshot was if Gen killed her, she wouldn't have to worry about Coco or the wedding.

CHAPTER TWENTY-THREE

The drawing room wasn't all that different from the sitting room. Yet another spot in the house that looked like it had been imported from Versailles.

This one done in creams and rose, everything was bordered with expensive, intricately carved wood and gold inlay. Chandelier overhead. A massive, ivory fireplace, its mantelpiece filled with bric-a-brac and a Chinese vase with rosebuds from the garden. In the middle of a sitting arrangement sat an oval coffee table with a pearl top that Miranda was afraid she'd break if she touched.

She found Gen waiting for her in the corner, sitting in the curvy bergère chair that was upholstered in a ruby pattern. With her almost white blond hair, her severe black pantsuit, and her tense posture, she reminded Miranda of one of those white tigers in Las Vegas. Eyes alert, body ready to pounce, claws ready to tear her apart. Stunning in a photo, but close-up? Deadly.

How about the breezy approach? "Hi, Gen," Miranda sang out as she entered the room. "So glad you could make it over." Might as well make the best of it.

"I'm sure you are." Wasting no time, she looked like she was about to snarl as she reached for the briefcase on the floor beside her. "As I'm sure you know, my father wants me to plan your wedding." She said the word *wedding* like she was talking about the plague.

"Yeah, I do." Nothing like having a planner who loved her work. This should go well. She took a seat opposite the woman on the pink silk settee. No need to get too close.

Gen closed her eyes and huffed. "Why on earth did you pick the first week in August?"

"What's wrong with it?"

"It's not enough time for a big wedding." Through those clenched teeth, Gen sounded a little like Edward G. Robinson. Her shoulders rose in a stiff inhale, as if she were reminding herself to behave. "I don't suppose I can persuade you to move it forward?"

"No."

Her dark eyes narrowed, and Miranda thought she could feel the laser piercing her forehead. She'd have to remember to check later for holes.

Gen sighed and snapped her briefcase open. She took out a notepad and pen, closed the case again and set it on the floor. "Okay. Let's get started. We'll have to work fast. And I mean really fast."

No screaming and shrieking in protest? No threats of firing? Parker had really done a number on his daughter this time. She wondered if Gen had talked to Estavez about the wedding. The two were close. But Gen wasn't about to offer a romantic toast like her surrogate brother had.

Miranda lifted her hands. "Fine with me."

"Let's start with the location."

Miranda frowned. "Location?"

"Where do you want the ceremony to be held?"

"Oh. Hmm. What's the biggest church in the area?"

"Saint Simon's Episcopal."

She'd been to St. Simon's during her last case for a funeral. But she didn't think that would bother Parker. He hadn't attended it. Well, he'd followed her there, but he'd stayed outside. "Sounds good."

"One decision down." Gen made a note on her pad. "Next, invitations. Where is your guest list?"

"Guest list?"

She slapped her hand on the pad. "You haven't started a guest list yet?"

Miranda shrugged.

Gen put her pen down, raised her hands to her face and groaned. "I don't know how you expect me to pull this off." Showing an amazing amount self control, she inhaled again through her nose, smoothed her hair, and straightened her shoulders. "Okay. We'll compile one. Whom do you want to invite?"

That was easy. "All of your father's friends and family. Maybe your grandfather can help with names?" Mr. P had come up with a guest list for the party she'd thrown in the mansion a few months ago. Though that was when she was trying to trap a murder suspect.

Gen scribbled something on her pad. Probably the word *bitch*. "What about your family?"

"Don't have any."

Gen looked up at Miranda, her eyes suddenly softening with what looked like sympathy. She shook it off. "What about friends?"

"Uh..." She was light in that department, too. The members of the road crew she used to work on probably wouldn't feel too comfortable at the high-class affair. "Some from the office, I guess. Becker and Holloway. Becker's wife is doing the food."

Gen had that funny, sympathy-like look again. No, honey, Miranda thought. I don't have a lot of friends, either. Maybe she had that in common with Parker's shrew-daughter. What'd you know?

105

Gen made another note. "I'll talk to my father about guests. What are you going to do about bridesmaids?"

That she had covered. "I've got two." Coco and Wendy. If Iris said yes.

"*Two?*" Gen rolled her eyes as if she were talking to an idiot. "A big wedding can have up to twenty bridesmaids. Who else do you have? And who is going to be your MOH?"

"MOH?"

"Maid or Matron of Honor?" Gen spoke the words slowly, as if she were talking to a five-year-old.

Sheez. Didn't she just indicate she was short on family and friends? There was Fanuzzi. She was the closest to a female best friend she had. But Fanuzzi was doing the food. She'd have to dig some more women up from somewhere. "I have to get back to you on that."

"You'll have to do it fast. We need to pick out the dresses and start the fittings right away."

"Okay." Dresses. Miranda scratched at her waist, that itchy feeling coming over her.

"Next. What sort of theme do you want?"

Miranda wrinkled her nose. "Weddings have themes?"

"Of course, they do. Spring, Fall, Fleur-de-Lis, Moroccan. Something that expresses the couple's, uh, tastes." Her tone said she didn't think Miranda had any taste.

Miranda sat back, scratched at her unruly hair. Tastes she and Parker had in common? She thought of the upcoming competition at the Agency and the intimate sparring match they'd had alone in the gym one night. "Martial Arts?"

Gen began to shudder, her dark eyes narrowed to ominous slits. She slapped her pad and pen down on the coffee table. "Look, Steele. I don't know how you've pulled the wool over my father's eyes, but you can't fool me. You haven't been dreaming of a big wedding since you were a little girl. If you had, you'd have all kinds of ideas. What are you really after? His money?"

Temper flashed through Miranda so fast, she had to hang onto the arm of the settee to keep herself from jumping up and socking the woman in the jaw. Wait. Parker told Gen that she'd been dreaming of a big wedding since she was a little girl? Maybe she should go practice her martial arts moves on him.

Instead, she rose and, hugging herself tightly, paced to the ivory fireplace. "You're a smart woman, Gen. You're right. I haven't been dreaming of a big wedding all my life. In fact, I hate big parties. But your father loves them, so I'm doing this for him."

Gen's face went from rage to shock to alarm. "Do you really expect me to believe that, Steele?" she scoffed.

Miranda lifted a shoulder. "Believe what you want. I'm telling you the truth."

"Why would you put yourself through all this if you hate big parties?"

"Because I love your father." She gave it a minute to let that settle. "And if you love him, too, you'll keep this between us and help me pull this wedding together."

Miranda had never seen an expression of confused stupor quite like the one spreading over Gen's face. She didn't blink. She didn't breathe. She didn't close her open mouth. Probably couldn't. But before the woman could recover enough to answer, there was a knock on the door.

"Am I disturbing anything confidential?" Parker stepped inside with an even more self-assured swagger than usual. He moved to Miranda's side and kissed her cheek.

Gen slapped a smile on her face and brushed at her lap. "Actually, you are, Dad. We were just getting to the wedding gown."

"On the contrary, Gen. I'm just in time."

"What?" With a laugh, she forced a cheery tone into her voice. "Your bride can't stroll down the aisle of Saint Simon's naked, can she? Or do you want to do a Lady Gaga thing, Miranda?"

Sensing the tension in the room, Parker turned on his characteristic charm. "Of course not, Gen."

"Well, then. Vamoose, Dad. We girls need to discuss this alone."

Miranda nodded to Parker. "He likes picking out my clothes." And she liked clothes shopping as much as she liked big parties. Though she'd have to make an exception this time, she guessed.

Gen snorted. "The groom can't pick out the wedding gown. You know it's bad luck for him to see it."

Parker held up the papers in his hand. "That's why I've selected four to choose from off Elegant Ensembles' website." He handed the papers to Miranda.

Elegant Ensembles. One of the ritziest dress shops along Peachtree Road. That was where Parker had bought her first dress. She'd paid him back out of her salary—at her insistence. Actually, she still had a few payments to go.

Miranda paged through the full-color pictures he'd printed. White satin with a contrasting fleur-de-lis accents at the pleats and bodice. A lacy, strapless creation with strands of silk roses down the back. Ruffles intermingled with floral mesh and a long, long veil. Draped silk over a bodice of embroidered lilies.

None of the frilly, girly-girl things he used to tease her with to get her to come around to his choice. Every dress was simply...breathtaking. "Wow."

"I've also spoken to Reverend Quigley at Saint Simon's. Our date is confirmed."

Miranda stared at him. "Saint Simon's?" How did he know?

He raised an elegant dark brow. "Were you thinking of somewhere else?"

It wasn't that hard of a guess. Big wedding. Biggest church in the area. And Parker's telepathic powers were pretty impressive. But just now, she couldn't resist rubbing it in a little. "Why darling," she sang in a syrupy voice. "You read my mind."

She had to grin at Gen's controlled grimace.

Looking amused, Parker strolled over to his speechless daughter and gave her a tender kiss on her forehead that spoke volumes about his affection for her. He handed her a pen drive. "I've written the announcement and chosen a photo of us for the paper."

Miranda gulped. "Photo? What photo?"

"One that we had taken when we were in the North Georgia mountains. It's very flattering. Would you like to see it?" He moved back to her side and showed her his phone.

She looked at the screen. The photo was flattering. Standing next to Parker, she stood on the veranda of the antebellum bed and breakfast where they'd stayed. The waiter who'd taken the shot had captured her wearing a mysterious, provocative smile, with her hair windswept and looking natural against the backdrop of green forest. And of course Parker had emanated his rugged-yet-sophisticated Southern charm.

"That'll do," she breathed, wondering where that sigh had come from.

He grinned at her with a sly, knowing wink and turned back to Gen. "Sweetheart, can you call Kevin Martin at the AJC and make sure that gets in tomorrow's paper?"

Gen looked like she was about to faint. "Sure, Dad. I'll get right on it."

Miranda leaned her head against Parker's shoulder, feeling smug. "I think I just decided on my theme, Gen."

"What?"

She wanted to say "Victory." She eyed the rosebuds on the mantle that were closing for the night, and thought of the fleur-de-lis and lilies and roses on those gorgeous gowns. And the way Parker made her chest ache every time he entered a room.

Instead, she tilted her chin sweetly and smiled. "Hearts and flowers." Corny, but she kinda liked it.

"Okay, then." With a nice sheen of humiliation on her face, Gen made a final note, packed her notepad back into her briefcase, and shut it with two sharp snaps. "I think I have enough to get started." She got to her feet, smoothed her slacks.

"Don't forget the announcement," Parker reminded her.

"No, Dad. I won't forget. I'll be in touch, Miranda." She turned and hustled out the door.

"Have a good night." With the glee of triumph, Miranda slipped her arms around Parker's neck and drew him close. "And that's why they call you the Silver Fox."

"Precisely." His warm laugh caressed her neck as he nuzzled her ear.

CHAPTER TWENTY-FOUR

He woke up horny.

His head groggy, he reached across the bed for Cora Beth.

Gone.

Rolling over, he groaned aloud in frustration. Even her scent wasn't on the sheets any more. He must've dreamed he'd smelled her. Touched her.

She liked to service him in the morning. Or pretended she did. If only she were here, where she belonged. Why did she leave him? Was everything they'd had together a farce? A joke? She must have thought so, the stupid little whore.

He ran his hands over his face, pulling himself up, and sat on the side of the bed until his head cleared. He had planning to do. But first, his ritual. He rose and plodded into the living room.

He stood there a moment, staring at the plain furniture, remembering the keyboard that used to stand in the corner. He'd sold it after he'd found out she'd been working at a club behind his back. Letting other men ogle her, drool over her. How could she? She deserved a good beating for that, and he'd given her one. Daddy always said the man had to show a woman who was boss.

He would have done more, if it hadn't been for Parker and Steele.

His teeth clenched at the thought of those two. He'd take care of them. He'd get Cora Beth back and take care of them for good. He just had to figure out how. And to prepare himself.

He moved to the middle of the floor and began his daily *kata*. Stretches first, pushups on his fists with one leg raised. Then straight punches. Step, step, punch. Step, double arm block. Quarter turn, hammer fist. Horse stance.

He uttered his guttural *kiai* as his blood pounded in his veins. Step, kick, step, stamping kick. Thrust, thrust. *Your body is a weapon.*

He was winded when he stopped but not like when he first started. He was growing stronger every day. He would need that strength to face Parker.

He shuffled to the bathroom and stepped into the shower. The exercise and the hot water did little to quench his arousal. God, he needed a fuck.

Soaping his chest, he thought of that hooker in Chicago. How she'd sucked him. How she'd struggled against his hands and couldn't get away—until she'd clawed him, the bitch. Those thoughts only gave him another erection. He had to focus.

He stepped out of the shower and dried off. The towel had a moldy smell. He gave his teeth a quick brush and tossed the toothbrush in the cup on the counter.

He got dressed and strolled to the kitchen for coffee. He grabbed a jar of instant and a spoon from the drawer that didn't look completely clean. He rubbed the bowl with his shirttail and jammed it into the brown crystals. Cora Beth always had hot coffee waiting for him in the morning.

He liked to catch her from behind, make her kneel on the linoleum, and love him with her sweet mouth. Soon, he'd feel her lips on him again.

On the counter was the loaf of bread he'd bought at a convenience store last night. He took some slices of out of the wrapper, popped them into the toaster and waited.

He had always been lucky. Lucky and charming. Most of the time, his charm brought him luck, especially with women.

That luck was playing into his hands now. He'd arrived in Atlanta two days ago and had come straight here to his old house.

He couldn't get in with his old key and had to call the real estate agent. Had to wait an hour for her to show up, his mind racing, his nerves driving him crazy.

He told her he was his brother, showed her the ID he'd had copied from Derek's. The photo matched his new darker, straighter hair and the altered nose done with latex and a bit of spirit gum and face paint borrowed from a makeup artist on one of Derek's sets. The agent bought it and gave him a key to the lockbox on the door.

The place was a mess. That stupid bimbo hadn't even kept up the yard, but at least he'd had a place to sleep. All he had to do now was find where Wade Parker was and he'd find Cora Beth.

The next morning, he got out the phone book and searched until he found the Parker Agency on Piedmont Road. He drove to downtown Buckhead in his rental car and found the fifteen-story Imperial Building. Then he'd waited. In the afternoon, he spotted Miranda Steele going to her ridiculous old Lumina. Why she drove that clunker when she was humping a rich bastard like Parker, he couldn't guess. Who knew the mind of a woman? As if they had minds.

He followed her out to the residential area called Mockingbird Hills, down Sweet Hollow Lane to Lakewood Chase. He would have nabbed her when she got out of the car, but he'd spotted the man in the Acura. Was that a guard? Had to be. Why else would he be just sitting there?

Hoping he hadn't been spotted, he'd pretended to be lost and hauled ass out of there.

Why was there a guard outside the Parker mansion? Parker couldn't know he'd come to Atlanta. He'd been too careful. No, he couldn't know. Maybe it was routine? Or a paranoid precaution. Or maybe they didn't know, but they suspected. Getting Cora Beth back wouldn't be as easy as he'd thought.

But he'd do it.

He'd have to come up with something else. He needed a plan. A good one.

The toast popped up. He pulled out the slices, laid them on a napkin, and took them to the kitchen table with his coffee.

He'd follow Steele around for a while and watch her habits. He needed to find a vulnerability. Maybe use a distraction of some sort. He'd pick his moment, make his move. Once he'd taken care of her, he'd go for Parker. Maybe negotiate a trade for Cora Beth—after he'd killed Steele.

Once he had Cora Beth back, he'd have to leave town. Go to Mexico, maybe. Or Brazil. For that, he'd need money. That agent had better get an offer on this house pronto. There probably wouldn't be time to close, but he might get a down payment.

He reached for the real estate agent's business card on the counter. Pretty and perky with red hair, a red suit, and a big, red lipstick grin. Fucking female agent. It was a man's job. A woman couldn't think like a businessman.

He ran his thumb over the photo. He'd love to fuck her. He'd love to see her red blood running over his hands. Too risky.

There was a single knock at the door and he jumped. Who the hell was that? He got up, hurried to the front door, yanked it open.

Nothing. He looked down and saw a copy of the *AJC* on the pretty welcome mat Cora Beth had bought when they first moved in here.

He'd never ordered the *AJC*, but the stupid delivery boy had always thrown the neighbor's copy over here, littering the yard. There had been a pile cluttering the porch when he'd gotten here.

With a grunt, he grabbed the paper off the mat and took it inside. He sat down at the kitchen table again to finish his meager breakfast.

Biting into his toast, he opened the paper and riffled through it. Local news, sports. Nothing interesting. Wait. What was this?

In the social section was a picture of Steele and Parker. His lip curled in a sneer. What a handsome couple they made. Steele looked better than usual, but that haughty air turned his stomach. Parker was just as cocky. That bastard.

"Atlanta's Most Eligible Bachelor Finally Ties the Knot."

The wedding date was the first weekend in August. He sat back, sipped his crappy coffee and smiled to himself.

Well, well, well. Someone ought to be "congratulated." And he was just the one to do it.

His mind began to whir with ideas. Lots of vulnerabilities when you're planning a wedding. Easy to get distracted, to let your defenses down, no matter what you suspect.

He laughed out loud. He *was* lucky. Parker and Steele's wedding would fit into his plan perfectly.

CHAPTER TWENTY-FIVE

Pop pop. Pop pop pop pop pop.

The IITs from the Parker Agency were getting to be regulars at the Aim-Right Shooting Range off Johnson Road, a few miles away from the office.

Frustration clamped Miranda's fingers tight around the handle of her Beretta as she fired off three rounds into the human-shaped target she was imagining as Gen. For the past two days, her sweet-tempered wedding-planner-slash-stepdaughter-to-be had been driving her crazy with a torrent of pushy emails.

Have you finished the guest list yet? Have you picked out the invitations? I sent you seven to choose from. Have you talked to your caterer? What about the cake? Where do you want the reception?

And the ever present, *Who are the rest of your bridesmaids? You'll have to decide by Saturday. I made an appointment at Elegant Ensembles.*

Saturday was tomorrow. Jeez.

She pressed the switch on the shooting stall and tapped her foot as the paper target rattled toward her. She studied her score. Two in the eight range. One in the three.

She sucked.

Hoping Parker had a good tab here, she tore off the target, clipped on a new one and sent it zooming back to its position.

She was about to fire again when Judd stepped up behind her. She could hear the buzz of his steady, monotonous voice through her earmuffs.

"Take it easy, Steele." He put his big hands around hers to relax her grip on the Beretta. "It's not wise to shoot with your emotions."

He sounded like Parker. Stay calm, collected. Yeah, yeah. She should save her rage for the dojo, though Parker thought serenity and control were the best approach there, too.

"Hold the weapon steady. Breathe. Then simply squeeze."

She followed his instructions and fired another round. Closer to the center that time. Maybe he had a point.

"That's better. Keep practicing." Judd strolled away to check on the other students.

"Right," she muttered. "No way I'm gonna win that shooting competition."

"You kicked my butt with your Muay Thai moves this morning." Beside her, Holloway squeezed off a few rounds himself. He got a lot closer to the bull's eye than she did. But then, he was an ex-Marine.

She had beaten him this morning on the mat. She'd studied a variety of martial arts since she left Leon years ago. She'd been obsessed about being strong enough to defend herself. Still was. And she'd gotten better after weeks in the IIT program.

"Your body is your weapon," she shrugged quoting a sensei she'd studied under once.

"This is an extension of my body," Holloway said dryly and fired. Looked like nine points from here. His military training sure gave him an edge. "You kicked my butt with those eavesdropping law questions, too." They had studied in her cube all morning.

She shrugged again. That was only because Parker had drummed into her head that some of her own tactics were inadmissible in court. "Becker's got a lot of catching up to do when he gets back from his honeymoon on Monday."

"Yeah. Hope he makes it." Holloway shook his head.

They both thought Becker was crazy for taking a week for a honeymoon just before exams. But love made you do crazy things. Didn't it, now?

She'd be glad to see Becker again. She'd really grown fond of her two best buddies at the Agency. Too bad they couldn't be bridesmaids.

Pop pop pop.

Miranda turned the other way. Through her goggles, she peered over at the flame-haired Janelle Wesson, who was grinning from ear to ear. Her body was extended, too. She displayed her target. Smack in the middle. Straight to the heart.

Bitch, Miranda wanted to say. Wesson couldn't hear her through the earplugs she preferred over the muffs to keep her hair from getting mussed, but she could probably read lips.

Wait a minute...

For a second, Miranda tried to imagine the lanky woman in a bridesmaid's gown. Nah, that was stretching it way too far. She must really be getting desperate.

Parker scanned the data on his computer screen, barely aware of the late July sunlight streaming in through his office windows.

From the information Miranda had provided, her mother had been around twenty-seven years old when her father abandoned the family. A two-year age difference would make Edward Steele sixty at the present. Parker had filtered for a range of fifty-eight to sixty-two to allow for error. The search results on his screen listed dozens of Edward Steeles.

The easy part was done. Now the real work began. Examining each candidate one by one.

After some initial research, more narrowing down, he'd begin contacts. If he found the information he wanted, he'd determine then just how it would affect Miranda to see the man in person.

There was a knock on his door. "Come in," he said without looking up. He smelled Miranda's delicious scent before she reached his desk, and his heart flooded with feeling. A feeling inflamed by the sight of her tempting backside as she slid herself onto the polished surface. Swiftly, he pressed a key to hide the screen.

"Didn't mean to disturb you."

"You didn't." He smiled at her tenderly.

Miranda eyed the sneaky PI, trying to read what was behind those seductive gray eyes. What was he hiding from her? Some kind of wedding present? Wedding present. Oh, hell. She'd have to get him one, too. Add another task to her list.

The lines on his face formed into a sexy half-grin. "Did you want something or did you come in for a quick love break?" His low drawl was dark and tempting.

Oh, how she wished. She eyed his tailored business suit and silk tie with its tiny blue diamonds and longed to tear those fancy duds off him. It wouldn't take long for him to get her out of the T-shirt and jeans she'd worn to the shooting range. They'd never made love in his office before. Wouldn't that get Gen's goat? But it wouldn't get the shrew off her back.

She let out a breath. "I need help. Bridesmaid help."

He raised a brow. "As in—?"

"As in I don't have any. Or enough of them. Gen thinks I should have twenty. So far, I've got two. Coco and Wendy. And Gen wants everybody to show up for a fitting tomorrow at ten o'clock."

"I see." It gave her some satisfaction to see Parker scowl at the way his daughter was managing things so far. "Gen should be in the bridal party."

She smirked. "She didn't mention that the other night. I don't think she's planning on it. Besides, she'll be running the show on the big day, won't she?"

"Yes, but it would be very bad form if she weren't included."

"Okay. Assuming she agrees with you, that makes three. I need seventeen more."

"Let's make a list of possibilities." He reached for a pad on his desk. "What about Joan Becker?"

"Who? Oh." She winced. She'd never get used to Fanuzzi's new name. "But she's doing the food."

"We can hire some staff to help free her up so she can be in the bridal party."

"Maybe. I'll call her." That would take care of the MOH, too. "Okay. So we're up to four." She groaned and went to the window to stare at the next building. "I just don't have girlfriends. You know that, Parker."

He was silent a moment, and she could feel his concern over her lonely lifestyle. But she'd chosen it. She'd preferred it that way. Since she'd met Parker, there had been more people in her life than in the last twenty years combined. "What am I going to do?"

"Surely you've met some women since you've been in Atlanta."

She thought a moment and remembered the classy criminal defense attorney who worked at Estavez' law firm. "There's Wilhelmina Todd." Miranda strolled back to Parker's desk and perched a haunch on it again, watching Parker eye her with delight.

She had liked Wilhelmina. She'd felt a connection with the woman the instant Parker had introduced them at a party a few months ago. But Wilhelmina was under the impression that she was some hotshot PI from out of state Parker had hired. What would the woman think if she discovered Miranda had worked on a road crew with Fanuzzi—who still worked on it?

And then there was Wendy. "No, that won't work because of Wendy."

"You're right." Parker said. "That would be quite awkward." The stigma of the terrible tragedies Wendy Van Aarle had been mixed up in two months ago still hung over her. But the one that ended with the death of Wilhelmina's younger daughter would be unforgivable to the lawyer. "Has Wendy committed to being in the wedding party?"

"Not yet." The kid had been pretty wishy-washy about it at dinner the other night. "But I think I can talk her into it."

"You've really grown quite fond of her, haven't you?" he said softly.

"Yeah. I don't know what it is about the kid, but I like her. Guess it's our history. You know, we have a lot in common."

Parker was silent, his face full of quiet understanding. He knew better than anyone that Miranda had once thought Wendy was her Amy.

The muscles in the back of Miranda's neck tensed. "Who else?"

Parker leaned back in his chair. "There's my sister, Evelyn."

"Your sister? I never even met her." He'd spoken of her only once before. She took that to indicate they didn't get along too well.

"I'll call her. I'm sure she would be delighted to help." There was just a hint of sarcasm in Parker's voice that made her wonder what sort of family history stew she'd be stirring up. That was all she needed.

"All right. That's five. I can't think of anymore. Gen will just have to be satisfied with that."

"I agree. That's just the number I had in mind for my groomsmen. By the way, who will be giving you away?"

She wrinkled her nose. "Nobody owns me. I'll give myself away."

He chuckled and got to his feet, his eyes shining as if he liked that idea. "How about my father?"

"Mr. P?" she grinned. "That would be cool." She had a fondness for the old coot. She shook a finger at him as he came around the desk. "Okay. But only because it's Mr. P."

"He'll be delighted to hear that. By the way, that reminds me." He strolled to the table that sat on the other side of his humongous office. "I took the liberty of ordering a sample invitation. Since time is so short."

Parker could plan a wedding as easily as a fancy dinner party for fifty. He had social skills coming out of his ears and coursing through his veins. On any other man, that might seem less than manly. But Parker oozed masculinity with everything he did.

He picked up a manila envelope from a stack of papers on the sleek glass table. "What you think?"

Miranda hopped off the desk and crossed the room. She reached for the package and peeked inside.

Hmm. Carefully she reached inside and pulled out a thick envelope lined with silvery paper. She drew out the card inside. Embossed on a silver card were two hearts entwined in a lily. It had all Parker's elegant class and style in abundance.

Hearts and flowers.

Odd emotions swirled inside her. "It's lovely."

Parker smiled tenderly. "I'm glad you think so. What do you think of the text?"

She opened the card and read.

The honor of your presence is requested
at the marriage of
Ms. Miranda Lynne Steele
and
Mr. Wade Russell Parker III
on Saturday, August the fourth
at four o'clock in the afternoon
St. Simon's Episcopal Church
Atlanta

Her throat tightened. "How did you know my middle name?"

"Lucky guess."

"Sure." It was that background check he'd done when they first met.

"So you're pleased with the design?"

"Pleased?" Her voice squeaked as she suddenly had a vision of herself waltzing down the aisle of St. Simon's in all the dresses Parker had picked out.

First the one with the fleur-de-lis accents. Then the strapless number. Then the ruffled one. Then the draped silk. With Fanuzzi and Coco and Wendy all lined up along the altar, grinning.

The reality of what she was about to do hit her. Her stomach began to quake like the San Andreas Fault. Sudden tears stung her eyes. She swiped at her cheek. She hated showing her feelings like this.

"Oh, Parker," she blubbered. "I don't deserve this."

"Of course you do, darling. You deserve anything you want. And I aim to spoil you and give it all to you." He drew her close to him and laid his lips against hers in a tender kiss.

Oh, my. Parker's kiss could always melt her like butter on asphalt in July.

He took the card from her hand and tossed it on to the table.

That did it. She threw her arms around his neck and kissed him back.

His lips curved into a smile. Whether he was more pleased with her response to the card or his kiss, she couldn't tell. But when he deepened the kiss and his tongue slipped inside her mouth, she knew he'd be pleased in a different way in a few minutes. And so would she.

His hands had just slipped down to explore her backside, and his breath was growing ragged against her cheek when the phone rang.

"Don't answer it," she murmured.

"It's still business hours." He pulled himself away from her reluctantly and crossed to his desk. As soon as he saw the number on the caller ID, his face grew somber.

Miranda tensed as the moment of passion drained away. What now?

Parker pushed a button on the phone. "Good afternoon, Sergeant Demarco. What can I do for you?"

Demarco? Was he calling to tell them Jeffries was going to trial? She rushed back to Parker's desk.

"Update on the Fleming case."

"Go ahead, Sergeant," Parker said. "I have Ms. Steele with me. You're on speakerphone."

"Good. Then I won't have to repeat this. First off, Diazepam was found in the bottle of bourbon discovered at the rental property. The substance was also in Jeffries' bloodstream."

"Valium?" She remembered that from the drug list she'd been studying for the exam next week.

"Exactly. Enough to put him out for several hours. The hours that cover Glenda North's time of death."

She couldn't believe what she was hearing. "So Jeffries was telling the truth?"

"Or some version of it."

"But we found the murder weapon that night." In the bushes at Jeffries' rental property.

"The lab finished with that test, as well. The size was right, but the screwdriver had no blood on it."

Parker leaned over his desk as if the voice on the phone was too soft. "Sergeant, are you sure the Luminol test didn't produce a false negative?"

"The lab ran it three times."

No blood on the murder weapon? How could that be? Miranda had never seen Parker speechless, but she couldn't form any words herself.

"Jeffries is being released this evening," Demarco continued. "So we're back to square one. We're looking into the rest of Jeffries' crew and his acquaintances, as well as random break-ins in the area."

Miranda blinked at Parker, hardly able to process the news.

Parker recovered first. "Ms. Hinsley—?"

"She's no longer a suspect. But as before, if she can remember any detail about her roommate that would help us out, we'd like to know."

"We'll certainly pass along any information, Sergeant."

"Appreciate it."

Miranda's brain was buzzing. "Uh, what about that guy Jeffries said he met at his property that night?"

"We're assuming he exists, but we don't have much to go on. Jeffries didn't even have a business card. He couldn't remember his name."

"Did he give a description?"

"Nothing helpful. Tall and on the muscular side, brown hair, mustache, knobby nose."

Her mouth opened. That didn't sound like Hinsley at all.

She and Parker stared at each other. "Thank you for keeping us informed, Sergeant," Parker said at last.

"No problem." Demarco disconnected.

Miranda held her breath as several minutes of stunned silence passed between them before she could speak. She lifted her hands and dug her nails into the back of her scalp. "I can't believe this."

"Facts are facts, Miranda."

She shook her head. "Random break-ins? Somebody breaks into Jeffries' house and hires a hooker and kills her?"

"Demarco also mentioned acquaintances. Perhaps Jeffries was in the habit of loaning his house out to friends. Perhaps it was an accident."

"And perhaps the man in the moon killed Glenda North." She paced over to the credenza. "Some 'acquaintance' or some random thief goes to the trouble of hiding Zelda Fleming's body in a wall? Come on, Parker. None of it makes any sense."

He sat down and picked up a pencil, tapped it against the glossy surface of his desk. "As much sense as Dexter Hinsley's flying in from California to kill Coco's roommate."

"It's not that far-fetched if he wants Coco back." And if he did, then Dexter Hinsley could very well be in town. She thought of the blank stare in Glenda North's dead eyes, the frozen terror on Zelda Fleming's lifeless face. Hairs on the back of her neck stood up.

Sitting back, the pencil still in hand, Parker eyed her carefully and read her thoughts. "Do you really think Dexter Hinsley is in Atlanta?"

"If he flew to Chicago, he could just as easily fly to Atlanta."

"I'll admit I thought the man at Jeffries' property might be Hinsley. But the description Jeffries gave to the police doesn't match."

"There's got to be an explanation for that." She just couldn't think of one at the moment.

"Why would he kill Coco's roommate and Glenda North instead of Coco?"

She thought a moment, glanced over at the wedding invitation on the table. Hinsley embodied everything Miranda feared about marriage. "When I first met

118

her, Coco told me Dexter had a bad temper. You saw what he did to her the night we convinced her to leave him."

He nodded, his eyes growing dark with the memory.

Coco wasn't in Chicago when Zelda was killed. "What if Hinsley found the roommate and wanted to know where Coco was?"

He tossed down the pencil and rose to pace a bit. "And she refused to tell him."

"So he got mad and killed her."

"And killed Glenda North to try to pin the murder on Jeffries? A lot of effort to go through." He leaned against the desk and rubbed his chin. "We have no proof of any of this. And your premise may be faulty."

"What do you mean?"

"Coco told us Hinsley agreed to their divorce without argument."

She hadn't bought that when Coco said it.

"Just because Hinsley left his job doesn't mean he left California," he added.

He had a point. Maybe she was overreacting. Maybe she was too sensitive about Hinsley because of Leon. Maybe she was barking up the wrong tree. But they wouldn't know anything for sure without some proof. "Did Coco's things from her apartment get here yet?"

"Not that I know of, why?"

"I'm wondering if she has anything with Dexter's DNA on it."

He was silent a moment. She watched his gray eyes calmly study her, not knowing if he thought she was brilliant or crazy. Finally he gave a decisive exhale. "I'll tighten the security on Coco. We know one thing for certain. The killer's still on the loose."

CHAPTER TWENTY-SIX

Dark clouds were gathering in the sky on the drive home, making Miranda wonder if they were in for one of those sudden southern windstorms like the one that had brought down half a tree in Parker's backyard a few weeks ago.

Traffic was horrendous and a case of the jitters had her glancing in the rear view mirror every other minute, unable to shake the feeling she was being followed.

Her thoughts were just as murky as the weather. Jeffries not the murderer? She remembered the night she found that screwdriver in the bushes. It was hidden, yet relatively easy to find, she realized in hindsight. Jeffries had time to hide it better. Maybe he didn't hide it. Maybe somebody planted it there. Jeffries claimed someone interested in his property had brought him that bottle of bourbon. Tall and on the muscular side, brown hair, mustache, knobby nose. That wasn't Dexter Hinsley. Unless…he used some type of disguise.

From what she knew of Hinsley, he wouldn't go to all that trouble. He acted impulsively. Out of passion and rage.

And why wasn't there any blood on the screwdriver?

She turned onto Lakewood Chase and had just spotted the bodyguard's half-invisible Acura and Antonio Estavez' red Ferrari parked along the curb—like it had been every night this week—when her cell went off. She jumped at the sound.

Scoffing at her own nerves, she reached for the phone and glanced at the display.

Wendy Van Aarle. She was surprised the kid hadn't texted her.

She pressed a button to answer. "Steele."

"Hi, Miranda."

"Hi."

"I uh, missed my ride home from the ice rink."

Oh, brother. "How'd that happen?"

"Mom was supposed to pick me up, so I told Brianna I didn't need a ride."

What had Iris pulled now? "But…?"

120

"But then Mom called and said she's stuck in a meeting. Can you come and get me?"

Anger rippled through Miranda at Iris's behavior. She was doing it again. Not too long ago, the Van Aarles could have been voted Most Dysfunctional Family in America. But they'd gone to therapy together to mend their ways. Things were supposed to be better now. Were they falling apart again so soon? Didn't Iris care about the pain her daughter had been through?

Her heart melted for the kid. "Sure," she told Wendy. "I can come and get you. Give me an address."

It took her over forty-five minutes fighting the delightful Atlanta rush-hour traffic to get to the ice arena that was all the way in bumfish Marietta. She found Wendy inside, leaning over the railing, attention fixed on a single, lone skater.

The young girl glided with ease along the far end of the rink, her dark hair pulled back with a band, her stretchy black tights showing her perfect form, her royal blue turtleneck making a blur of color.

Miranda rubbed her arms. It was chilly in this place. "I'm here, Wendy."

"Shhh." The girl was spellbound.

Graceful as a swan, the skater sped up, raising her arms as she glided over the ice. Then she turned and lifted off the ground in a nimble spin that seemed to go on for a full minute. She landed on the ice backwards, arms and one leg poised in the air.

Impressive.

"Isn't she incredible?" Wendy's voice crackled with excitement. "Her spins and jumps are outrageous. I can hardly do a spiral without falling on my butt." She rolled her eyes in disgust at herself.

"Yeah. Beautiful." Her moves were breathtaking.

"She's been skating since she was five. She won the Atlanta Open last month, and she's going for the Regional in August. I bet she wins."

"Who is she?"

"Mackenzie Chatham."

Chatham? "As in Chatham, Grayson, and McFee?"

"Uh huh. Her father's Mr. Estavez' boss. Kind of funny, huh?"

A real laugh. The girl skimmed over to the edge of the rink to be hugged by an older woman. Her mother, Miranda presumed. Wendy stepped off the ice and went to a bench to remove her skates. "You want to go say goodbye?"

Wendy shook her head vigorously, her hair swirling around her face. "Oh, no. Mackenzie doesn't like to be disturbed after practice. She did let me carry her skates once. She says she's used to criminals because of her father's line of work."

"I see." Sounded like a new spin on *prima donna*. She hoped Wendy wasn't getting close to someone who'd snub her again. When her former schoolmates ostracized her, it had ended in tragedy. "Well, let's get going. It's freezing in here."

"Sure."

Miranda watched her charge out the front door to the parking lot, where the ninety-degree heat suddenly felt wonderful. The clouds were gone, and the late July sun had returned in full force for a final blast before setting.

They got into the Lumina and began the trek back to Mockingbird Hills.

As she merged onto I-75 and hit the brakes before she rammed into the back of a smelly semi, Miranda thought of Gen's appointment at Elegant Ensembles tomorrow morning.

"What time is your mom coming for you?"

"She didn't say."

Hmm. "So what's this meeting about?"

"An advertising campaign for a new line of cosmetics. Press releases, radio, maybe some TV spots. And the Internet of course."

Internet? Might as well ask the question sooner or later. "Is Isaiah Todd involved?"

"I think so."

God, no. Wendy wasn't stupid. She might pretend not to understand what her mother was up to, but she had to have her suspicions about what might be going on between her mother and her web designer again. That's all the kid needed right now. A broken family.

Miranda decided to drop the subject. She put on a bright smile. "Did you ask your mom if you could be a junior bridesmaid in my wedding?"

"Yeah." Wendy's attention was on a frisky poodle hanging out the rear window of a Toyota a few cars down.

"What did she say?"

"She said I could if I wanted to."

The semi moved a few feet and Miranda inched up. "Well? Do you want to?"

She shrugged. "Guess so."

The kid had about as much enthusiasm for the wedding as Miranda did. "We're supposed to pick out dresses tomorrow morning. Wanna come?"

"Seriously?" She wrinkled her nose, but Miranda couldn't tell if it was from the idea of going dress shopping or the black puff of smoke coming out of the semi's tailpipe. She eased off the gas and turned a knob on the dash, glad that Parker had insisted on getting the AC on her jalopy checked.

"Yeah. Seriously."

"Sure," Wendy said at last.

Miranda couldn't explain the flip her heart did at that response. "Why don't you stay overnight then?"

Suddenly, the kid's eyes lit up. "At your place?"

"Yeah. My place." Parker kept saying the big, fancy pile of stone was her place. Why not act like it?

Wendy smiled. "Cool."

"It's not going to be a party, though. I've got studying to do."

She looked like Miranda had grown a third eye. "You don't go to school. You're an adult."

"It's training for my job."

"Seriously? As a detective?"

"Seriously."

Wendy gave her a wide grin. "Beastly. I could help you study."

Beastly? Better than another *seriously*. "Okay."

"Awesome. Hey, maybe I could go to work with you one day."

"Would you like that?"

"I'd love it." She even bounced a little in her seat. "Beastly," she said again.

Something she'd love? Maybe as much as she loved figure skating? Seriously, that was pretty beastly.

Dinner was coffee and sandwiches à la Parker, which meant the just-ground coffee beans were imported from St. Helena and the sammies were expensive cold cuts and cheeses on freshly baked bread from a gourmet deli. Still, it was quiet and subdued around the dining table, the conversation not more than idle chitchat.

Miranda talked about tomorrow's trip to the dress shop as if she were really looking forward to it. Coco chimed in, and Parker remained mum about Demarco's phone call. Which was just as well, in Miranda's opinion. Especially when Coco announced FedEx had delivered the things from her apartment late that afternoon.

Estavez was working a case, so he left early, while Parker headed upstairs to do some work on the computer. Coco went to her room to sort through the boxes from Chicago.

That left Miranda and Wendy alone in the dining room to spend the rest of the evening in a rousing study session. The kid was relentless as she quizzed her on DNA profiling, illegal search and seizures, and the many ways of getting a fake ID. After three hours, Miranda had had enough.

She took Wendy upstairs and put her to bed in a room down the hall from the master. The third floor was supposed to be for guests, but she didn't want to leave the girl up there by herself.

This guest room wasn't really suited for a thirteen-year-old. Like all the rooms in the house, the décor was pompous and overdone. But the style was sort of fanciful, furnished with a richly carved, cream-colored armoire, matching nightstand and dresser, and a rosy chair in the corner. And the four-poster bed had a pink ruffle around it and was topped by a dainty crocheted canopy.

It was what she had to work with.

"Exciting day tomorrow," Miranda said, pulling the thick quilt over the girl.

Wendy wrinkled her nose. "I'd rather just study detective stuff with you. That was way cool."

Little Nancy Drew. "Maybe we can study more later. For now, let's get some sleep." She reached over and turned off the light.

"Miranda?"

"Yeah?"

"Thanks for letting me stay here."

"You're welcome." Resisting the urge to kiss the kid good night, she tiptoed out and down the hall.

As she headed for the master bedroom, her path illuminated by the soft glow of wall sconces, her thoughts went back to Demarco's phone call that afternoon—and to Jeffries and the DNA in Glenda North's stomach.

In front of Coco's door, she hesitated, stood there, tapping her toe, studying the panels. Parker wouldn't approve of this move, but he was still upstairs. This was as good a time as any for some serious "girl talk."

She drew in a breath and knocked.

"Who is it?"

"It's me. Can I come in, Coco?"

"Sure, Miranda."

She stepped inside and found Coco on the floor, open boxes and piles of clothes all around her. Her long legs sprawled on the Tibetan rug, she had changed into sky-blue shorts and a pink top with spaghetti straps and a big blue butterfly on the front. Her perfume made the place smell like peaches. If only Estavez could get a load of her now.

This room had a regal air about it that fit someone as naturally elegant as Coco. Done in tans and greens and blues, it had bedding and drapery that looked like it had been hand embroidered. The headboard and dressers were cherry and rosewood, carved in an elaborate design. A small chandelier hung from the ceiling.

Coco grinned at her. "You must be so excited about tomorrow. I remember when I picked out my wedding gown." Her smile faded and her blue eyes grew troubled. Miranda knew she must be thinking of the disaster her marriage had turned into.

"You must've been a beautiful bride," Miranda said softly, hoping to raise her spirits a little. She gestured toward the bed. "Okay if I sit down?"

"Sure, it's your house."

Miranda looked at the antique Ottoman bench at the end of the bed. It had a stack of mail. "What's this?"

Coco stretched her neck to see. "Oh, that's just my mail that was forwarded from Doon."

"You left a forwarding address at the post office in Iowa?"

"Sure. Isn't that what you're supposed to do? It's all right that I gave them your address here, isn't it?"

"Of course."

"It's mostly junk mail, anyway."

Miranda grabbed the papers, laid them on the dresser and took a seat. "I need to talk to you."

"Oh, there's a gift for you there."

"Gift?" Miranda turned and spotted a package wrapped in silver sitting on the foot of the bed.

"It's sort of a wedding present. I got it when I went shopping today."

"You went shopping?"

"Of course. I'm a big girl."

She hoped the bodyguard had followed her all the way. She made a mental note to check with him to make sure.

"Well, open it."

"Okay." She picked up the box and tore the paper away. Inside she found a designer handbag. It was on the large size and looked like leather, with a gold and silver giraffe print. She was speechless.

"You never carry a purse, so I thought you could use one. Especially on your honeymoon."

Honeymoon? Purse? "Gee, thanks, Coco. That was really thoughtful." She set it beside her on the bench. Maybe she could use it once in a while. "Like I said, I need to talk to you about something."

Coco reached for a pile of clothes and began folding blouses. "What is it? These really should be hung up."

"Help yourself to hangers in the closet. We can get you some more if you need them."

Coco got up and shuffled to the closet to poke her head in. "No, there are enough in here. You were saying?" After a minute, she returned with a stack of them in her arms. She set them on the bed and reached for a blouse from one of the piles.

Miranda took a deep breath. "Sergeant Demarco called this afternoon."

"Again? What did he want?" She reached for a hanger and slipped a yellow ruffly lace thing onto it.

"He told us the evidence against Jeffries didn't stick. They had to let him go."

Coco's blouse slid off the hanger and dropped onto the polished hardwood floor. "Let him go? They don't think he killed Zelda or that other woman?"

"No, they don't. They couldn't hold him any longer."

Her blue eyes grew wide. She put a hand to her face. "Am I in trouble?"

"No, Demarco said you were no longer a suspect. But the killer is still at large."

"In Chicago."

"Maybe."

Coco picked up the blouse and rearranged it on the hanger. "What you mean by maybe?"

Miranda gave her a steady look.

"Do you still think Dexter's involved?" She shook her head, making her blond curls shimmer. "That's just crazy. Sure, he could get nasty, but he'd never do anything like that. He'd never kill anybody." She hung the blouse in the closet.

Miranda ignored her and gestured at the FedEx boxes. "Think there's anything in there that belonged to him?"

Coco looked confused. "No. I didn't take anything of his when I left. You know I hardly had time to think."

That was true. Coco must have bought most of that stuff after she left. Bummer. "What about the house?"

"Which house?"

"Your old house. Where was it?"

"Doraville."

That was right. "Would there be anything there?"

Coco got another hanger, hung another blouse and stuck it in the closet. "Dexter said he was selling it. I can't go back there. You can't make me."

Miranda raised her hands in protest. "No. I wouldn't ask you to go there."

"Why are you asking me these questions?" She scowled at Miranda. "Do you think you can find fingerprints or something to pin those murders on him?"

Miranda pursed her lips in irritation and stared at the girl, seeing distress behind her blue eyes. She wasn't over that bastard. Not by a long shot. Counseling or not, Dexter Hinsley was still in her head. Miranda ought to know. "If Dexter's innocent, some evidence would get him off the hook."

"Is he on the hook, Miranda? Does Sergeant Demarco think he killed Zelda and that other woman?"

She closed her eyes and let out a breath. "No."

"So it's just you who thinks he's the killer." She got to her feet and brushed off her shorts. "I think I need to look for my own place."

Miranda felt a stab of panic. "Coco, don't say that."

She spun toward her, her blue eyes moistening with tears of anger. "I can't keep staying here with you and Parker. I've got to live my own life. I was going to tell you, I called Frankie at the Gecko Club today. I've got an audition next week."

Miranda felt like ants were crawling over her skin. "I don't think that's a good idea."

"I didn't know I had to ask your permission." Her nose turned a little red. She reached for a tissue off the nightstand to daub it. "I know Dexter was a lousy husband. I know he cheated on me with those middle school teachers he sold textbooks to. I know you were right about that. But you can't convince me he's capable of murder."

With a huff, she hung some more blouses in the closet. Then she grabbed a FedEx box and pulled it to the side of the room.

Miranda pulled at her hair. Gosh, she was screwing this up. She couldn't let Coco leave. Not now. "Okay, I'll drop the subject. Look, Coco. I've got a lot on me right now with the wedding and studying for exams and now Wendy."

That got her attention. Coco stopped messing with the box and straightened. "What's wrong with Wendy?"

Miranda chewed on her lip a minute, considering what to say. "I didn't want to mention it, but it looks like her folks' marriage might be on the rocks again."

Coco's expression turned from anger to compassion. "Oh, that's too bad."

"It would really be nice if you could stick around and help me out."

Coco nodded, all her irritation forgotten. "Of course, I'll help."

Relieved, Miranda got up and gave her an awkward hug. She was less than an expert at comforting people. "I'm sorry I made you mad. I won't talk about Dexter again. Promise." For now, anyway.

"Okay. I forgive you."

Miranda released her. "Everything's going to be okay," she reassured her with her best smile. "Wendy's here with us tonight, and we're all going dress shopping tomorrow."

That made Coco grin.

CHAPTER TWENTY-SEVEN

By ten thirty the next morning, Miranda had a migraine the size of Connecticut.

Despite Elegant Ensembles' muted chandeliers, the draped velvet bordering its walls, and the soft baroque music playing in the background, among the Parker-Steele wedding party, war was brewing.

Coco said the gown Miranda had been leaning toward, the one with the fleur-de-lis pleats, made her look fat. She tried on all three of the others but was already too irritated to decide on one. Why couldn't she just wear jeans and a halter-top?

Then Gen and Coco started arguing about the color of the bridesmaids' dresses while Wendy sat in a chair in the corner with a scowl, playing games on her phone. There had been tension between the two women since they arrived here and Miranda had introduced Coco as a nightclub singer. Good thing Gen didn't know she was dating Estavez.

Coco held up a long dusty pink gown made of supple jersey. "This is pretty."

Gen rolled her eyes. "Not enough style." Her tone had a not-too-well-hidden note of condescension.

Coco made an angry face. "What do you mean, Gen? It's very classy. And look. It's got a convertible bodice. Each of us could wear it a different way."

Stubbornly, Gen shook her head. "The color is wrong."

"It's perfect. We should do light pastels," Coco insisted. "We're both blondes, after all."

And they were both about the same height, Miranda noticed, not that it mattered to Gen.

"We have to stick with the *theme*. And there will be a lot more than you and me in the wedding party. Besides, the gowns need to be more chic, if you even know what that word means."

That did it. Miranda stomped over to Gen. "Hey, don't insult her. She's my friend."

Gen glared at her. "Where are the other bridesmaids?"

"They're on their way."

"They're late."

"They'll be here. And only one is coming. The MOH is out of town." If she even agreed to it. Miranda's call to Fanuzzi last night and had gone to voicemail. "I only have five total."

"What?" Gen's face twisted with emotion. "Isn't it bad enough that my father roped me into being one?" Parker had called his daughter last night and insisted in that stubborn way of his, that Gen be a bridesmaid.

Miranda raised her hands. "Apparently not. Your father said five was good enough."

That shut her up. For the moment.

Miranda eyed the big giraffe purse Coco had given her that she'd set on one of the fancy chairs earlier. Inside, it had a pocket that held her Beretta. If Gen gave her any more guff, she might just use that weapon on her wedding planner. Of course, she'd have to enlist the three bodyguards waiting outside to help drag out the body.

Humming a tune, Coco sidled up to them and held up another creation. "This one is just gorgeous," she gushed. "You really need to consider pastels, Gen."

"Look, Steele," Gen hissed under her breath, "if you want me in charge, make her put a lid on it."

Miranda opened her mouth, about to tell Gen she could take a slow boat to Madagascar, when a bell jingled at the entrance.

"Sorry I'm so late. I just got back in town this morning."

Miranda's spirits soared to the ceiling at the sound of that Brooklyn accent. "Fanuzzi?"

She spun around in time to catch the bouncy swagger of her old road crew buddy as she climbed the salon's red-carpeted steps and headed toward them.

She looked great. Healthy and tan, she wore sandals, bright blue culottes, and a flowery shirt. It looked like she'd had her almost black hair cut and styled, too.

"I left a message on your cell yesterday."

Fanuzzi gave her a tight hug. She smelled like she'd come from the beach. "I got it. Parker answered when I called back last night and gave me all the deets. He said you were asleep. The kids were getting bored at Disney World, so we decided to come home a day early."

"You didn't have to do that." Now Miranda felt guilty.

Setting down her purse in the chair next to Miranda's, Fanuzzi waved a hand. "Oh, it's all right. Dave was getting antsy to get home. He's got that big exam coming up next week. Well, you know that," she laughed. "And when Parker said you were coming *here* today, I said, 'Dave, pack the car.'" Fanuzzi was gaga over Parker and his ritzy style.

Miranda grinned. "Did Parker tell you he was going to hire staff to help you out with the food?"

"Yeah. I can manage that now and be in your bridal party, too." She leaned forward and whispered. "I'd be happy to be your matron of honor. I'm thrilled you asked me."

Technically, it was Parker who'd asked, but Miranda wasn't being picky. She'd just enjoy the relief. "You're a godsend, Fanuzzi."

"Just doing what girlfriends do."

Guess she did have girlfriends, after all.

"Did I hear 'matron of honor?'" Miranda turned and found Gen in her face, her black eyes flashing.

She put on her best posh party smile. "You did. Fanuzzi, this is Gen. She's going to be my new stepdaughter. Gen, this is Joan Fanuzzi, an old friend of mine. She's going to be my MOH." How was that for elegant manners?

As if she were picking up a dirty sock, Gen extended a hand. "Glad to meet you."

With glee, Miranda watched Gen fight a quiver in her lip. Must have been the Brooklyn accent that impressed her.

"Likewise," Fanuzzi said. "I'm a big admirer of your father. Atlanta wouldn't be the same without the work he does."

Gen blinked, suddenly looking almost sheepish at the compliment. "Thank you," she managed to say. Then she shifted back to Nazi mode. "Now can we get on with this exercise? We haven't got all day." She turned toward the rack of dresses she'd been studying and chose one. "I'm thinking something muted and sedate like this."

"Oh no," Fanuzzi cried. "You got a go with bold for this showstopper of a wedding. Reds and cobalt blues. That's the way I see it."

Gen managed not to raise her eyes to the ceiling. "We have to keep with the theme. Hearts and flowers. This is a wedding. Not the Fourth of July."

The saleslady, who had been standing on the sidelines out of the fray, dared to step forward. "Let me show you ladies several ensembles that might work for you."

Gen was about to run the poor woman off when the door jingled again. "Hello."

Everyone froze and as if programmed. Then they all turned toward the door and the imposing figure that had just entered.

Tall and elegant, dressed in a tailored teal business suit with lapels embossed in a fancy design, a perfect string of pearls at her neck, more pearls on her ears, steel gray hair piled on her head, and familiar piercing gray eyes that looked like they could strip you to your underwear with one glance, the woman studied the party. She was as foreboding as Margaret Thatcher. Or maybe Queen Elizabeth.

Moving like a steamship sailing out of the dock, she crossed the carpet heading toward Gen.

"Genevieve," she sang out in a voice as musical as Julia Child's. "How is my favorite niece this morning?" She gave Gen a peck on the cheek. Miranda had to stifle a laugh at the wince on Gen's face.

"I'm your *only* niece, Aunt Evelyn. And I'm fine. Thanks for showing up."

So this was the great and powerful Evelyn Parker.

The woman dismissed her niece's sarcasm with a regal wave and turned to Miranda. "And is this my baby brother's bride to be? Please introduce us, dear."

Miranda had never imagined Parker as anyone's baby brother, but this woman was in charge of Mr. P's vast real estate empire. How tough did you have to be to run a business like that?

"Aunt Evelyn, this is my father's fiancée, Miranda Steele." Gen got the words out without choking. Miranda was impressed.

She took the woman's hand. "It's good to meet you, ma'am."

"Oh, please. Call me Evelyn. And welcome to the family."

"Thanks."

"I've heard you're quite the rising talent in my brother's Agency."

Miranda looked down at the carpet and rubbed her nose. "I guess."

"Oh, she is," Fanuzzi said. "She's already solved two murders."

Time to change the subject. "This is my matron of honor, Joan Fanuzzi." These formal introductions could come in handy.

"How nice to meet you," Evelyn sang.

"Likewise."

While Gen fumed and Miranda introduced Evelyn to Coco, the persistent saleslady rolled in a rack with a dozen gowns on it and nearly gasped when she saw the newcomer. "Ms. Parker. I'm so glad you've arrived. Perhaps you can help the ladies make their selections."

Evelyn turned to her with a smug smile. "Why I'd be happy to, Heloise."

"What do you ladies think of these creations? They're some of our latest."

Ignoring her aunt, Gen studied the dresses a moment, then picked one up. "Now this is what I'm talking about." It was a straight-line indigo of shimmering silk with a slit up the side and a high waistband that looked like it was made of diamonds. Miranda had to admit it was classy and would look great on Gen's tall, angular body.

"But you said hearts and flowers." Coco reached for a lacy chiffon creation with a floral design of fanciful plums and blues that really brought out the color of her eyes. "I like this one."

Gen curled a lip. "It's a peasant dress."

"So?"

Fanuzzi grunted. "Neither of those would look good on me." She reached for a draped gown in solid amethyst with a silvery belt and matching clasp at the shoulder and held it up to her. "This one's for me."

"And for me, this." Evelyn stepped to the rack and lifted a classy suit of satin magenta with silvery buttons.

"It's knee length," Gen protested.

Evelyn ignored her. "So then we're set."

Gen bared her teeth. "Set? All these dresses are different."

"But they go together," Evelyn countered. "They all have the same color scheme. See?"

She made a gesture like an orchestra conductor, and everyone held her choice of gown up to her chin. Suddenly, it was like a dress symphony. The colors and shades, the flowers, the swirls, the silvery accents, all flowed together like a song. Hearts and flowers.

Miranda grinned. "I like it."

Gen was still scowling.

Aunt Evelyn shook her head. "There's no rule that says we have to wear the same gown. Have some imagination, Genevieve."

Gen's taste in her work wardrobe did run toward the predictable.

Miranda glanced over at Wendy, who was still in the chair, as if cemented there. Why her eyes weren't bugging out from staring at that little screen, Miranda didn't know. "We forgot my junior bridesmaid. Hey, kid."

Wendy raised her head. "Yeah?"

"Come pick out your dress."

Reluctantly, she rose and shuffled over.

Miranda bristled when she heard Evelyn whisper to Gen. "Is that the Van Aarle girl?"

"I'll explain later," Gen replied curtly.

Heloise pointed out the end of the rack. "Here are some of our gowns for younger girls."

Wendy stood staring at the dresses for a long moment.

Miranda mulled over the selections. "Which do you like?"

Wendy shrugged. She was probably looking for one with a cell phone pocket.

"Coco, what do you think?"

"Oh, they're also pretty," she laughed. "That's why Wendy can't decide."

Finally, Fanuzzi reached for a lavender dress with multi-color swirls and a beaded pattern of hearts at the shoulders and waistline. "Picture yourself in this one, honey."

That got half a smile. Good enough.

"That's it," Miranda declared.

Gen clapped her hands together. "All right, everyone. Time to try everything on."

Amazingly, nobody changed her mind about her selection, but there'd be tweaks and adjustments by the seamstress—which meant fitting in fittings. Ugh.

But Miranda was happy the worst was over. Peace at last. And progress. By the time they left the shop, she had even decided on her gown—the draped silk over embroidered lilies.

Things were definitely looking up.

He sat in a rented car across the street on the second story of the covered lot of a bank building, peering through the high-powered binoculars that had taken far too much of his remaining cash.

One by one, he watched them leave the bridal shop.

When Cora Beth appeared in the door, he sucked in his breath. His stomach turned as he watched her cross the asphalt and get into that ugly old car.

She was there.

Right there in front of him. With Steele and that child. He could have been behind them, could have nabbed them, could have had her back right then. If it weren't for the three cars idling along the edge of the Peachtree Road parking lot. Damn Wade Parker and his bodyguards.

Damn him and all those stupid, fucking bitches.

He slammed his fist against the steering wheel. He wanted to kill them. Kill them all.

He put his stinging hand to his lips, caressed it. Oh, Cora Beth. Why did you leave? He had to find a way to get her back. But he could hardly think. The need for a woman was consuming him.

In the bridal salon parking lot, the cars started up and drove away. He didn't bother to follow them this time. It would do no good. Parker's men were always there.

There had to be a way to get to them. He would find it.

Desire swelled within him. God, he needed a fuck. If only he could clear his mind. If only he had more of the pills the doctor in California had prescribed for him. He had only a few left and he'd need those later. He didn't dare refill the prescription here.

He turned the key in the ignition and backed out of the space. Slowly he wove around to the exit, paid the fee and turned onto the street. He hated the idea of going back to that dingy hotel room.

He'd had to abandon the house. He'd hired a cleaning crew to clear out the furniture and shampoo the carpets so there would be no trace of him. He was sleeping in a rundown, fleabag roach motel along the interstate now.

His mind filled with images of the teachers he used to visit when he was a textbook salesman.

There was Jenny, the hot little number at Dogwood Academy. He could look her up. No. After the scandal at that school, that would be too risky. There was the babe across the border in Alabama. But the last time he saw her, she'd pushed him for commitment, and he'd intended to drop her. Besides, he couldn't even remember her name.

He did remember Elizabeth Lane. Petite, sweet, sassy. All she ever wanted from him was sex. He wondered… She was far enough out of the city. Should he risk it? Between his legs, the need throbbed. He didn't have much choice.

At a stoplight, he reached for the cheap cell phone he'd bought so the real estate agent could keep in touch. His fingers trembled as he dialed Elizabeth's number. He was surprised he remembered it.

"Hello?" said a soft, low voice.

"Did I catch you on a break?"

He heard her gasp with delight. "Dexter? Is that really you? I haven't heard from you in so long."

"I've been busy."

"Really? Too busy for me?" There was a pout in her voice that turned him on.

"I'm not busy now."

"Oh? Do you have any more of those *special* sales?"

"I think I might have one just for you."

She uttered a low, sensuous laugh that made his mouth water. "How soon can you get here?"

He glanced at the time on the dash. "Forty minutes. Same place?"

"Of course. That's *our* spot. I'll be waiting for you."

He had to force himself to slow down as he took the interstate and drove the familiar route. It only took him thirty-five minutes. He found Elizabeth's lemon yellow Camry outside the room at the Mableton hotel they'd used so many times before.

He got out of the car and knocked on the door, nervous as a schoolboy on his first date.

When she opened it, he discovered she was wearing that lacy black negligee he liked, her blond bangs drooping over one eye.

"What took you so long?" She laughed, pulling him inside and closing the door. Then she pulled the hair out of her eyes and her mouth dropped open. "Dexter? Is that really you? You look so different."

"It's me, babe."

She studied him a minute. "I kind of like it." Her gaze lowered. "What's with the gloves?"

He glanced down at the latex on his hands. "I thought we'd play doctor."

Another low, sexy laugh rang in his ears. "Oh, Dexter. You are too cute. It's been way too long. I've really missed you. Come here." She took a step toward him.

He didn't say another word. Grabbing her by the hair, he moved toward the bed and pressed her face to his lips.

CHAPTER TWENTY-EIGHT

It was Sunday evening. Iris had picked Wendy up around noon and Miranda and Parker had stolen a few hours on the third floor, savoring the pleasures of the Taj Mahal room.

She lay beside him, sated and intensely comfortable, letting him run a hand down her side until she was ready to drool all over the jacquard pillow. She sighed out loud.

Parker chuckled. "I'm glad you feel that way."

She smiled at him. "Do you think sex will be this good once we're married?"

His brow rose in a wicked arch. "I intend to make it better."

Oh, really? She narrowed an eye at him. "Have you been holding out on me?"

"You'll find out soon enough."

She laughed. Hard to imagine anything better. Sex with Parker was like no experience she'd ever had. It was one of the things she would miss most when their relationship fell apart, as all relationships did. But that was years off. She hoped.

She stretched, forced herself up and reached for the red silk robe he'd given her recently. "I'd love to stay here all night, but I've got a big exam and two competitions coming up."

He stood and tied the robe's silky belt around her waist. "So I hear."

"Yeah, my boss is a real ogre."

He ran his hands up her arms, leaned in to nuzzle her neck. "How awful for you."

Shivers skimmed over her body. If she stayed here much longer, the robe was coming off again. Uh uh.

She pulled out of his embrace. "Sorry. I've got a hot date with my books and the gym." She tightened the belt of her robe. "But you could join me for a workout later. How about that? In the gym, that is."

He looked tempted but shook his head. "I have pressing work."

135

She put a hand on her hip. "You've been doing a lot of that lately."

He shrugged as he headed for the shower. "Busy season."

She didn't buy that for a minute. He was up to something. But she'd let him have his little secret for now. She gave him a peck on the cheek, then headed for the other bathroom down the hall. No sense getting in the tub together. They'd never get out.

When she was clean, she found a quiet room with a couch and dug into her books. Two hours later, her eyes were crossing. She stood up and yawned.

She'd never studied so hard for an exam in her life. But she'd never wanted anything so badly. She had to pass it. And she had to do well in that martial arts competition.

She closed her book, slipped into a jersey tank and a pair of fitness pants, and headed downstairs for a workout.

A few weeks ago, Miranda had discovered the old mansion had a basement that had once been used for servants' quarters. She and Parker had decided to convert part of the area to a small gym. Now it held mirrors and mats, punching bags and weights, and an assortment of other equipment Parker liked to use.

Taking a position on the mat, she did some stretching, some sit ups, some pushups. Then she went to the bag and concentrated on her Chok and Thip, punches and foot-thrusts. She watched her form in the mirror. Cross, hook, swing. Straight, sideways, reverse.

Not bad. Pretty good, in fact. Much smoother than she used to be.

She might be good, but was she good enough to place in that competition next week? If she didn't, she'd never live it down.

Not wanting to overwork and strain herself, she ended with some cooling off exercises and climbed back upstairs. She needed another shower, but first, a snack. As she made her way toward the kitchen, she found Coco strolling down the long hallway.

The girl eyed her warily, then held something out to her. "Here, Miranda. I found this in my stuff."

She took it from her. It was a picture of Dexter. She studied in a moment. Wavy, dark red hair. Flirtatious eyes. A movie star smile. She despised the man, thought he was a murderer, but he was a looker. No wonder he could woo any woman into bed with him, the bastard.

"Thanks. This could help."

Coco shook her curls, making them shine under the lights. "No, it won't. I'm sorry, but I just don't believe you."

Miranda sighed. "I know you don't."

She straightened her shoulders. "I promised to stick around and help you with your wedding, and I will. But I want you to know I'm leaving as soon as it's over. And I'm going to that audition next week at the Gecko Club."

Miranda suppressed a groan. "I wish you'd rethink that, Coco."

Coco frowned with annoyance. "Stop treating me like a child, Miranda. This is my time. My career." She spun around and headed toward the living room.

Miranda followed her. "I'm not trying to hinder your career. I think you've got incredible talent. It's just that things might be dangerous right now."

"Only in your suspicious mind. It must be part of being a detective."

"Maybe, but it's because I care about you."

"You don't know what you're talking about." She plopped down on the big leather sofa and switched on the big screen TV with the remote.

Miranda ran a hand through her hair. She didn't want to fight with Coco, but she couldn't let her go out and do a late night gig. Not now. "Look, maybe we could work something out. If you want—"

The newswoman on the television caught Miranda's attention. She turned and stared at the screen.

"The body of the young woman found this afternoon in a hotel room outside Mableton, Georgia, has been identified as Elizabeth Lane, a local middle school teacher."

Middle school teacher?

"Police state Lane was raped and brutally murdered by an unknown assailant. The teacher, who was popular among the students..."

"Oh, my God." Miranda shot a finger at Coco. "Stay right there. I'll be back."

"Where are you going?" Coco asked, but Miranda had already rushed out of the room.

She dashed into the great hall and against the protests of her thighs and calves, took the grand staircase two at a time. She was almost too winded to speak when she reached Parker's office. But she managed.

"Parker, turn on the TV. Quick."

Working at the middle of the three computer screens, Parker spun around as soon as she entered the room. "Miranda, what's wrong?"

She waved a hand at the screen. "Hurry. Channel eleven."

"I can do that right here." He pressed a button on the keyboard.

A window appeared on the screen on the right. One of the local cops was being interviewed. Parker pressed more buttons to turn up the sound. "The Mableton police force is doing everything in our power to find the perpetrator of this vicious crime. Unfortunately, so far we have no leads."

There was a shot of the schoolyard where kids were playing ball. "Needless to say, Ms. Lane's students and her parents are beside themselves." The camera cut to a middle-aged woman clutching a handkerchief. Her short, gray-brown hair was tangled, her face lined with grief.

"I don't understand it. She was so young. She had so much to live for." A picture of the smiling victim flashed on the screen. A pretty, youthful blond with long bangs. A headline emerged below the picture. *Middle school teacher killed in Mableton hotel.*

Miranda squeezed Parker's shoulder. "Is that her, Parker? Is that her?"

Parker went rigid beneath her grasp. "Are you talking about the middle school teacher in Mableton Dexter Hinsley was having an affair with?"

"The one we discovered when we tailed him a few months ago."

He pressed a key and the news story froze with the picture of Elizabeth Lane. "The photos we took that day have been scanned into the Agency's database. I have a secure access to it here." Again he worked some more magic on the keyboard, and after a minute, dozens of thumbnails appeared. Quickly, he scrolled through the photos and found the ones from Mableton.

The first was a shot of the school parking lot. The next one captured Hinsley and the teacher getting into her yellow Camry. It didn't show her face very well. But the third one caught the teacher's face full front as she'd turned toward Hinsley.

Miranda took in her features, compared them to the TV screen. "That's her. Dexter Hinsley's lover." One of them. "She was raped and murdered in a hotel room yesterday."

"It is her, indeed." Parker's voice was dark and angry. He picked up his cell phone.

"Who are you calling?"

"Lieutenant Erskine."

Miranda was surprised when Parker got hold of Estavez and asked him to stay with Coco while he and Miranda went out. He didn't tell him why, but she suspected Estavez could guess from his tone that something dreadful was up. He came over right away.

It was after ten o'clock when Miranda stood with Parker outside the Mableton hotel room talking to Sergeant Dan Grogan of the local police, Lieutenant Erskine, and Inspector Francine Whitman of the Georgia Bureau of Investigation.

"Here's all the data the Parker Agency collected on Ms. Lane this past May." Parker handed the inspector a folder of the pictures and everything else he'd printed out from his files. Plus a copy of the photo of Hinsley that Coco had given Miranda.

Inspector Whitman opened the folder and leafed through it. "You say you had this Dexter Hinsley under surveillance for a client?"

"That's correct, Inspector. His wife suspected him of cheating."

That wasn't exactly true. Miranda had caught him cheating.

The inspector studied one of the photos, then moved to her car and did a check on the computer inside. She stood up again. "The license of the Camry in your photo and the one found on the premises match, Mr. Parker."

Even though she knew they would, a chill went down Miranda's spine.

Erskine studied Parker carefully with his dark eyes, then addressed Whitman. "You also have access to Dexter Hinsley's arrest record last May for domestic abuse," he offered.

That wasn't quite the truth, either. Parker had told the police Hinsley was a suspect in a local murder so that they'd hold him long enough for Coco to get away.

Sergeant Grogan scratched the side of his head, looking like he wasn't sure what to make of this new information. "We don't even have the perp's description yet. The hotel records confirm Lane checked into the room around two p.m. Saturday," he said. "There was a *Do Not Disturb* sign on the door, but this afternoon, a maid entered the room anyway and discovered the body. My men are still canvassing the other guests."

Parker stepped toward the yellow crime scene tape. "May we take a look at the crime scene?"

Inspector Whitman eyed him for a moment. "Your call, Sergeant Grogan."

"If a new set of eyes can find us a clue, I'm all for it."

Everyone slipped on disposable plastic gloves and crime scene booties. Miranda climbed over the tape and into the room right behind Parker. They took in the scene.

Nasty.

There was blood spatter along the walls, on the headboard of the single bed, the lampshade. A large, dark stain was in the middle of the mattress.

"The sheets, and of course the body, have been taken to the lab for analysis," Inspector Whitman said. "The mattress will go once we've finished."

Grogan strolled over and switched on a light. That only made the room more gruesome. "No shoeprints or fingerprints except Ms. Lane's have been found so far. Evidently, the killer wore gloves of some type."

Miranda wondered what kind of excuse Hinsley used to get away with that. "No murder weapon?"

"None." Grogan exhaled in disgust. "He slashed her up pretty good. Hit the carotid artery. Cut up her face pretty bad, too."

Miranda's gloved hand slid to her chest, where her own knife wounds had healed. "Sick SOB." She stepped over to the bathroom and peeked inside, hoping for something with some DNA on it. "Did they use any towels?"

"The towels are being analyzed as well, but so far, nothing." Grogan planted himself in the corner. "There were no body fluids from inside the victim, either."

The sicko used protection? So there was no DNA to match against Demarco's evidence.

Parker turned to the officers with a stern look. "We have reason to believe Dexter Hinsley may be involved with two recent murders in Chicago."

Grogan folded his arms, looking skeptical. "Chicago?"

Miranda came out of the bathroom. "Hinsley's ex-wife was working in Chicago when her roommate and another woman were killed," she told them. "We think Hinsley may have been hunting her down. She's in Atlanta now."

Miranda watched the inspector's face grow dark.

"Sergeant Demarco of the Chicago police has been keeping us informed on the cases," Parker added.

Inspector Whitman was quiet a moment, taking in the new data. Then she gave a quick nod. "We've picked up a local man the victim's mother identified as Lane's boyfriend. The couple had been dating for some time and recently broke up. But I'll contact Demarco."

Parker turned to Erskine. "Hosea, you didn't take Hinsley's DNA when you arrested him in May, did you?"

"Unfortunately, there wasn't cause."

"I was afraid of that."

By now, Miranda's stomach was churning. Not just from the gore in the room, but from frustration.

As they climbed over the crime scene tape again and pulled off their gloves and disposable shoe covers, a uniformed officer trotted up to them. "Sergeant Grogan?"

"Yes, Casey. What do you have?"

"I just spoke to one of the residents, sir. He said a man came to Lane's door shortly after she arrived yesterday."

"Did he give you a description?"

"Tall, dark-haired. Sloppy dresser. He didn't have much else. Only saw him from the back."

Grogan nodded. "Good work. I'd say that description sounds like the boyfriend we picked up."

Miranda watched Parker stiffen as her heart fluttered down to the pavement. Another boyfriend? And one with a possible motive. That description didn't sound like Hinsley any more than the visitor at Jeffries' property had. If only they had something to match with the semen in Glenda North's stomach.

Their only hope was getting some of Dexter's DNA.

CHAPTER TWENTY-NINE

The next morning, Miranda left the mansion after Parker and made a detour before heading for the office. She pulled off the road near Chastain Park, picked up her cell phone, and dialed the number she'd entered last night.

While Parker had been busy gathering their surveillance records on Dexter boy, she'd noted the Hinsleys' old address in Doraville on Hickory Lane. This morning, she'd taken a few minutes to do some research of her own and found the property was for sale and was being handled by the Mountain Real Estate Company. Surely something in that house had Dexter's DNA on it. She was going to find it, if it killed her.

After two rings, a soft, friendly voice answered on the other end. "Mountain Real Estate. How may I help you?"

"Hello. I'm interested in buying a house in the Doraville area. I saw one on your website that really looks perfect. I know it's short notice, but I'm on my way to work, and I'm wondering if someone could show it to me this morning." Miranda put some pretty-please-with-sugar-on-top in her voice. Must be Coco's influence.

"Oh. Let me look that up." The voice sounded surprised. Probably most customers weren't so pushy. "What's the property you're interested in?"

She rattled off the address.

She heard typing on the other end. "Why yes, ma'am. I can show you that property." The agent sounded like she'd won the lottery. "Can you be there in fifteen minutes?"

That was quick. Miranda glanced at the traffic on the GPS. "Might take twenty. But please wait for me. I'm really excited about this."

"Oh, I will, Ms—. I'm sorry I didn't catch your name?"

Name? "Uh…Groth. Louise Groth." Jeez, couldn't she think of anything better than Leon's and her aunt's names?

"I'm Donna Davis. I'll see you shortly, Ms. Groth."

"Thanks." Miranda clicked off. Excitement kicking up her heartbeat, she pulled back onto the road and headed for I-85.

It took her seventeen and a half minutes. By the time she pulled up to the curb in front of the two-story frame with the neutral siding, the hairs along the back of her neck were doing their tap dance number. She couldn't help thinking of the night they'd rescued Coco here.

The "under contract" sign on the lawn caught her attention. Now what did that mean?

The real estate agent was waiting for her on the driveway. Miranda got out of her jalopy and made her way across the lawn. She hoped the lady didn't give her any flack. She'd hate to have to come back here tonight and do some B and E.

Donna Davis wore cherry red pumps, a white skirt, a red coat and red lipstick over a big, saleslady grin. She held out her hand. "Ms. Groth?"

"That's me." Miranda shook the hand and pointed toward the sign. "It says under contract."

"Well, yes. We got an offer yesterday. But these things have a way of falling through, if you know what I mean. If the deal doesn't happen, you'll be first on the list." She smiled as if she were giving Miranda a gift.

Miranda acted disappointed. "Gee, I really had my heart set on this one. Can I see it anyway?"

"Certainly. That's why we're here."

Miranda blew out a breath of relief as she followed Donna Davis to the front door and watched her open the big padlock. She recalled banging on the door with Parker the night Hinsley beat up Coco.

The two women stepped inside.

There was a short hall alongside a staircase and an arched door that opened into a living room. Donna hit a light switch and Miranda strolled into the room, as if she were browsing. In truth, she was fighting the memory of Coco sitting in the middle of the beige carpet with a gash in her head.

But the room was different now. It was empty. Every stitch of furniture was gone. The place smelled of cleanser.

"It's very roomy," the real estate agent cooed. "And the bay window has a charming view."

Miranda sidled over, peered out the pane without seeing anything and nodded. There was nothing she was looking for in here. "I'd like to see the kitchen."

"It's right in here."

She followed Donna Davis down the hall and to the right. There was an average sized kitchen painted a cheery yellow with white cabinets. She began opening them one by one. She was hoping for a cup or a glass Hinsley might have handled before he left for LA, but there was nothing. She opened cabinets under the sink thinking she might find a used Styrofoam cup in the trashcan. But it was just as empty.

"I'm a stickler for space," she laughed.

"Oh, I am, too. A lot of space here. It's a three bedroom, two and a half bath, as I'm sure you know. Would you like to see the upstairs?"

Miranda nodded enthusiastically. "Oh, yes."

She followed Donna Davis back down the hall and up the steep, carpeted staircase to the upper floor and headed for the master bedroom. The sight of it, and the idea that Dexter and Coco had slept here together, sickened her.

But there was no trace of Hinsley here. No sheets, no bed, no furniture, nothing in the closet. Growing disgusted, she marched to the master bath.

While the agent remained in the bedroom, chatting about the floor plan, Miranda scoured the linen closet. Empty. Not even a stray towel or washcloth left behind. She turned around and opened the medicine cabinet, hoping for toothbrush or cup. Also empty. She ran her hand over the shelving. If only she could find a razor blade. But the surface was clean as a whistle.

Her heart sinking, she yanked open the top drawer of the vanity. Nothing. She tried another drawer. Nada. Last one. Everything had been cleared out. She was just about to slam it shut when she spotted something in the back of it.

She leaned down and peered inside for a closer look. Her heart stopped. Was that what she thought it was?

Wedged in the very back, in the corner seam of the drawer, was a short black comb. A man's comb. A comb with red hair in its teeth.

She called out to the real estate lady. "Uh, I think I need to use the little girl's room. Hope that's okay."

"Of course, help yourself."

She shut the door and laid the clunky giraffe purse from Coco down on the counter. Being careful not to disturb her Beretta, she dug for the baggie she'd found in the mansion's kitchen and for Parker's monogrammed handkerchief that she'd pinched from his drawer this morning.

Carefully, she draped the hanky around her hand, reached into the drawer and touched the comb. It took a bit of pressure to pry it loose, but finally it came free.

With a steady move, she wrapped the hanky around the comb, put both into the baggie, sealed it, and shoved it into her purse.

She closed the drawer, gave the toilet a flush, and exited the room. She found Donna Davis at the window. "This place is nice. Too bad it's not readily available."

"Oh, but like I said, you'll be next on the list. I promise."

Miranda nodded, as a thought struck her. "Is the owner in town? I mean, maybe I could talk to him."

The agent's pupils dilated and her painted smile faded. "No. I mean, uh, he's not here. He's out of state. His brother's handling the transaction. He has power of attorney."

That was interesting. "I see. Well, I really have to get to work now."

"I can show you some other properties if you'd like to make an appointment, Ms. Groth."

"I really had my heart set on this one." Miranda hurried past her and down the stairs. "But call me if the deal falls through. Or if you can arrange for me to talk with the owner."

"But I'm sure I can find something you'll fall in love with…" Her voice sounded desperate.

As she went out the front door and down the walkway, Miranda wondered why Donna Davis had suddenly seemed so frightened.

CHAPTER THIRTY

Parker leaned back and smiled with satisfaction at his computer screen. His work this weekend had finally paid off. He'd narrowed his search for Edward Steele down to two states. One of them was Hawaii.

Just the perfect place to take Miranda on their honeymoon.

He minimized the program, rose and strolled to the window as the murder of Elizabeth Lane overshadowed his thoughts. It was hard for him to believe the killer was Dexter Hinsley. The former textbook salesman had lost his job and been away from Atlanta for weeks. Why would Lane see him?

Besides, he'd heard on the news this morning that Ms. Lane's boyfriend had threatened the victim after she broke up with him and was now the chief suspect.

In addition, Ms. Lane's friends indicated the teacher had been seeing several men recently, all of whom were now being questioned by Sergeant Grogan. The killer could be any of them, or one of her colleagues, or a hitchhiker she picked up along the road. In short, anyone.

With the lack of evidence, unless someone confessed, it would be a long time before that case was closed. He hated that and felt for the family.

He reached for his jacket and pulled it on. He had a meeting with Judd and Gen this morning to go over the future assignments of the graduating IITs. Both of them would be shocked by his plans for Miranda. After Sylvia passed, he'd lightened his caseload and had been only dabbling at his work at the Agency. Now he had grown tired of that. After mourning the loss of his deceased wife for three years, he'd decided to come back to work in full force. After he and Miranda were married, he intended to offer his services to agencies all over the country.

He chuckled to himself. And, if she found the idea agreeable, and he knew that she would, Miranda would be at his side.

As she hurried up the back entrance to the Agency, Miranda felt her cell vibrate in her pocket. She yanked it out and glared at it. A text from Gen. *You need to decide on favors. And gifts for your bridesmaids. And the rehearsal dinner.*

Good grief. Later. Without replying, she shoved the phone back in her pocket.

She was breathless when she burst through Parker's office door and found him staring out the window at the cloudless sky.

"Got a minute?" she asked him.

He turned and smiled at her with that gorgeous grin of his. "Just a few. I have a meeting soon."

She closed the door and plopped her big giraffe purse on the table. "I visited the Hinsley residence this morning."

His smile vanished. "You did what?"

"I went to their old Doraville address on Hickory Lane. It's for sale. I called the real estate agent and got her to let me in."

"You went there alone?" His voice was threatening.

"I had my Beretta with me."

She could see Parker wrestling with stunned admiration and his protective nature. "The police have already checked out the property. They found it vacant."

"Actually, it's under contract now. And the police didn't find this." She pulled out the baggie and held it up.

"What is that?" he said, as if he had already made a guess.

She couldn't help grinning. "Hinsley's comb. With hair in it."

The angry expression on his face melted into pure pride. "You found something with Hinsley's DNA?"

"I hope so. The hair's red." She set it down on the table.

For a moment both of them just stared at the baggie, not wanting to touch it for fear of disturbing the evidence.

At last Parker spoke. "Excellent work, Miranda. We'll send this to Inspector Whitman at the GBI right away."

"Can't our lab analyze it?"

"Not as quickly."

"What about Demarco? Wouldn't he like first crack?"

"As grateful as I am to the sergeant in Chicago, I don't think his lab would be faster."

He was right. "Then he'll just have to understand." The hair wouldn't be admissible in court, but if they got a match, it would be enough for the cops to get a warrant for a DNA swab on Hinsley. Once they captured him.

Parker lifted his gaze and studied her face a moment. "You have to be prepared that the results may be disappointing."

Miranda frowned. "What do you mean?"

"That Hinsley's DNA may not match the DNA found in Glenda North."

She was stunned. "You don't think Hinsley killed her?"

"Let's just say I'm not as convinced as you are. My men haven't seen anything of Hinsley while they've been guarding Coco."

She gave him a scowl. "That's probably because Hinsley got wise and avoided them."

"It could be. Or it could be because he wasn't there. You have to admit that possibility."

"Sure, it's a possibility, but we can't assume it."

He stepped away from the table, picked up a folder on his desk. "Just why I still have bodyguards in place. Did you see any signs of occupancy at his house?"

She shook her head. "Nada. Everything was cleared out. The real estate agent said Hinsley's brother is handling the sale. That he has power of attorney. I didn't believe her."

"That could be true. Hinsley could still be in California, for all we know. He could have taken another job without giving notice to the carwash."

She slumped down into one of his cushy blue chairs. Parker sure knew how to take the wind out of her sails. "Somebody ought to check the flight records from Chicago to Atlanta."

"Already done."

She sat up. "Really? What did you find?"

"I checked the day of our flight and the entire week after it. No Dexter Hinsley was a passenger on any flight."

"He could have traveled under an assumed name," she said.

"Or taken a bus or a train."

"Or driven, or hitchhiked, or taken a slow boat from China." She put her head in her hands. God, this was maddening.

Parker laid down his folder, came around to her chair and gently pulled her hands away. She looked up at his handsome face. "I will admit from what little we know, Hinsley does have characteristics of a sociopath. Untruthfulness, irritability, aggression."

That was better. "Don't forget charm. I wonder how he'd score on the Hare Psychopathy Checklist."

He grinned. "You have been studying."

She shrugged.

"You're going to do well on your exam."

"I hope so." But if Parker thought she was off base about Hinsley, she wondered if she'd pass.

If only they had a way to know for sure if he was the killer. The DNA test, even at the GBI, would take time. Even if it turned out positive, they still had to find him. Hopefully before he struck again. If only they had a way of drawing him out into the open.

"I'm late for my meeting." He kissed her on the cheek, reached for his folder, and started for the door.

She wondered how long they could keep Coco under wraps. The girl was getting restless. Then an idea struck her. She stood up. "What if we set a trap?"

He turned back. "What kind of a trap?"

"Coco is trying to get her old job back at the Gecko Club. What if we have her do just that and advertise it in the newspapers? If Hinsley's hunting her down, he'll come after her there."

A slow, lazy grin spread across his handsome face. "My darling, that's a brilliant idea."

CHAPTER THIRTY-ONE

He sat on the end of his ratty bed in his cheap hotel room along the interstate, staring at the beat-up television. The newscaster blabbered on and on, just as she had for two days. His heart stopped when his own picture appeared on the screen.

He shot to his feet. No. How could they suspect him?

He listened to the words. They didn't know his whereabouts. Anyone who knew any information about the man in the photo should call the number on the screen.

He dug his nails into his scalp. Parker and Steele had to be involved in that investigation. They had it out for him. Where had they gotten that picture? He recognized it. It had been taken when he and Cora Beth were first married.

Cora Beth. *She'd* given it to them. She'd betrayed him.

He'd have to teach her a lesson for that.

He shut off the TV and stomped to the bathroom. Leaning over the sink, he stared at himself in the mirror. He was safe. No one could identify him.

His hair was straight and black as night. His complexion was dark from the liquid tanning solution he'd been using. He didn't look at all like the photo on TV. He looked like Miguel Rodriguez, just like his new ID claimed he was.

And he'd filled out since he started training with his sensei in California. The police would be looking for a thinner man with curly red hair.

He was safe.

He lifted his hand and stroked his mustache with a forefinger. Thick, but not dark enough.

He reached for the kit he'd bought at the drugstore on the corner. He pulled on a new pair of latex gloves and patiently mixed the color with the activator. The smell was awful. Ignoring it, he took the small brush from the kit, dipped in the mix and slowly stroked it on his mustache, from root to tip, being careful not to touch his skin.

The funny thing was that he'd changed his mind about killing Elizabeth. After fucking her eyes out for three hours in the Mableton hotel room, he'd gotten dressed and was simply going to leave. It was too risky, anyway, he'd decided.

But she wouldn't let him go. She wanted more from him. Promises. A relationship. At first, he'd laughed at the stupid bitch. Then she started screaming at him. She called him a coward, a jerk, a son-of-a-bitch. She struck him across the face.

No woman had ever dared to strike him.

He didn't remember much after that. Just the blinding rage pulsing through every nerve in his body.

He'd had a knife in his belt. A small survival knife he'd bought for protection when he moved to the hotel. He must have grabbed it. Must have slashed her with it. Must have kept slashing until she shut the fuck up.

When he came to, he was standing over her, the bloody knife in his hand. Her lifeless body lay naked on the bed. Blood was everywhere.

But it didn't matter. He'd taken care of it. He'd driven south toward the airport and stuffed his clothes and shoes in a dumpster behind a Goodwill store. Then he'd changed into the extra set he carried with him. The police would never find them, much less trace them to him.

He was safe. He was Miguel Rodriguez now.

He put the mustache brush down and pulled off the gloves. Twenty minutes to set.

He turned off the bathroom light and shuffled over to the cheap pressboard nightstand. He opened a drawer and pulled out the sleek, compact Ruger .380. He ran his hand over the barrel. No waiting period for him. Not in this location. The upside of living in a sleazy hotel. He got the gun from the same guy who sold him the fake ID.

He'd use this bad boy soon. But first, he had to get rid of those bodyguards.

He put the gun away and went to the desk. He sat down and reached for the Priority mail envelope he'd purchased. He scratched out his brother's address on the label, then used a piece of notebook paper to dash off a quick letter.

Hi bro,

Sorry I haven't been in touch. Can I ask you a favor? I need you to mail this card.

He picked up the postcard. "Greetings from sunny Los Angeles." It even had the Hollywood sign on it. He'd picked it up in an LAX gift shop, hoping to use it in Iowa to convince Cora Beth to come back to Los Angeles with him by feeding her dream of becoming a star.

He turned it over and wrote on the back of it. He even used that ridiculous stage name of hers.

Coco, I hope this finds you well...

He told her he'd found a new job. That he was starting a new life in LA. He even threw in that he'd found a new girlfriend. That would make her want him again.

He signed the card and slipped it into the envelope along with the note to Derek. He'd mail it off later today.

He and Cora Beth had moved twice after they married. Two apartments before they'd bought the house. Both times, she had insisted on leaving a forwarding address.

She would have done the same in Iowa. That meant his postcard should arrive at the Parker residence just before the wedding.

He picked up the announcement he'd clipped from the paper. A little more than a week away.

Yes, the Hollywood postcard was just the thing to set Cora Beth's empty little mind at ease. To set all their minds at ease.

Then Parker would call off his bodyguards, and everyone would let down their defenses.

They'd all get ready for the big day. And no one would enjoy it more than he would.

He smiled to himself. Everything was falling into his hands. He was lucky. Killing Parker and his bride just before their wedding day would be a better payback than he could have hoped for.

Best of all, he would finally have his Cora Beth back.

"Oh yes, Cora Beth," he whispered as if she were here already. "You will belong to me then. We'll always be together. I'll hold you in my arms and you will be forever mine."

CHAPTER THIRTY-TWO

The next three days were the most insane Miranda had ever lived through.

The RSVPs from the wedding invitations started coming in. So did the gifts. Miranda didn't know what to do with the linens or the cutlery or the chafing dishes—as if they needed any of that stuff. Gen knew. She insisted that Miranda open each one and write thank you notes. Good grief.

Mr. P stopped by the mansion to say how excited he was about giving away the bride, but Gen kicked him out after half an hour.

She wanted decisions on seating arrangements and the food for the reception. And the cake. Oh, the cake.

They had to go to three different bakeries and taste twenty different types of freaking wedding cake. From dark chocolate to strawberry to butterscotch to some kind of foie gras mixture. Parker suggested the cake be baked with jalapenos and topped with Red Hots.

Grunting her exasperation, Miranda told the baker it would be yellow cake. Five heart-shaped tiers iced with white buttercream and decked with white magnolias made out of sugar and purple-tinted gardenias.

She wanted to escape the bakery before she broke out in hives. Whose idea was this wedding, anyway? Oh, right. Hers.

But that was only the beginning of Gen's list. The only way to get it over with was to go into overdrive. So Miranda started making decisions with a vengeance.

The rehearsal dinner would be in the restaurant atop Parker Towers, where Parker had fed her that first five-star dinner. For the reception, they'd use a downtown events center owned by Mr. P that had a large ballroom. After she and Parker had auditioned bands until she thought her eardrums would bleed, she chose the seven-piece jazz combo. For favors, she selected soap carved like roses for the ladies and silver pens for the men.

Then it was off to the florist. After just half an hour, she picked out a heart-shaped bouquet of ivory honeysuckle and roses in every tint of the bridesmaids dresses. And matching rose bouquets for the bridesmaids. Lilies draped in tulle for the pews at St. Simon's. Gardenias and peonies dyed in fuchsias and pinks and plums for the reception.

Done.

Next, the jeweler. She picked out a sleek hand brushed tailored platinum band for Parker, while he chose a diamond-and-sapphire one that fit perfectly under the rock of her engagement ring.

When he wasn't looking, Miranda selected a pair of onyx-and-diamond cufflinks for him as a wedding present. Not too original, but she couldn't think of anything else he'd like.

Then it was the men's shop. Here they decided Parker and his groomsmen would be in black cutaway jackets, matching vests, white wing tip shirts, and coordinated striped pants set off by solid gray ascots at the neck and a single rosebud boutonniere on the lapel.

Then came more fittings for the ladies.

And in between was study, study, study. Study at home alone. Study at work with her buddies Becker and Holloway. Study in her sleep. Practice at the shooting range. Workouts in the company dojo and the home gym.

On top of that, she had to pick Wendy up at the skating rink again when her mother was too busy to get her.

But that was a welcome break. Miranda liked taking care of the kid. She kept her overnight again and took her to work the next day, as she'd promised. It was fun having her around. But while trying out the fingerprinting kit Miranda had given her to play with, Wendy had asked if Miranda was after the guy who killed the teacher in Mableton.

Perceptive kid. She told her she couldn't say and got a scowl in return.

She couldn't let Wendy in on the plan because Coco wasn't in on the plan.

When Miranda told her she'd changed her mind about the Gecko Club, Coco acted like she'd won a game show. She hopped up and down, hugged her, slobbered her cheek with kisses. Jeez.

She promised she'd be careful and swore Miranda wouldn't regret it.

Not if they got Hinsley.

Miranda bit her tongue and pretended to be excited when Estavez escorted the girl in his Ferrari to her audition, followed by the three bodyguards. Parker was prepared to grease Frankie's palm, but the owner hired the talented singer right away. Her opening night would be three days before the wedding. That should wrap things up nicely.

And then one sunny afternoon, she found herself in her IIT classroom taking the three-hour written exam.

Some questions were easier than she'd expected, others harder. Covert surveillance was a breeze after hanging around Parker all these weeks. Search and seizure was tricky. By the time she got to Firearms, she was sweating shotgun shells.

She was the last one to finish, and when she turned in her paper to Detective Judd, she wasn't at all sure she'd passed.

"I think you did just fine," the stodgy instructor called after her as she shuffled out of the room.

What if she didn't make eighty percent? What if she couldn't become a private investigator in Georgia? Once she'd entertained the idea of going to another state where the licensing laws weren't so strict. But if she were married to Parker, that would be kind of awkward.

And tomorrow she had to face the gun range and martial arts competitions.

The next morning, after the class drove out to the Aim-Right Shooting Range and got their equipment, her buddies Becker and Holloway were still sweating over the exam.

"Did you get that question about the GPS on a car?" Becker whispered while they were getting in place.

Holloway shook his head. "It stumped me."

Miranda was stunned. If her buddies had a hard time on the test, where did that leave her? They had real investigation-related experience before they came to the Agency. She'd been a construction worker. But she'd known the answer to that question.

She lowered her voice. "The roads are public, so there's no expectation of privacy. But if you trespassed when you put the GPS on the suspect vehicle, the court will throw out the evidence."

Becker hit his head with the heel of his hand. "I knew that."

"Too late now," Holloway muttered.

Judd called the class to order and read off the rules.

Each IIT was to shoot one-handed at twenty-five yards. Rapid fire, two five-rounds strings. A couple of senior investigators from the Agency were on hand to help keep score. Judd assigned everyone a number and they would go in that order.

This was it.

One by one, the eight students stepped up to the stall and fired. Miranda was last, right after Gordon Granger, who had been with the New York Police Department. She tried her best, but her palms were as sweaty as a drug addict going dry. She flubbed it. She just couldn't get her aim close to the bull's eye.

She came in fifth out of eight. Becker took third place and Holloway came in second.

Janelle Wesson took first place and was gloating like a peacock. Miranda thought she might sprout feathers any minute. She couldn't wait to kick her ass in the martial arts competition.

That afternoon, the IITs met back in the Parker Agency's gym, where a large mat had been set up.

This time Judd paired the students against each other by weight. Bill Taylor was matched with Jose Vega. They both had military backgrounds. Becker got

Gordon Granger. Holloway wound up with Amir Khan, a big dude who had the same name as a professional boxer. Miranda was glad she hadn't been pitted against him. But that left her with the only other female in the class.

Janelle Wesson.

Noreen Tan, Parker's Chief Assistant, would act as referee, and each of the four bouts would be judged by Judd, Kay Carson, an investigator who'd been with the Agency for a decade, and Ray O'Neill, head of Protection.

Tan was a good choice for ref, in Miranda's opinion. She was tough but fair—she treated all the IITs like equal piles of dung.

None of the contestants could win an MMA championship, but if you couldn't defend yourself in a fight with a criminal you might meet in a dark alley, you'd be a goner. So doing well was mandatory to become a Level One Investigator. The judges were not going to go easy on the IITs.

Parker didn't show on purpose so as not to distract anyone. Or to embarrass Miranda, now that everyone knew they were an item after the wedding announcement in the newspaper. She'd gotten razzed pretty hard at first, but it was old news now.

Taylor and Vega were up first. They were evenly matched, but the contest didn't last long. Vega got a submission in the second round with an arm bar.

Next up, Becker and Granger. Miranda held her breath when Becker took an uppercut to the chin that broke his lip open and bled all over the mat. She was glad Fanuzzi wasn't here. Her MOH might climb in the ring with her new hubby and give Granger a few slugs. Hey, it was all Miranda could do not to join them herself.

But Becker recovered and held his own. He went all three rounds. The winner would be up to the judges, but Miranda thought Becker made it by at least five points.

Holloway's jump kicks against Khan were smooth and precise. Khan was an excellent fighter, but by the second round, Holloway had him down on the mat. Just before the bell, he got a tap of submission with a joint lock to the arm. That had to hurt.

And then it was Miranda's turn. As she climbed into the ring, she felt like somebody had her stomach in a chokehold.

She was wearing her red boxing shorts and a black tank top, while Wesson was all in white. Like she thought she was an angel? Or some kind of freaking knight in shining armor?

She sneered at Miranda as they touched gloves.

Tan gave the signal and the bell rang.

Now or never. Do or die. And a few other not-so-nice clichés came to mind as they glared at each other.

They hung back along the ropes, dancing clockwise, counterclockwise, and clockwise again. Pretty soon, *The Blue Danube* would start playing.

Finally Wesson made a move. She rushed across the mat like the wind and threw a sharp jab at Miranda's jaw.

Miranda did her classic last-minute sidestep. Wesson flew past her and hit the ropes. She spun around, fury on her face. "You can't get by with that sissy move, Steele."

"Just did." With a smirk, Miranda gave her a kick to the chest, followed by a chambered punch to the head.

Wesson blocked it. She was quick. She returned the punch and followed it with a left.

Miranda returned with an elbow slash to the forehead.

Blocked again.

Deep down, Miranda wanted to respect Wesson. She was tall and lean and smart. She was only thirty-two, but she'd worked for a small police department out West and was the only one in the class with real investigative experience.

If only she weren't such a bitch.

"You're nothing but a suck-up, Steele."

"And what do you suck, Wesson?" Miranda heard Becker cheer.

They danced some more and exchanged a volley of punches that winded both of them.

Wesson leaned against the ropes, gasping. "You think you're such a hotshot. I'm gonna show you you're not."

"Oh, yeah?"

"That's right. You're only here because you're screwing the boss."

That got boos from the class. And almost distracted her from Wesson's foot flying toward her face. In the nick of time, she threw up her arm and blocked, but it stung like hell.

Keep your head, she told herself. Wesson was just talking trash, trying to piss her off. She was succeeding. Miranda's relationship with Parker was a sore spot. But she'd beaten guys twice her size before she came to the Agency. She'd been locked up for fighting. She could put men under the table in jalapeno eating contests.

Come on. Get serious.

She went on the attack. Leading with jabs and hooks, she backed Wesson up several feet. But Wesson bobbed and slipped, dodging Miranda's fists. Finally, she executed a nice flying knee kick that smacked Wesson right under the chin.

Wesson flew back and caught herself against the ropes, shock on her face.

Miranda had to gloat. "What were you saying about my relationship with the boss?"

Wesson ignored her. The trash talk was done. Fire in her eyes, she hurled herself at Miranda and hit her with a head butt to the stomach that knocked the wind out of her.

Miranda lost her footing and stumbled backwards. As she went down, Wesson got her in the shin with a low kick.

She landed hard on the mat with the bitch on top of her. Not good. Grappling wasn't her strong suit. That's when she usually had flashbacks of the night she was raped.

But this time, there was nothing in her head but pain. And the sense of impending loss.

Somehow she managed to wrap her legs around Wesson's waist and lock her ankles together. That gave her a little leverage, but Wesson kept punching at her face and her ribs.

It hurt like crazy and though she blocked most of the blows, Miranda was losing steam fast. They couldn't be more than three minutes into the round. She couldn't hold out until the end of it.

She was going to lose. She wouldn't be a Level One Investigator. She'd be doomed to paperwork for the rest of her life.

Anger pulsed inside her. And sharp disappointment. Then, in the swirling emotion came a new burst of determination. Lose to *Wesson?*

Like hell.

With adrenaline that must have come out of her backside, she shoved Wesson away with her elbows, got a knee around her and in her stomach. She twisted, pushed. And with one gargantuan pull, she turned Wesson around. Now she was the one on top.

Wesson's cheeks burned with rage.

Now what? Miranda didn't like chokes. Didn't have the stomach for it. But just now, she had no choice. She leaned forward and pressed her forearm against Wesson's neck.

Wesson went red in the face. Mostly from anger, Miranda hoped. "Ease up," she hissed.

"Give it up, Wesson."

"Why? You're the loser."

"Not at the moment." She added a little pressure.

Wesson's eyes went wide, as if she couldn't believe Miranda had the guts to do her in.

There was dead silence in the gym. Tan would stop the fight any second now. But Wesson wouldn't quit. Then from the corner of her eye, Miranda saw her opponent's hand shoot out and give the mat three taps.

She let go, got to her feet, and reached out a hand to help Wesson up. Rubbing her throat, she sat there on the mat and glared at her.

"Good work, Steele." Tan tucked her hands under Wesson's armpits and lifted her to her feet. The gym shook with roars.

Looking around at her cheering classmates and teachers, Miranda was amazed. She couldn't believe it. She'd done it. Submission in one round. The longest five minutes of her life.

CHAPTER THIRTY-THREE

"Did I make it?"

Miranda lay on her back next to Parker in the big, luxurious bed in the mansion's master bedroom, basking in the delicious afterglow of intimacy. It was amazing how making love to Parker could soothe and relax sore muscles.

He turned to her, satisfaction on his face. "Make what?"

She grimaced and rolled over, leaning on one elbow. "You know what. Tell me if I passed."

"Passed?" He was playing dumb.

"Passed the tests? The ones I took yesterday and today? At the Agency you own?"

He feigned confusion. "You think I know the results of those tests?"

"You have to. You're the boss. So spill." She poked him in his muscular chest.

He gave her a horrified look. "That would be unethical."

She grunted and socked him on his bare bicep. "Screw ethical. I want to know. It's killing me. C'mon, Parker. Tell me if I'm a Level One Investigator."

He chuckled with amusement. "I don't think you'll have to go back to working on the road crew, if that's what you're worried about."

That didn't tell her much. Fighting her frustration, she studied the stubborn man. "I thought you didn't know anything."

His smile grew wicked. "You're right. I have no way of knowing that. But I heard you've mastered the chokehold."

She narrowed an eye at him. "I think you know more than results."

Ignoring her remark, he slipped an arm around her. "And you shouldn't be afraid to use it. You might have to in a real situation some day."

"Oh, yeah? I'll get those test results out of you." She pivoted quickly, centered herself atop his muscular frame, and leaned in to lay her forearm across his neck.

Before she could blink, Parker's hand caught her wrist. He spun around and laid her flat on her back, pinning her arms over her head on the mattress. He began to kiss her face.

"What are you doing?" she sputtered under his lips.

"Demonstrating one of my own techniques."

His mouth moved to her neck and her breath fluttered out of her. Her whole body shivered with sensation. "No fair. You're a lot sexier than Wesson."

He laughed against her throat. "I should hope so." He began to work his way down her neck to her collarbone. Then down further down to her breast. "And about those test results?"

"Yes?" she gasped before she lost verbal capability.

His laugh turned soft as his tongue grazed her nipple. "You'll find them out tomorrow along with the rest of the IITs."

The next morning Miranda crept down the hall of the Agency to Judd's office, her stomach as jumpy as a kangaroo.

She found Becker, Holloway, and the rest of the IITs perched in front of Judd's door, gaping at the paper posted there.

She stood there eyeing them, her arms wrapped tight around her middle. She couldn't look. Oh, God. What if she didn't make it? What was she going to do?

But she couldn't stand here forever, either. She had to deal with it sometime. Might as well get it over. Mustering her courage, she took a deep breath, stepped forward, and dared to look.

The firearms results were first, which everybody already knew. Wesson had scored one hundred, beating out everyone else. Holloway was second. Miranda's score was painfully low.

The written exam was next. Her breath caught when she saw her name. Was that right? *Ninety-eight percent?* She'd scored ninety-eight percent on that bear of an exam? She'd never scored that high on a test.

What about the martial arts? The bout with Wesson gave her a perfect ten. Wow. And Becker had come in second.

Quickly, she scanned the rest of the page. The four winners were listed at the bottom. Curt Holloway. Dave Becker. Janelle Wesson. And…Miranda Steele.

Really? She couldn't believe it. She gave a little gasp and started to prance. She'd done it.

She'd made Level One Investigator.

And so had Becker and Holloway. She was thrilled for them. It was their dream. She was even happy for Wesson. But what about the others?

She stopped dancing as she glanced at her classmates. She shouldn't celebrate in front of them. They must be humiliated.

Beside her, Granger shook his head. "Sorry you didn't make the cut, Steele."

"What?" Had she read the paper wrong?

Granger gestured toward the door. "You and your buddies here are Level One Investigators."

"Yeah?" What did he mean?

He nodded at the others who weren't on the list. "We get to work at a nice, safe desk in a cushy office while you all have to risk your necks on the street."

She scowled at him. "You *want* to do all that paperwork?"

"Sure. That's what I signed up for."

Khan, Vega, and Taylor nodded their agreement.

Miranda did a double take. "You mean you four didn't do your best? You held back?"

Granger appeared shocked by her question. "I wouldn't go that far."

"Are you kidding?" Khan said. "And look like a wimp on purpose?"

"I sure didn't hold anything back," Taylor agreed. "But if I'd made Level One Investigator, I was going to ask Judd if I could change spots with somebody."

Guess she didn't have to feel bad for them after all. With a happy grin, Miranda lifted her hands. "To each his own."

That evening, Parker held a party in one of the Agency conference rooms in honor of the graduates. There were saucers of expensive canapés, flutes of Dom Pérignon, and a big cake with *Congratulations* written on the top. The instructors and staff even joked and conversed with their students like they were real human beings for a change.

Miranda was munching a blue cheese celery boat and teasing Becker about his nerves over the written exam when the door opened and Parker strolled into the room.

The whole place went silent. At least her half of it, as all former-IIT eyes zeroed in on the CEO and President.

Oozing his confident charm, Parker sauntered through the area greeting his staff members. He was flawlessly dressed in a charcoal worsted suit and a red, paisley silk tie that set off the salt-and-pepper of his perfectly styled hair. Every inch of him was gorgeous and suave, right down to his Gucci wingtips.

After finishing the niceties with the faculty, he made his way over to the graduates.

He shook hands with each of them. "Congratulations, Mr. Vega."

"Th—thank you, sir," Vega squeaked in reply.

"Mr. Granger. Mr. Khan. Well done, Mr. Taylor."

It took a minute for Taylor to find his voice. "Thank you, Mr. Parker."

Then Parker turned to his four new Level One Investigators, beaming proudly.

He shook hands with Becker first. "Excellent tenacity in the third round of your bout, Detective Becker."

Turning beet red, the poor guy could only nod.

He turned to Becker's tall buddy. "That was some fine shooting, Detective Holloway."

"Thank you, sir," Holloway coughed and looked away.

Next was Wesson. "And I was impressed with your perfect score on the range, Detective Wesson."

Military-like, she straightened and returned a curt nod. "I did my best, sir."

Finally, he took Miranda's hand and gave it a shake devoid of any passion. "Fine work on the mat, Detective Steele."

"Thank you, sir." Miranda shot him a sidelong glance. *You sly devil, you.* He had known the scores all along. And the details, too. But she was glad he was treating her like one of the guys and not like a fiancée.

"Are you ready to go to work?"

Becker came to attention. "We are, sir."

"Then I'll see all of you in my office in ten minutes for your first assignment."

Parker's classy blue-and-silver office had an edgy feel tonight under the fluorescent lights, with the glow of offices in the neighboring buildings twinkling through the floor-to-ceiling windows. As Miranda settled into one of the blue swivel chairs, she thought of the night she'd snuck in here to do some "research" and discovered Iris Van Aarle was having an affair with Isaiah Todd.

"Close the door, please," Parker said to Holloway as he took a seat behind his big glass desk.

"Yes, sir." Holloway shut the door and stood by it, like a sentry.

Parker gestured to the four chairs he'd arranged in front of his desk. "Please take a seat, everyone."

Becker sat down next to Miranda and Wesson grabbed the next chair, leaving Holloway the one at the end. Anxious over what she knew Parker was about to announce, Miranda resisted the urge to chew on her thumb.

"What's this about, sir?" Wesson asked, her face full of excitement.

Kind of ironic, but Miranda was glad to have Wesson on board for this assignment. It called for someone who was tough.

Parker reached for a copy of the *AJC* and held it out to the new investigators. It was turned to the entertainment section. "Have any of you seen this?"

It was an ad for the Gecko Club's returning singer, with a picture of Coco in all her stunning glory. They all studied it for a moment.

Becker was the first to nod. "I noticed it, sir. Holloway and I went to see that singer at that club a couple of months ago." He glanced at Miranda. "She's a friend of Steele's, isn't she?" He knew that from Fanuzzi.

"Yes," Parker said, as casually as if he were talking about his shoe size. "Coco is her stage name. Her real name is Cora Beth Hinsley. We suspect she could be the target of a serial killer."

Becker's mouth fell open. Holloway stiffened.

Wesson's green eyes glowed. "A serial killer? We're taking down a serial killer, sir?"

Excitement trickled through the group.

"Don't get ahead of me, Detective Wesson. One of the purposes of Ms. Hinsley's performance at the club is to draw out the killer."

Becker sucked in his breath. "A sting operation?"

Everyone grinned.

Parker regarded his new graduates with a mixture of pride and caution. He remembered how it felt when he was new at this game and every case pounded adrenaline though his veins. He still felt that way at times. But it wasn't wise to lose one's head.

He reached for a folder and took out copies of Dexter Hinsley's photograph, the police mug shots, and a summary of the data they had on him. He handed them to Miranda to pass out. "These are the best likenesses we have of the suspect. His name is Dexter Hinsley."

"He has a record," Holloway noticed as he examined the papers.

"He was incarcerated for a short time last May. The charges were dropped," Parker said flatly. "Coco's first performance is tomorrow night at eight. This is the man we expect to show up. I want all of you to study the photos and be ready to apprehend."

"What's he done, sir?" Holloway wanted to know.

Miranda watched Parker inhale slowly, wondering how much he was going to tell them. "We don't have conclusive evidence of anything," he said at last. "But he's wanted for questioning in several murder cases."

Becker's eyes grew round. "That teacher who was killed in Mableton?" The story was still on the news.

Parker nodded. "Yes."

"Hinsley," Wesson said thoughtfully. "Is he a relative of the singer?"

"Her ex-husband."

"Oh." Wesson looked down at the floor with an expression that made Miranda wonder if she'd had a violent man in her past.

Parker gave everyone a moment to take it all in. "All of you will be posing as patrons of the club, there for drinks and the show. Of course, you are to drink non-alcoholic beverages during the duration of the assignment."

"Understood, sir." Holloway half-saluted.

"Does everyone feel up to this task?"

"Absolutely, sir." Everybody nodded vigorously.

"Excellent. Any questions?" After no one said anything, Parker rose.

Everyone stood. Becker put a finger in the air. "Sir?"

"Yes, Detective Becker?

"Are we to carry firearms?"

Parker's stern nod shot chills down Miranda's spine. "I want everyone locked and loaded. We assume Hinsley is desperate. He may be armed and dangerous."

CHAPTER THIRTY-FOUR

The Gecko Club seemed larger than Miranda remembered it. With its sweeping, salmon-colored bar of mahogany, its wide, shiny mirror lined with gleaming glasses, its softly lit elegance, the club had become one of the hot spots along the Buckhead strip, attracting hoards of designer-clad patrons.

Of course, the ads proclaiming the return of the beloved Coco had filled the place tonight. As she crossed in front of the stage, which also seemed a lot bigger now, Miranda wondered how they were going to spot Hinsley in this crowd. No, that was just her nerves talking.

Becker, Holloway, Wesson, and Parker were spread across the room in strategic positions where each of them could keep a close eye on both the door and the stage. If Hinsley stepped inside and tried anything, he wouldn't get far. Tonight was the night that bastard was going down.

The noise died down as she slipped through a door behind the stage and into a narrow, darkened hall. Frankie, the owner, had cleared out a small room here where the entertainment could dress and get ready. She knocked on the door and found Coco in her glittery loveliness, Estavez by her side. Of course.

"Ready?"

Coco put her hands to her cheeks, her silvery nails catching the light. "Oh, Miranda. I'm so nervous. I haven't played in public since Chicago."

How could someone so beautiful and talented be so insecure? "You'll do fine."

Miranda was excited for her and wished they didn't have to pull off an operation under her nose. But once Hinsley was in jail, Coco would really have her freedom back.

She shook her blond curls. "I don't know. What if they don't like me?"

"They'll love you. Just think about the music. Think about Estavez, here."

"She's right, *mi querida*. You know when you play, you make my heart soar to Heaven." He took her hands and kissed them.

Coco's cheeks turned pink, but she was smiling now.

"It's show time," Miranda grinned. "Go knock 'em dead."

163

"You're right. Both of you. And I will." She straightened her shoulders, lifted her chin and headed down the hall.

Miranda gave Estavez an "okay" sign with her fingers and followed.

Making her way to a tiny table in the corner that gave her a good view of the entire place, Miranda settled in and ordered a glass of non-alcoholic White Zinfandel as the singer appeared on the stage.

The crowd cheered and whistled. She smiled coyly and sat down gracefully at the baby grand on the stage. Then she started to play and fell into her rendition of the jazzy and, in this case, ironic "Lady Sings the Blues."

She filled the air with her gorgeous voice and impressive piano playing. She'd gotten even better. She was so talented. Miranda caught a glimpse of Estavez mooning over her from the floor and hoped with all her heart her friend could have her dreams and live a life free of fear.

Maybe after tonight, she could.

Coco was three songs into her set when a dark-haired figure appeared, beer mug in hand, making her way toward her with a familiar bouncy swagger.

Without invitation she set her mug on Miranda's table and sat down. "I finally found you."

"Fanuzzi," Miranda hissed, her nerves going into overdrive. "What are you doing here?"

"What am I doing here? What is everybody doing here? I came to see Coco's debut. She's really hot, isn't she?" Grinning with excitement, she turned toward the stage.

"You shouldn't be here."

Fanuzzi's head snapped around with a scowl. "What the hell? You sound just like Dave. What's up with you two?"

Miranda tapped her hands on the table. "It's just that—that this isn't a good place for you now."

Fanuzzi shook a finger at her. "Look, missy. I'll tell you what I told Dave. If I want to come, I'll come. It's a free country." Fanuzzi's eyes twinkled with something. Miranda was stunned when she realized it was tears. "God, who'd of thought we'd have had our first fight over something like this?"

Oh, hell. She couldn't let Fanuzzi think she was unwanted. She leaned over and whispered. "You're a *civilian*, Fanuzzi. We're not supposed to tell you." She hoped that would be enough for her friend to get the picture.

Her brown eyes grew round as the words sank in. "There's something going down here tonight?"

Miranda nodded. "We're on assignment."

She sat back. "I wondered why Dave didn't order his normal brewski."

"Which is why you should go home. It could get ugly."

Her dark brows drew together. "Excuse me, Miss High-And-Mighty Parker Agency Detective, but I can hold my own in a fight."

Miranda recalled the night they went barhopping together. Fanuzzi was one tough chick. She guessed she could hold her own. "Okay," she told her. "But if all hell breaks out, promise me you'll get under a table or something."

Fanuzzi leaned close with a conspiratorial grin. "What's going down?"

Miranda blew out a breath. She could never keep a secret from her stubborn friend. "It's Coco's ex. We think he might be after her."

The grin disappeared. "Really?"

Miranda put her head close to Fanuzzi's and spoke quietly. "When we were in Chicago, two women were killed. One of them was Coco's roommate."

Fanuzzi gasped. "And you think her ex did it?"

"We're not sure, but he could be the killer. If he is, and if he followed her to Atlanta, he could show up tonight."

Fanuzzi leaned back, took a sip of her beer to steady herself. "And do what?"

"No telling what he might try if he wants her back." Miranda reached for her big giraffe bag, which did not have her Beretta tonight because her weapon was tucked into a holster under her sweater for easy access. She opened the purse and dug out Dexter's photo. If Fanuzzi wouldn't leave, might as well recruit her. She slid the photo across the table. "That's him."

Fanuzzi picked up the picture and studied it. "He's a good looking guy. A real charmer."

"Yeah. He liked to charm Coco with his fists when she was married to him."

Alarm had her jaw dropping. "God, that's awful."

"Keep an eye out for him."

"You got it."

Miranda sat back, sipped her faux wine and watched the crowd. Becker was at the bar munching peanuts and nursing what must have been tonic water. Holloway was near the door in his Marine stance. Wesson was near the back, fighting off the guys trying to hit on her.

Miranda smiled like she was having a good time, but her stomach was in knots. If only Hinsley would show up soon. She'd relish taking that jackass apart. Though Frankie would be upset if she tore up his bar again.

Coco finished her set with a heart-felt interpretation of "People" that left everyone teary-eyed. She had just left the stage for a short break when Miranda's cell rang.

What now? "Steele."

"Where are you?" It was Iris Van Aarle.

"Excuse me?"

"Didn't we agree that Wendy would stay the night at your place? There's no one home." The woman sounded like she was beside herself.

"Uh, that was tomorrow night, Iris."

"Did I tell you tomorrow night? Oh, I'm so sorry. I have a late staff meeting and Wendy's terribly tired and bored. Well, you know how she gets."

She knew all right. "I'm out. I can't leave."

"That's all right. I'll take her to you."

"I'm at a club in Buckhead." A club that didn't allow minors?

"Well, isn't there someplace she can stay there?"

"Iris." Wendy couldn't come here. There could be a fight or a shooting or God knew what.

"I really don't know what to do," Iris whined.

How about start behaving like a mother? Selfish, self-absorbed woman. Irritation twisted in Miranda's gut. If she didn't say yes, Iris might leave the kid in the street for all she knew.

Miranda closed her eyes and thought. There was Coco's dressing room. She could have Parker talk to Frankie. He'd talk him into letting the kid in. She'd be safe back there.

She glared at her cell, then drew in air to steady her voice. "Okay, Iris. Bring her over." She gave her the address.

"I'll be there as soon as I can."

She clicked off. "God, I'd like to murder that woman."

"What's going on?" Fanuzzi asked.

"That was Wendy's mother. She needs a babysitter."

"Tonight?"

"She's bringing Wendy here."

Fanuzzi looked more shocked than if Miranda had stripped off and started dancing naked on the table. She shook her head. "I hate to say it, but that woman seems kind of derelict to me."

"That's an understatement. Next to her, my mother could have won Parent of the Year. I really feel for that kid." With a huff, she got to her feet. "Save our table. I've got to go talk to Parker."

"Sure thing."

She found Parker at the bar with Estavez and whispered in his ear that Iris was bringing Wendy over.

Parker's eyes flamed. "She can't bring a child in here. Not now."

"She wouldn't take no for an answer. Said she had a late business meeting." Miranda thought she knew what kind of business Iris was up to.

"Irresponsible women," Parker muttered. "And where is Shelby?"

"Off on some golf course somewhere. I have to take her, Parker."

He nodded. "Of course."

"I can take care of Ms. Wendy," Estavez offered.

"No, you're here to watch Coco. I'll handle it."

Parker leaned toward her and whispered. "If Hinsley shows up, take Coco and Wendy to the back immediately."

Miranda nodded. "I'll take care of both of them."

"Sorry about this, kid." Miranda handed Wendy a pillow.

With a grimace, the girl took it and tossed it down beside her on the couch. She had on new gray sneakers, a pair of ratty jeans, and a short-sleeved olive green shirt that looked like it came from the Army surplus store. She'd kicked off her sneakers and tucked her bare feet under her.

Coco's shimmering dress rustled as she bent down to stroke the girl's hair. "Do you think you'll be comfortable here, sweetie?"

Setting the blanket Frankie had provided on the arm of the couch, Miranda eyed the big plate of nachos, the large soda and the store-bought cookies set out on the small table. "I think she's got enough to eat."

Fanuzzi fluffed the pillow. "I can get more from the kitchen, if you need it." She sounded more like a mother than any of them. "One of the staff used to work for me."

Wendy shook her head and groaned. "I don't see why I have to stay here. Why can't I be out there with the grownups?"

Miranda put a hand on her hip. "Because the owner says so. You have to be eighteen and Coco's voice can't hold out that long."

Wendy rolled her eyes at the lame joke and lay down on the pillow with her phone, which she began to punch with her finger, tuning everyone out.

Coco looked apologetic. "I have to get back out there."

"Sure," Miranda said. "Fanuzzi, why don't you take Coco out and watch our table."

Fanuzzi seemed surprised. "Dave's doing that, but okay."

Miranda gave her a look that said she needed a minute with the kid and Fanuzzi nodded. She took Coco by the arm and her two friends left the room.

"Coco's only singing for a couple more hours, and then we'll go home to my place. Your room's waiting for you."

Wendy nodded without looking up from the screen. She looked so sad. She might be playing a game on her phone, but Miranda knew she was thinking about Iris. Miranda thought about Hinsley.

"Look. If anything happens tonight. If you hear any commotion or anything? Don't go anywhere. Just stay right here and wait for me to come and get you. Okay?"

Wendy lowered the phone, her eyes growing round. "Are you on a sting operation? Are you trying to catch that guy who killed the teacher?"

Gosh, she was sharp. The kid ought to enroll in Parker's next IIT class. Miranda guffawed and waved a hand in the air. "I was talking about bar stuff. You know fights and such. It can get ugly."

Wendy twisted her lips. "Right. Okay, Miranda. Don't worry about me. I'll be safe and sound right here." She went back to playing Irate Pigeons or whatever the heck the game was.

"Call me if you need anything. I've got my cell."

She didn't answer.

Miranda turned and left the room, closing the door behind her.

With all her being, she hoped Wendy would be okay. If Miranda lived through this night, she might go to jail for strangling Iris Van Aarle.

CHAPTER THIRTY-FIVE

Miranda was back at her tiny table in the corner with Fanuzzi, sipping her drink, which tasted like lighter fluid by now.

She scanned the crowd. It hadn't thinned much. Coco's return had attracted a roomful of adoring fans.

Still no Hinsley.

Her talented friend worked the crowd, banging out a soulful melody that tore at Miranda's heartstrings, then switching to an upbeat toe-tapper that had everyone singing along. Miranda swelled with pride. The girl was born to entertain.

Coco was nearing the end of her last set. Miranda squinted at the patrons along the bar and at the tables. No tall guy with wavy red hair and a lady-killer smile. Hinsley hadn't shown up. Had she been wrong about him all along?

Fanuzzi tapped her arm. "Listen, Murray."

Coco was working her magic on the keyboard, filling the club with a gorgeous tune. A love song. "*Nuestro amor*," she said to the crowd in her sultry voice. "That means 'our love.'" She opened her mouth to sing the chorus.

Nuestro amor is like no other.
Nuestro amor can transcend time.
Nuestro amor can transport us to another realm...
Where nothing fills our minds but nuestro amor. Nuestro amor. Nuestro amor...

She finished with a flourish and the crowd broke into hoots and cheers.

"That's Estavez' lyrics." Miranda stole a glance at the lawyer, who was leaning at the bar, staring up at Coco, his face beaming.

Beside him, Parker stood gazing at Miranda across the room, heartfelt emotion on his handsome face. *Our love.* She locked eyes with him, and her heart did that flippy-floppy thing that she'd come to expect every time she caught him looking at her.

In three days, they'd be married. She hoped this feeling wouldn't die with her vows.

Fanuzzi produced a tissue from her purse and blew her nose. "That song was so beautiful. Dave and I are going to make up as soon as we get home."

Miranda smiled. Fanuzzi was such a marshmallow inside. "I'm glad you two are happy," she sniffed as Coco went into a quiet number.

"It's a crazy life, but we are." She lifted a shoulder. "Dave wants me to quit the road crew."

"Really? Are you going to?" It hadn't been a barrel of laughs spreading hot mix on the Georgia highways, but the job had given her money and independence. Didn't Fanuzzi need that, too?

"I'm thinking about it. Oh, I'll still keep my catering business."

"That's good." Miranda thought of Fanuzzi's happy marriage and her three kids, and her mind wandered to the kid in the back room. "Did I ever tell you why I came to Atlanta?"

Fanuzzi's lips went back and forth as she thought. "No. You just showed up on the paving crew one day. I was glad for the help. But I took one look at you and thought, 'Now here's one tough broad with a chip on her shoulder.'"

Miranda grinned. "Yeah, guess I did have an attitude." Working for Parker hadn't exactly tamed it, but he'd steered it in a healthier direction. She ran her fingers over the condensation along the side of her glass. "I was looking for my daughter."

Fanuzzi dropped a hand on the table with a thud. "You have a daughter?"

Miranda took a sip to wet her throat that had suddenly gone dry, and nodded. "She'll be fourteen in November."

"Where is she?"

Miranda shrugged. "I don't know. Leon stole her from me when she was little."

Fanuzzi's mouth jerked open, her jaw dangling in stunned shock. "You're crazy ex? What do you mean he *stole* her?"

"I woke up one morning and she was gone. Leon said he took her and put her up for adoption. He got a judge to sign the papers somehow."

"How old was she?"

"Three weeks."

"Three weeks?"

Miranda nodded and stared down at the amber liquid in her glass. "Then Leon beat me up and threw me out of the house. I've been looking for my daughter ever since. On and off." Taking in air, she lifted her gaze and met her friend's stare.

Fanuzzi looked at her like she'd grown a third eye. "Oh, my God, Murray. That's horrible. It's criminal."

"Yeah, and he was a cop."

They went for a long moment without speaking. Just listening to the mournful tune that matched the mood. Then Fanuzzi spoke gently. "So I take it…you never found her?"

Miranda inhaled with heaviness. "No. That's why Parker and I went to Chicago right after your wedding. We petitioned a judge to open the adoption records, but he refused."

"Oh, Murray. I'm so sorry." Fanuzzi reached over and gave her arm a squeeze.

Miranda shook her head. "What I wanted to tell you was that when I got to Atlanta the first time, I found Wendy Van Aarle."

Fanuzzi took a drink from her mug and set it down. "You saved her from your crazy ex."

"Yeah. For a while there, Fanuzzi, I thought Wendy was my daughter."

Fanuzzi wiped a hand over her face in disbelief, then grew thoughtful. "She does kind of look like you."

"But then I found out she wasn't my daughter. Parker even dug up her birth certificate."

Now Fanuzzi reached across the table and took Miranda's hand. "You must have been devastated."

Tears welled up in Miranda's eyes as old memories swirled inside her. Her hatred of Leon. Her terror when she found Amy's empty crib. The years of agony and hopeless searching. And her feelings for Wendy.

Her hand shot to her mouth as she fought back the rush of emotion. It was several long moments before she could talk again.

She took a breath and attempted it. "Yes, I was devastated. But you know what? Right now, I love that kid as if she were my own. If Iris and Shelby would let me, I'd adopt her."

Fanuzzi sucked in her breath. "Really? You two do get along. You seem to be the only adult she responds to. What do you think Parker would say?"

"I'm sure he'd go along with it. He cares about her, too. But there's no chance of that happening."

Coco's lovely voice fluttered over the loud speaker. "That's all for tonight, folks. Thanks, everyone, for welcoming me back. Hope to see you all next week."

As she rose and left the stage, all the patrons got to their feet, wild with applause.

Then the place went dead and started clearing out. Miranda spun around and glared at the door. Holloway was still there, doing his soldier act. He raised his hands, palms up.

No Hinsley.

Wendy. Coco.

She jumped up and barked at Fanuzzi. "Find Becker and get somewhere safe."

She turned and shot across the floor and through the door where Coco had exited. She sprinted down the hall to the dressing room. She heard Coco gasp as she came around the corner.

"What is it?"

Coco stood in the doorway, both hands on her face. "Oh, no."

Miranda raced up to her. "What's wrong?" She peered inside. "Where's Wendy?"

"She's gone."

The food hadn't been touched. The blanket had been shoved aside on the couch. The pillow was gone. Was somebody going to smother her?

Did Wendy have her phone? Had to.

Her hands shaking, Miranda pulled out her cell and dialed. "Listen for 'The Eye of the Tiger.' It's the ringtone she gave my number." She let it ring five times, but there was no sound of another cell. It went to voicemail. Miranda left a message. "Hey, kid. Where are you? It's time to go home." She hung up.

Parker came up behind her. "What's going on?"

She turned to him, feeling as if she were about to break out into hysterics. "Oh, God, Parker. Wendy isn't here. She's missing."

"What do you mean, missing?"

She pointed to the empty room. "We left her in here and now she's gone."

He stepped inside, his investigator's eyes taking in every detail. He felt the couch. "It's not warm, but she couldn't have been gone long."

"Did anyone else have access to this room?" Parker asked.

"The staff, I suppose."

"We'll search the place." He raised a hand. "Stay calm. We'll find her."

They scurried around like crazed mice for what seemed like forever. Combing the labyrinth that was the back of the Gecko Club, they called out Wendy's name, searched in all the nooks and crannies, racked their brains.

Miranda's mind raced. Was it Hinsley? Had he kidnapped her for spite? But why would he do that? He was after Coco. Or so she thought.

She went through the cabinets along the floor of the kitchen. The storage room, the closet. Nothing.

There was only one person who'd want to harm Wendy—to get back at her. She slipped along the hall and back to the empty dressing room. Quietly, she closed the door and took out her cell. Pacing the worn carpet, she dialed Brandywine-Summit Memorial Hospital.

It rang three times before someone picked up the phone. "Third floor."

"Uh, hello. I'd like to check on the condition of a patient?"

"Which patient, ma'am?"

"Leon Groth. I'm his sister. I've called before. I just want to know if he's still in a coma."

There was the familiar sound of a keyboard being typed on. After a moment, the voice said, "I'm sorry, ma'am. There's no change in his condition."

"He's still there in his room?" She bit her lip, hoping she didn't sound too obvious.

"Why, yes. I checked on himself not five minutes ago."

"Thank you." She hung up and let out a long breath as relief rippled through her. But that was only one crazed killer she didn't have to worry about.

The door swung open. It was Parker. "What are you doing in here?"

"Nothing."

"One of the bodyguards just told me he saw Wendy getting into a cab just before the crowd started to leave."

"A cab? Where would she get money for a cab?"

"I'm sure Iris gives her a generous allowance. My father used to do that in lieu of real attention."

Parker'd had a rough time with Mr. P growing up, though that wasn't exactly Wendy's relationship with Iris. Still, she must have had the money. "Can we contact the cab company?"

"Holloway's doing that right now."

As soon as the words were out of his mouth, Holloway stepped around the corner, cell to his ear. "Thank you. I appreciate the information." He hung up and looked at Parker. "The cab dropped her off in Marietta a few minutes ago."

Miranda raised a hand to flatten her forehead, digging her fingers angrily into her scalp. "Let me guess. The skating rink."

Holloway blinked at her in amazement. "How'd you know, Steele?"

Her only answer was to grunt aloud and stretch both palms to the ceiling. She wanted to strangle the kid.

"Good work, Detective. You can join the others." Parker turned to Miranda. "Let's go."

"Where's Coco?" Miranda asked as they raced down the hall, heading for the entrance.

"With Estavez. He's taking her home. Becker and Wesson and the bodyguards are following."

Another relief. As she raced out the door and hopped into Parker's souped-up Lamborghini, she wished it had wings.

CHAPTER THIRTY-SIX

The outline of the Marietta skating rink seemed grim and imposing under the sparse nightlights.

As they pulled into the empty parking lot, Miranda spotted a dark form at the entrance. She could just make out Wendy's shape lying on the front stoop. Facing the other way, the girl had her head propped on the pillow she'd taken from Coco's dressing room, which she'd rested against the railing.

"Do you want me to go with you?" Parker pulled into a space at some distance from the door. Couldn't risk spooking the kid. But she seemed oblivious to the car's presence.

"I'd better handle this alone." Miranda got out of the car and strolled up to the entrance, fighting back angry tears.

Absorbed in the game on her phone, Wendy didn't notice her.

"If you wanted to camp out, we could've pitched a tent in the backyard."

Wendy lifted her head and turned, shock on her face. Then she scowled. "What are you doing here?"

Miranda smirked. "I'd say the question is what are you doing here? It's the middle of the night."

"So?"

Miranda was getting a little tired of that perpetual sneer. The girl turned around and went back to her game.

Moody kid. What in the heck was wrong with her? "You know, a good detective would face the road to see if someone was sneaking up on her."

Wendy kept punching her phone with her finger. "I don't want to be a detective. I want to be a figure skater."

A chorus of cicadas chirped in the nearby trees. Even though it was after two in the morning, the early August heat made the air muggy.

With a sigh, Miranda put her hands in her pockets and strolled around to see the child in the light. Redness around her eyes and nose revealed the kid had been crying. "So what are you doing here? Showing dedication to your art?"

Wendy rolled her eyes.

Miranda exhaled. She'd had enough. She extended her hand. "Okay, kid. Let's go home."

Wendy glared up at her. "I'm not going with you."

"What? Are you going to sit out here all night?"

"They open early. When they do, I can wait for Brianna inside."

And freeze her little hind end off. "No, you're not. You're coming home with me." She reached for Wendy's arm.

The girl pulled away. "Leave me alone, Miranda. I said I'm not going with you."

"Yes, you are." She tried to snatch the phone out of Wendy's hand, but the kid was quicker.

She got up stuffed her pillow under her arm, shoved the phone in her pocket and headed down the walkway.

"Where are you going?" As she trotted after the girl, Miranda heard the door of the Lamborghini shut and Parker's steps behind her. Wisely, he held back.

"You think I'm just going to leave you here?"

Wendy brushed her hair back over her shoulder. "Why not? You don't care about me."

What? Miranda stopped in her tracks. That hit her harder than Wesson's punches the other day. "Wendy, what are you talking about?"

Coming to a halt, Wendy spun around in angry defiance. The light caught the glisten of tears streaming down her cheeks. "You know what I'm talking about."

"No, I don't."

"I know how you feel, Miranda. I heard you."

"Heard me?"

"At the club." Wendy wiped her nose with her bare forearm. "I wanted to watch the show. I wanted to sit at the table with you. So I left the dressing room and snuck inside. I came up behind you so you wouldn't see me until I was already there. That was when I heard you talking to Fanuzzi. You told her how your ex had stolen your daughter from you. That you've been looking for her ever since. That you and Mr. Parker went to Chicago to try to find her. About how much you hoped I was your daughter. And when I wasn't," her chest began to heave, "you were *devastated.*"

Miranda tugged at her hair, trying to remember her conversation. "Yeah, okay. I said that."

"You should've seen the look on your face." The poor kid started to bawl. "My mother doesn't care about me. My father doesn't care about me. And now you don't care about me."

Now she understood.

Oh, the poor kid. She wanted to laugh with relief and cry along with Wendy at the same time. She wiped a tear away that had rolled down her own cheek with her knuckles. "I know you said you didn't want to be a detective. But if you change your mind, you're going to have to learn to get all the facts straight."

"What do you mean?" Wendy blubbered.

"I mean you left too soon. You didn't hear what else I told Fanuzzi."

"What did you tell her?" She dared to take a step toward Miranda.

She looked into the girl's eyes, seeing yearning and a little bit of hope. "That I'd adopt you if I could."

Her mouth opened. Then her face curled up in a snarl. "I don't believe you."

Miranda inhaled, trying to conjure up the patience of Job. "It's true, Wendy. Don't you get it?"

"What's to get?"

"Ever since I first saw you. I felt something. A connection."

"You thought I looked like you. You thought I was your daughter."

"Yeah, I did. But then we started talking...and now? God, it would break my heart if your mother took you off to Paris or someplace again for weeks on end. I don't know what I'd do without you in my life. I care about you. I really do."

She still looked like she didn't buy it.

"Wendy, what you overheard was true. I've been looking for my daughter for years. Sure, I was devastated when I found out you weren't her. But..." She studied the pavement, not understanding the emotions swirling around inside her a bit. "But I don't really know my daughter, and I probably never will. I do know you. And as crazy as it sounds, I don't think I could feel any more for her than I do for you."

"Really?" There was still doubt in Wendy's tone.

"Yes, really." Now Miranda's voice broke. "I love you, kid. Don't you know that?"

That did it.

Wendy dropped her pillow and rushed into Miranda's arms. Heaving with sobs, she hugged her tight.

Miranda stroked Wendy's dark hair, trying to keep her own tears from falling on her head. Was this what it felt like to be a mother of a young girl? It felt good. Real good.

"Wendy, I don't know whether your folks don't care about you, or if they're just wrapped up in their own lives. But I care about you and I always will. Please believe me. It would really hurt me if you didn't."

Wendy nodded her head against Miranda's chest. "I believe you. I...I love you, too."

Relief and joy shuddered through her. And in that single moment, for the first time in her life, Miranda felt complete.

Gently Parker touched her shoulder and spoke in his tender, elegant Southern voice. "Shall we all go home now?"

"What do you say?"

The kid raised her head and smiled through her tears. "Yes."

Miranda swiped her hand under the girl's eyes. "Glad you said that. 'Cause we've got a wedding to get ready for."

Miranda tucked Wendy into bed under the lacy canopy where she belonged and tiptoed slowly down the hall, lost in the emotions still swirling around her very full heart. This was happiness, wasn't it?

In her pocket, her phone buzzed. She took it out and looked at the display. An email sent to Parker and copied to her, from Inspector Whitman at the GBI.

She read it carefully.

The lab had been able to extract only a partial follicle from the hair in the comb Miranda had taken from Hinsley's house. Technicians had run several tests against it, but couldn't get any DNA. Whitman was sending the sample on to Chicago, but the color didn't match hairs found at the crime scenes there.

In addition, Elizabeth Lane's boyfriend was being charged with her murder.

Suddenly, her chest felt like a tire with a slow leak. She pulled at her hair. Why couldn't they get this guy?

The sound of happy humming coming from Coco's room shook her out of her thoughts. She needed to tell Coco that Wendy was okay.

Shoving the cell back in her pocket with a growl of disgust, she knocked on the door. "Can I come in?"

"Of course, Miranda."

She found Coco in a pink bathrobe with a towel around her head, prancing around getting ready for the night.

Miranda let out a breath. "The kid's in bed. Safe and sound."

"I'm so glad she's all right. She gave us such a scare." Coco waltzed across the blue Tibetan rug and into the bathroom, removed the towel and began drying her hair with it, using a styling brush on her curls.

"Yeah." Miranda sank down onto the Ottoman bench, glad that Coco was all right, too. "You did really great tonight. I was proud of you."

"Thanks," she called.

"I really loved the song you and Estavez wrote."

She giggled. "I do, too. And what's more the crowd loved it." She poked her head out of the bathroom, her eyes sparkling with light from the chandelier. "I'm thinking of wearing my hair pulled back for the wedding. What do you think?" She held her wet locks straight back with her hand.

She looked like Princess Grace. "You could wear your hair any way and still be gorgeous, Coco."

Her blue eyes went wide. "Really?"

"Of course. Doesn't Estavez tell you that?" Miranda was sure Dexter never did. Probably told her she was stupid and ugly, like Leon used to do. That could make even a beautiful woman insecure about her looks.

Her cheeks went as pink as her robe. "Yes, he does. But I wanted a woman's point of view."

"You look great."

"Terrific." She returned to the sink. "See, Miranda? Everything went fine tonight. Dexter didn't show up at all, did he?"

Miranda stiffened, cleared her throat. "What makes you think I expected Dexter to show up?"

Shaking her still damp curls, she returned to the bedroom laughing her musical laugh. "All those detectives from the Parker Agency spread out all over the room like armed guards?" They were armed guards. "I'm glad they all had a good time."

Coco was more observant than Miranda thought. On the other hand, the secret sort of came out when Wendy went missing, Parker started barking orders, and everybody fell into line.

Miranda's shoulders slumped. "We're just trying to protect you, Coco."

"I know and I appreciate it. But Dexter's in California and I can prove it." She blinked at her. "Prove it? How?"

She danced over to the carved rosewood dresser and picked up a card. "With this. It came in the mail today." She handed it to Miranda.

Cautiously, she took it. A postcard from LA. Hollywood. She turned it over. The postmark looked legit. It had been forwarded through Doon, Iowa. No return address. It had gone through Los Angeles seven days ago. A few days after the Mableton teacher was murdered.

She read the writing. He was doing well. Had a new job, a new girl. God help her. He was happy and wished Coco the best.

Coco plopped down beside her on the Ottoman bench. "See what I told you, Miranda? Everything is going to be fine. There's no one after me."

Miranda just looked at her. There was no evidence that pointed directly to Hinsley at any of the crime scenes. No record of him traveling to Atlanta from Chicago. No DNA from the hair on the comb in his house. And now this postcard. Could she have been wrong?

Coco put her arms around her and gave her a heartfelt hug. "Oh, Miranda. Don't look so glum."

Miranda opened her mouth, but she didn't know what to say.

With a big smile, Coco took her hands in hers and squeezed them. "I'm happy. I'm finally happy. And you should be happy, too. You're getting married in a few days."

"Yeah."

"So forget about Dexter. Let's just relax and enjoy your wedding. Okay?"

Forget Hinsley. Get married. Sure. It took all the energy Miranda had to nod.

CHAPTER THIRTY-SEVEN

Did Coco say *relax*?

Miranda didn't see how. There was too much to do.

The limo company canceled, and Gen was having fits trying to find another one to usher the bride and her bridesmaids from the Parker mansion, where they would dress, to Saint Simon's. Guests were arriving from out of town, all of them loaded with questions and wanting to chat. The soloist for the church music came down with laryngitis and had to be replaced. Coco volunteered, but Miranda couldn't lose a bridesmaid. Luckily, Aunt Evelyn found a friend from the Atlantic Opera Company who would sing "O Promise Me." Well, she had wanted to go with traditional.

They had their last fitting at Elegant Ensembles, and Gen arranged for the gowns and the shoes and the veil and accessories to be delivered to the mansion the morning of the wedding. And the cake to go to the reception hall. And the flowers to go everywhere. And the food for the reception, including the special treats Fanuzzi insisted on making herself the day of the wedding in the Parker kitchen. There would be an army of temporary staff on duty at the house that day.

And now Gen was after Miranda and Parker to write their vows.

Somehow, Gen pulled it all together, and they got through the final days. The evening before the Big Day, the rehearsal at Saint Simon's and dinner at Parker Towers went off without a hitch.

"I'm exhausted." Miranda flopped down onto her bed, still dressed in the shiny red number she'd worn tonight. She let her toe-eating three-inch heels drop to the floor. "Who knew all this social make-do could be so tiring?"

Along with the minister, Mr. P had invited half of the out-of-town members of the Parker clan. She'd met and made meaningless chitchat with more people in the last three hours than in her entire life.

Parker chuckled as he loosened his tie. "You'll be able to get a good night sleep tonight. You'll have the bed to yourself."

She shot up, her heart pounding. "Where are you going?"

He strolled to the closet, hung his tie on a rack, and began to unbutton his shirt. "It's bad luck for the groom to see the bride on the wedding day. I'm sleeping downstairs."

She had only a moment to glimpse his magnificent muscled chest before he disappeared into the closet. The huge walk-in closet was as big as the bedroom of her old apartment, with mirrors, a dressing bench, and enough clothes between Parker's things and the stuff he'd bought her to start a small boutique.

"Where downstairs?" she called after him.

"The guest bedroom."

She frowned. "There's a bedroom on the first floor?"

"You've seen it. It's at the back of the house."

"Uh huh." For the life of her, she couldn't remember it. This house was too big.

"I'll leave in the morning, and you ladies will have the house to yourselves." He emerged from the clothes cave dressed in a polo shirt and chinos, pajamas and another set of clothes over an arm, a small suitcase in his hand. He laid the suitcase on a rack near the dresser.

She didn't know why the idea of sleeping alone had her so flustered. She got to her feet and began wrestling with her party dress. She got the zipper halfway down, then sat down on the bed again. "The wedding isn't until four. What are you going to do until then?"

Parker strolled over to the bed, pulled the zipper down the rest of the way. He eased it off one shoulder, kissed the nape of her neck. She could feel both the passion and resistance in his breath as he pulled away and returned to his suitcase. He opened it and began packing his things into it. "Estavez is taking me out for my 'bachelor breakfast,' as he calls it. I suppose he wants to give me some honeymoon advice."

Mesmerized by his charm, she had to laugh at that. "Have you come 'round about Estavez and Coco?"

He laid several of his monogrammed handkerchiefs in the suitcase, then sauntered to the bathroom for his cologne. "Let's say I'm getting used to the idea."

She grinned. "You're doing better than Gen." Her wedding planner had been about to have a hissy fit tonight when she realized the two were truly a couple. That was, until Estavez took her outside and set her straight.

Parker returned to his suitcase and put the cologne into a side pouch. "I'd say so. Coco does seem to make Antonio happy."

"And that's what's important."

"Yes." He snapped the bag shut. "My tuxedo is already at Saint Simon's, so this is all I need. Have you finished your wedding vows? Reverend Quigley needs them tomorrow morning."

Miranda groaned. "I've tried, Parker. Really I have. But I'm afraid I don't have Estavez' panache with poetry."

"What do you have so far?"

She opened the drawer of the nightstand and pulled out the small writing pad she'd scribbled on. She handed it to him.

He took it and looked down at the paper. She winced as he read her words. *For better or worse. I'd like to try better. I've already had worse.*

His lips went back and forth. He tried to be angry, but he had to smile. He laid the notepad on the dresser. "Why don't we go with the traditional vows?"

Traditional? She lifted a brow. "Without that sticky 'obey' part?"

He laughed. "Wouldn't hear of it."

She gazed up at that strong, tall body leaning with that seductive pose against the dresser, that outrageously handsome face, that exquisitely styled salt-and-pepper hair, those penetrating gray eyes scanning her like an x-ray, and tried to make herself believe they were really getting married tomorrow afternoon. Married.

She put her hands to her face. "Oh, God."

His gut in a knot, Parker studied his fiancée. She was so lovely, even half dressed in that scarlet cocktail dress with the v-neck and the fabric draped interestingly around her slim waist. A stylist had pulled her dark hair up and away from her stunning face. She didn't realize her own beauty. Or her own tenacity. Or her own transparency. Her nerves fairly danced on her frame.

Compassion flooded him. He knew what she'd been through. He knew how hard this step was for her. "Miranda," he said softly. "Would you like to call this off?"

Slowly, she lifted her head, her deep blue eyes gleaming with emotion. "What did you say?"

"I'm not so naive as to think you chose this date because you were eager to get married."

Miranda's head started to pound. Parker could always see through her. Might as well fess up. "Okay. You're right. When I said I'd marry you, I wanted to do it in three weeks because if I waited any longer, I knew I'd lose my nerve."

"And the big wedding?"

He wanted it all, didn't he? "You know I hate big parties. The wedding was for you."

"I'm touched. Truly." He crossed to the bed and sat down beside her. He took her hand in his, rubbed a finger over her knuckles. "I'll cancel the ceremony tomorrow."

"What?"

"I understand how you feel, Miranda." He kissed her fingers. "I'm not letting you go, by any means. But if you want to go back to the way we were before, if you want to live together without vows, I'm willing to do that."

Without vows? Call it off?

She yanked her hand away and shot to her feet, her heart swirling with feelings she didn't understand. "How dare you suggest that we call it off? How dare you second-guess me, Wade Parker? Don't you dare cancel my wedding. That would be...grounds for divorce."

Parker stared at her, looking more surprised than if she'd socked him in the solar plexus. "Are you sure, Miranda?"

"Of course, I'm sure. I made a promise and I'm going to keep it."

"As I just said, I'm not going to hold you to that promise."

"Hold me to it. I'm going through with this."

His brow creased into his most intimidating investigator mode. His voice became dark. "You won't leave me standing at the altar?"

"Why?" She gasped in a half-laugh. "Just because I walked out on you twice before?"

"That might have something to do with it."

She raked her fingers through her hair to loosen it from the sticky gel she'd worn tonight. She took off the earrings she'd worn and laid them in a jeweled glass on the dresser. "But I didn't get very far, did I?"

"No, you didn't. Those times."

He was infuriating. She shook a finger at him. "Mark my words, Parker. I'm going to be there tomorrow. With wedding bells on my fingers and my toes."

"Very well." With a sigh that was almost resignation, he rose and took his bag.

"You don't believe me?"

He strolled to the door. "I believe you mean it at this moment. But will you mean it tomorrow afternoon?"

Anger rose up in her gut. She had no idea where it came from. "I'll mean it," she grunted through gritted teeth. "And I'll be there."

"We'll see." He closed the door and went downstairs.

CHAPTER THIRTY-EIGHT

Miranda woke the next morning to Sarah knocking on her bedroom door and bringing her breakfast in bed.

"Oh, the house is all in a hubbub, Miss," she sang out in a cheery voice setting the silver tray over Miranda's lap.

Miranda eyed the eggs and toast and orange juice. She reached for the coffee and took a sip. "Should I guess where this came from?"

"No, Miss. Mr. Parker ordered for you, of course."

There was a single rose in a vase and a large greeting card on the napkin. With a jaundiced eye, she reached for the card and opened it. It was covered with glitter and silver flowers. Inside was a beautiful verse about love and forever. And a note.

I couldn't find a card with a martial arts theme. I hope this will suffice, Parker had written. *You'll see this waiting outside the church for you. We can take a test drive after the ceremony.*

He was referring to a photograph enclosed in the card. She turned it over and gasped. It was a hot, shiny red Corvette ZR1. The key was taped inside the card. She squealed aloud. Supercharged V-8 engine? Zero to sixty in under four seconds? Hot dog.

That man. He knew how to push her buttons.

Sarah started fluffing the pillows. "Mrs. Becker arrived at six o'clock. She's been baking all morning."

Poking at the eggs, Miranda frowned. "Who?"

"Your matron of honor?"

Oh. That's right. Fanuzzi's new name. "What's she making?"

"Brownie pops for the reception. Oh, they're delicious. She's dipping them in white chocolate and sprinkling each one with silver sugar crystals and tiny red candy hearts."

Heck of a lot of work. She owed Fanuzzi big time.

"Ms. Genevieve is here, too, bustling about, taking care of everything."

"Guess I'd better get a move on." She took a sip of the orange juice, downed the coffee, and jumped out of bed to hurry to the bathroom for her last session with the octopus shower as a free woman.

The spray from the eight jets caressed her body in an invigorating water massage, and she moaned with pleasure. Life with Parker did have its perks. *Free woman.* The thought made her shiver, even though the water was hot.

No, she wasn't going to think about that. She'd been in denial this long, and she'd stay in denial. Stay there all day long—right up until she said "I do" and walked out of that church. She'd deal with the consequences of her folly later.

She finished her shower and dried off and pulled on a pair of jeans and a zip-up cotton shirt. Then she climbed the stairs to the third floor where Gen had rooms all fixed up and ready for nuptial preparation. She submitted herself to the hairdresser and makeup artist Gen had hired. The hairstylist slopped a handful of gooey, strawberry scented gel on her unruly hair, which Miranda had decided to wear down, making it look almost like a normal person's.

The makeup lady spread more goop that smelled like gardenias all over her face, then covered it with base and powder. Miranda forced herself to hold still while she applied eye shadow, liner, mascara and lipstick. The makeup went down her neck in the area the woman called her *décolletage*. But Miranda was happy she managed to cover the scars on her chest that Leon had given her.

In the large dressing room, furnished with an elegant dresser and cabinets and large, velvet covered ottomans for sitting, she tugged on the flesh-colored thong, the sheer, silvery pantyhose and the strapless push-up bra that made her boobs look half again their size. How had she let Gen talk her into that one?

There was a knock on the door, and Fanuzzi and Coco appeared, with Wendy at their side. The women filled the room with delicious scents of roses and chocolate.

No privacy today. At least she wasn't naked, Miranda thought, eyeing the scowl on Wendy's face. She put a hand on her hip. "What's wrong?"

Fanuzzi set the paper plate of goodies she was carrying down on the dressing table. "Today, she doesn't like her dress."

Miranda studied the beaded hearts along the girl's shoulders and waistline and the colorful swirls of the skirt. In her dark hair, somebody had fixed a lily with a bit of lavender tulle to match the flowers at the church. Miranda thought she looked adorable, but she knew better than to use that word.

She chucked Wendy under the chin. "Cheer up, kid. This'll all be over in a couple of hours."

Wendy's lips curved into a smirk. "You look funny in your underwear."

"Hey, it's not polite to insult the bride."

Fanuzzi reached for one of the sticks on the paper plate. "Here, Wendy. Have one of my brownie pops. I brought some for everyone."

Gen marched into the room wearing her shimmering indigo gown with the slit up the side, and misery on her face. "You can't eat those now," she barked. "You're already dressed."

"I'm not." Miranda took one.

Fanuzzi scoffed and waved a hand at Gen. "I brought plenty of napkins." She was wearing a full-length apron over her amethyst chiffon gown.

Miranda bit into the lusciously rich brownie dipped in white chocolate, holding her napkin to catch the silver sugar crystals. It was heavenly. "Man, these are good. You sure can cook, Fanuzzi."

"Thanks," her friend beamed. "There'll be more at the reception."

Sweeping over to the dressing table in a pink robe, Coco picked up a stick. "I'll try one." She took a ladylike nibble and her blue eyes glowed. "They are good."

Fanuzzi handed one to Wendy. "Now be very careful or Miss Gen might throw you out the window."

Wendy giggled. "I will." She sat on the velvet ottoman in the corner to devour her goodie.

Gen refused the treat and stood with her arms folded, grunting like a bulldog until everyone was finished munching. Then she tromped to the closet and retrieved Miranda's wedding gown. "Time to do the deed. I hope everyone's hands are clean."

"They are." Fanuzzi held hers up.

Coco did the same. "Mine, too."

Miranda lifted her arms and they all helped to slide the silky fabric over her head.

After Coco anchored her veil, she pulled on the fingerless to-the-elbow gloves, with their lace-and-pearl embellished satin, stepped into the satin open-toed heels with the heart-shaped crystal accents, and turned to look at herself in the French style tri-fold full-length mirror Gen had set up.

The ruched silk over the bodice of embroidered lilies flowed to the floor like a cloud from Heaven. Her veil was two-tier, fingertip-length, edged with satin and pearls and fastened to the back of her head with a silver comb shaped in a row of hearts. It gave her an angelic look that she hardly deserved.

She didn't know what to say.

Fanuzzi was the first to voice an opinion. "Absolutely stunning." She stood on tiptoe to give her a peck on the cheek.

"You are dazzling, Miranda," Coco purred.

Gen cocked her head. "I must say I did a good job."

Coco nodded enthusiastically. "Oh, you did. You really did. Oh," she sniffed. "I'm crying already."

"You'll muss your makeup," Fanuzzi warned her.

Ignoring the fuss, Gen went into command mode. "We'll all be leaving in fifteen minutes. Coco, Wendy, and I will ride in the first limo. Joan and Miranda will ride in the second." Aunt Evelyn had elected to dress at Saint Simon's, foregoing the staff with the handheld steamers that Gen had arranged to meet the bridal party in the vestibule. "Everyone got it?"

Joan? Oh, Fanuzzi. Miranda nodded. "Got it."

"Sounds good," Fanuzzi agreed.

Coco did a little girlish hop. "Wait. We can't forget the garter."

Fanuzzi pointed a finger at her. "You're right, girl. Where is the garter?"

With a huff, Gen went to the closet and returned with a small box. She opened it and drew out the piece of ruffled satin with two silver charms in the shape of hearts dangling from it. "Who wants to do the honors?"

"I will. I'm the MOH." Grinning from ear to ear, Fanuzzi took the garter from Gen and gestured like she used to do on the job site. "Hoist 'er up, kid."

Miranda shook her head, but she reached for a chair, kicked off a shoe and lifted her leg. Fanuzzi bent down and slipped the garter over her foot and up her leg to her thigh. "There. Just perfect. Oh, I almost forgot. This is for you to tuck under the garter." She produced a small piece of paper.

"What is it?"

"My recipe for the brownie pops. It's my Something Borrowed." She folded the paper then scratched her chin. "Hmm. It would probably fall out of the garter. Put it in your shoe. Remember, it's borrowed, so you have to give it back after the ceremony. It's a family secret."

"Sure." Miranda certainly wasn't going to use it. But she appreciated the thought. She took the paper and laid it on the sole of the torturous high-heel, then slipped the shoe back on. "Thanks, Fanuzzi." She gave her a gentle hug, so as not to mess up makeup, hair, or clothes.

"What's a matron of honor for?"

Coco waved her delicate hands in the air. "I've got something for you, too, Miranda. It's your Something Blue." She pulled a small package out of the pocket of her robe and handed it to her.

"What is it?"

"Open it and see."

Miranda pulled the paper off and found another box. She opened the lid. It was a piece of jewelry, all silver and blue. Costume, no doubt, but the thoughtfulness warmed her heart. She took it out and draped it over her wrist. "It's gorgeous. It is a bracelet?"

Coco laughed. "It's an ankle bracelet, silly. Here." She took it out of her hands and bent down to clasp it around Miranda's ankle.

Miranda lifted her skirt and gazed at the string of stones. "It's cool." The only ankle bracelet she'd ever worn before was when she'd been arrested.

"What about her Something Old?" Coco said as she rose.

"I know that one." She went to the dresser and pulled out a string of pearls. "Parker wants me to wear these." He'd had Sarah put them up here for her last night.

Everyone oohed at the two strands, one greenish-blue, the other pink. Fanuzzi came around to fasten the clasp. They were the Tahitian pearls that belonged to Parker's mother. He'd given them to Miranda, and she'd given them back one time when things were testy between them. The symbolism of this gift on their wedding day wasn't lost on her.

Miranda saw Gen's face grow cold as she stared at the pearls. "Those were my grandmother's," she murmured half to herself.

"Yes." Uh oh. Maybe that wasn't such a smart move.

Coco clapped her hands, oblivious to Gen's mood swing, though Gen's grouchy and sulky were hard to differentiate. "Now we need her Something New. What are we going to do for that?"

Miranda lifted her hands. "My underwear's new. Actually, everything I've got on today is new."

Coco shook her head, her curls shimmering. "Oh, those don't count."

"Gen hasn't had a turn," Fanuzzi said.

"Oh, yes. Gen, don't you have a Something New for Miranda?"

Gen looked like she was about to snort fire. "I'll have to find one. I'll look downstairs. I have to check on the bouquets, too." She turned toward the door.

"Wait a minute, Gen," Miranda said. She took in the woman's annoyed scowl and braced herself. She had something to say and she was determined to say it. She looked at Fanuzzi and Coco. "I'd like a word with my wedding planner alone for a minute."

"Sure. I've got baking to finish." Fanuzzi raised a hand. "Don't worry. I'll be done in ten minutes."

Coco suddenly looked panicked. "I've got to finish getting ready. C'mon, Wendy."

"Oh, no."

Everyone turned toward the corner. "What?"

Wendy rose, tears in her eyes. "I've ruined it." She looked down at her dress. There was a big smear of dark chocolate in the middle of the skirt.

"That's just what we need," Gen growled.

"We'll get it out," Fanuzzi insisted.

"Soda water. I know," Coco said. "I've had accidents before going on stage before. You go finish your baking. I'll take care of her."

"Make sure she gets the rings," Miranda said. It would be just her luck to forget something like that.

"We will." And the two women hustled Wendy out of the room, shutting the door behind them leaving Miranda and Gen by themselves.

"What do you want, Miranda?" Gen snapped. "I'm busy."

Taking a deep breath of air, Miranda steadied herself as she turned to face her new stepdaughter. "I know we haven't gotten along in the past. But I want to thank you, Gen, for everything you've done for me these past three weeks."

Still eyeing the pearls at Miranda's neck, Gen shrugged.

Miranda tried to smile. "In a couple of hours, this will all be over and we can relax."

"That's what I'm supposed to say to you. Is that all?"

Miranda dared to take a step toward her. "I was hoping maybe…when things settle down we could be…I don't know…friends?"

Gen glared at her a long moment, her lips twisting, contorting her face, her eyes darting from the corner to her grandmother's pearls. At last she opened her mouth with a tight jaw. "Miranda Steele, you're the last person I want to be friends with. I have no idea why my father's marrying you. I'm only going along to placate him. But I do know one day he'll wake up and realize what a mistake he's made. I doubt your marriage will last a year. And when it breaks up and you're out of his life, I'll be damn glad."

Her eyes suddenly filling with tears, Gen turned and rushed out of the room with a stifled gasp of anger.

Well. Didn't that beat all the other wedding presents?

Miranda stood, shivering as if a cold blast from the Antarctic had blown over her. She felt like someone had dumped a wheelbarrow of cement blocks on her chest.

Gen sure had great timing, didn't she? Couldn't she have made something up?

Nausea flooding her stomach, shakily she turned and looked at herself in the mirror. The gown, the veil, all the trimmings. Everything seemed ridiculous on her now. *She* was ridiculous. What made her think she belonged with someone like Wade Parker the Third?

Who was she kidding?

"You're nothing but a lowlife," she whispered to her image. "A woman who was raped and beaten up by her ex-husband." Parker must be out of his mind to think he was in love with someone like her.

She'd always agreed with Gen about their relationship. This time, she was spot on the money. It wasn't going to last. How could it?

But what Miranda had never considered before was how much the breakup would hurt other people. Parker, Gen, Mr. P, Wendy. If the kid got used to thinking of them as a couple, like a family, and they split? What would that do to the girl?

She wouldn't have it. She reached around her neck, unclasped Parker's pearls and laid them on the dresser.

Cell phone. Where was her cell? She'd left it in the bedroom. She started for the door. No, Parker would be at the church now. She'd tell him in person.

But the first person she'd tell was Gen.

Reaching for some tissue to catch the tears suddenly dropping onto her gown, she lifted her skirt and hurried out the door to make her way downstairs.

CHAPTER THIRTY-NINE

At last, the day was here. Finally, he'd found his chance. The planning, the waiting, the agony was over. Soon, very soon, he'd have everything he wanted.

"Fill those cups and take them out to the limo drivers. It's going to be a long afternoon for them."

He stared at the obnoxious curly-haired housekeeper who'd been ordering him about for the last half hour, wishing he could backhand her.

But it wouldn't be wise to second-guess his luck. Beside, this is just the opportunity he'd hoped for.

"Yes, ma'am," he bowed demurely, pleased with the touch of a Hispanic accent he'd mastered.

Carefully, he filled the china cups from the urn on the marble kitchen counter, barely able to contain his excitement. The staff was too busy to notice that he grabbed a third cup and filled it, as well. He reached for some creamers and sugar packets, laid them on the silver tray. Then he headed out the door.

No one saw him take a turn toward the deck where he set the tray down on a table and reached into his pocket. He drew out his prescription bottle and the pills from the LA doctor that he had ground to powder that morning. He had just enough left to keep Cora Beth under until they crossed the Mexican border.

Forcing his hand to remain steady, he measured out equal portions into the three cups. He slipped the bottle back into his pocket, stirred the liquid, then lifted the tray and headed around the house for the waiting limos.

He tapped on the window of the pale green Acura. "Coffee, sir? Compliments of Mr. Parker."

Without hesitation, the man rolled down the window. He eyed him a moment, then reached for the cup. "Sure, thanks."

"Cream and sugar?"

"No, thanks."

"Very good, sir." He bowed and moved away as the man rolled his window back up.

He waited until he turned his back to smile. There was still one bodyguard, but Parker had dismissed the others. It wouldn't be long before that one was as sound asleep as the two snoring limo drivers.

He made his way around the house to the backyard and ditched the silver tray in the bushes. Then he squatted behind a row of roses while he watched the back door and waited for the staff to leave.

He laughed to himself. The idiots thought they could draw him out with that ruse at the Gecko Club, but he was too smart for them. He'd known it was a trap, especially when he'd seen the bodyguards again. Besides, he had a better plan.

And his plan hadn't been as difficult to execute as he expected to pull off. A little research and asking around gave him the name of the staffing service associated with one of the hotels owned by Parker's father. The manager was only too happy to find another body with a driver's license who'd work for cheap.

They'd given him a uniform of black slacks and shirt, with the logo etched on the breast pocket. He couldn't have looked more authentic if he'd sewed the outfit himself. The fools had even given him the schedule for the wedding day.

When he'd arrived a few hours ago, he'd blended in perfectly with the rest of the staff in the kitchen, preparing food for the reception under the direction of an annoying bitch with a Brooklyn accent.

He'd been disappointed to learn that Parker had already gone to the church, but it was probably for the best. The man was tricky. He could handle the women. How would the *AJC* describe the bloody deaths of the Parker wedding party? Too bad he wouldn't be here to read about it.

The back door opened and two women hurried out carrying trays. They were followed by another three. Then four young men, all of them dressed in the same outfit as himself.

That was all of them. His heart began to pound. Now was the time. There was no one in the house but the bridal party.

They were his.

He took a deep breath. Slowly, he rose and strolled to the back door.

He drew his Luger as he stepped inside the kitchen. There was a woman at the stove. What was she still doing here? She was dressed in a long purple dress and wore an apron. Was she in the wedding party? He couldn't remember.

He put his gun behind his back as she turned around and spotted him. "Oh, I'm glad you came back," she said in that awful Brooklyn accent. "I just finished the last one. Can you take it out?" She gestured toward the tray on the island.

"Don't move." He lifted his gun.

She sucked in her breath. "What do you want?"

He wanted to kill her. But not yet. If Steele and the rest of them heard the gunshot it would tip them off. Instead he rushed at her, turning the gun over in his hand, and gave her a hard rap on the side of the head.

She jabbed at him, hit him hard in the stomach as she went down. It hurt like hell. He wanted to give her a kick, but she was already out and sprawled on the floor like a child's discarded doll.

He crept out of the kitchen and down the hall. They'd be upstairs, no doubt. All he had to do was find them.

The hallway opened up to a large foyer with a huge staircase. Luck was with him. As he passed a room, he heard a noise. He peeked inside.

It was a beautiful room, filled with palatial-like furniture and piles of wedding gifts. Wasn't that nice?

But it wasn't any of those things that had his attention now. It was the woman in the lavender gown bending over one of the packages. Her blond hair was shorter and lighter than before. His heart stood still. He couldn't be any luckier. It was *her.*

He slipped inside the room, moving silently. He crept up behind her, slipped his arm around her neck in a *hadaka-jime.* The naked stranglehold. "Cora Beth," he whispered in her ear.

She tensed, struggled, tried to kick out at him.

In response, he held the gun where she could see it, then pressed it to her temple. She went dead still.

"Don't be afraid, Cora Beth. I'm here for you."

He loosened his grip just a tad. He longed to hear her speak to him again. But what she croaked out was not what he expected.

"I'm not Cora Beth."

CHAPTER FORTY

Why on earth women like Coco liked to dress up in long skirts and heels, Miranda would never understand. Wrestling with the fabric of her skirt and her evil shoes, she fought back the hot tears stinging her eyes and made her way down the grand staircase.

Gazing over the mahogany banister, she scanned the foyer, with its chandelier, its high walls lined with exquisite paintings, its gold inlayed furniture and urns.

Empty.

"Gen?" she called out. Where in the world would that shrew-devil have gone to get her Something New?

She reached the bottom stair, stepped onto the marble tiles, her heels clicking. Oh, God. Gen could be anywhere in this maze of rooms. It might be an hour before she found her.

She started toward the left, then heard scuffling and turned back. The sound was coming from the sitting room just off the staircase, where the wedding gifts that came in during the last few days had been stashed.

They'd all have to be returned, she thought vacantly as she headed for the room. "Gen? I need to talk to you. You'll be happy to know—" she stepped inside the door and stopped dead in her tracks.

She could barely process the scene before her.

The windowless interior room was done in a Revival style with paintings of castles and cottages on the walls, a settee and chairs in teal brocade, wallpaper that matched the deep red Persian carpet on the floor, and heavy, ornate furniture. The credenza, the end tables, and most of the floor space along the walls were stacked with packages wrapped in silver or gold or pastel prints of flowers or swirls, each one tied up with pretty ribbons and tulle.

And in the corner, one of the servers had Gen by the neck and had a gun pointed to her head.

Miranda fell back on her training, forced her nerves not to go haywire. "Take anything you want," she said in a strong, steady voice. "Just let her go."

The man stared at her like she was a piece of wedding cake he'd like to devour. Then his lips twitched in disgust. "Stupid, fucking bitch. I don't want your things. I want my wife. Where is Cora Beth?"

Wife? Cora Beth? Only one person called Coco "Cora Beth" now.

Her heart stopped cold.

He didn't look at all like the smiling, wavy-haired charmer in Coco's picture of him. His hair was black and straight. He had a mustache of the same shade. His skin was the color of chocolate milk. He was dressed like one of the servers Mr. P had hired. And his face was hard and lined with evil.

"Hinsley?" she gasped.

"That's right," he sneered, hatred pouring out of him. "The man you and your illustrious fiancé put away three months ago."

Put away? The few days in jail had hurt his pride, but what Parker had done to him had hurt worse. He had a grudge, she thought, panic prickling her insides.

Keep him talking. She caught Gen's eye and tried to steady her with a look of assurance, but the woman's flesh had turned as pale as her hair. Miranda saw the shimmer of her gown as she shivered with fear.

The man's lips twisted with madness. No, he didn't look like Dexter Hinsley. He looked like a crazed killer. Apparently bent on revenge.

"And there you are, all dressed up in your wedding gown. Just as I imagined you."

Imagined? He must've been planning this for a while. Her mind raced. Where had he gotten a uniform? Stolen it off a worker? Or gotten hired? And the gun? From this distance, it looked like a Luger, medium caliber. He'd probably come through the kitchen. Her heart spasmed. Was Fanuzzi still in there?

"Give me my wife," he demanded.

Coco was still upstairs with Wendy. Please God, let them stay up there. Her Beretta was in her purse in the master bedroom. Crap. Got to keep him talking.

"It's been a long time. Hasn't it, Dexter?"

"Long enough for me think hard about what you did to me. What you took from me. I want my wife back."

Might as well use the opportunity to get the truth out of him. "You've been busy. You've turned into quite the traveler. You followed her to Chicago, didn't you, Dexter?"

He blinked. His lips parted in shock. He'd been unaware of how much she'd guessed. "Chicago? I don't know what you're talking about."

"Sure you do. Let's start with Coco's roommate. Why did you kill her?"

Suddenly he seemed confused and even angrier. "That wasn't my fault. The stupid woman wouldn't tell me where Cora Beth was."

She'd been right. He did kill Zelda Fleming. "So you stabbed her with a screwdriver and hid her body in the wall. Pretty fast thinking." She risked another step toward him.

His dark eyes flashed. "Stay back." He pressed the gun closer to Gen's head, and she winced. But now he couldn't resist talking about himself. A smile of pride drew his lips up as he nodded. "That's right. She deserved it. She'd be alive if she'd done as she was told."

Miranda took on the air of a news reporter. "What about the girl in Jeffries' house? What was that all about?"

"I needed her to frame Jeffries. She was just a worthless whore."

She nodded and took another step. Closer now, she could see his eyes were bloodshot, his pupils dilated. From drugs or booze or just plain insanity. "Hmm. It worked for a while. But Jeffries is free now. The cops up there are looking for you, Dexter."

The pride turned back into rage. "You lying bitch. Stay where you are, I said." He waved the gun.

Gen gave a little squeal.

She was starting to rattle him. If she could just create a distraction. She gambled another step. "What about that teacher in Mableton? Elizabeth Lane?"

He scoffed. "She was nothing but a plaything."

She clucked her tongue. "You can't get away with this, Dexter."

"Don't tell me what I can't do. Stay where you are, or I'll blow this bitch's brains out."

Miranda froze. She eyed a long, sharp letter opener on the antique desk. If she could just get to it. She had to think of a way to distract him.

Just then, a soft, sweet voice came from behind her. It was broken and tearful. "Dexter? You *murdered* my roommate and those other women?"

Oh, God no. How did Coco get in here?

Hinsley turned toward the door. "Cora Beth," he whispered, as if speaking to a saint.

Now. She grabbed one of the wedding gifts—thank God it was something heavy—and hurled it at him with all she had, aiming for the hand with the gun.

The silvery package hit square on the target. His arm flew back. The pistol fell to the flowery red carpet with a thud.

"Run!" Miranda screamed at Gen.

She did, dashing for the door and pulling Coco out with her.

Bewildered, caught off guard, Hinsley snatched at the air. But he was too late. His confusion didn't last long. The next second, he recovered and stooped down to scoop up the gun.

As fast as she could, Miranda kicked off her heels and leapt toward him, thrusting out her foot in a forward kick that would have landed a nice uppercut.

But Hinsley dodged it.

Her foot connected with nothing but air and she landed right in front of him on her stocking feet.

Leaving the gun where it laid, fury in his eyes, he rose, formed what looked like a karate stance, and lunged at her, hands outstretched in two fists.

She tried to block but wasn't fast enough.

"Hai." He hit her hard in the chest, knocking her backward.

Kiai. She fell, her forearm scraping against the sharp corner of the credenza. Yow, that hurt.

As she hit the floor with her butt and saw the blood from her arm ooze onto her satin glove, she realized she was facing a trained martial artist.

He glared at her with disdain, his features contorting in surprise, as if he was just as stunned to learn he was battling a woman with some skill, a woman who dared to fight back.

What the heck was she doing with satin gloves on? She yanked them off and tossed them in the corner. Just as he came toward her, reaching for her hair to pull her up by it.

Before his fingers touched her, she ducked and rolled, her veil and dress wrapping around her, constricting her. Not good. She'd banged against another table, knocking several wedding gifts down and sending an expensive Victorian figurine crashing to the floor.

The noise distracted Hinsley long enough for her to get her feet under her and untangle herself.

Wasting no time, she yanked off her veil, wrapped it around her hand. She took two leaps, faked a left which he blocked, and struck him with a right hook on the side of his jaw.

She heard the smack. The material was too thin to be much protection. God, her hand stung. But it did the trick. Hinsley went flying over the antique sofa.

She looked around. Where was the gun?

There. Just behind the carved leg of the wingback chair. She crouched and lunged for it, hand outstretched. Hinsley recovered too fast. He crawled up beside her. She saw she'd bloodied his lip as he grabbed her hand and shoved it away. She clawed at him.

He cried out, her nails digging into the flesh of his arm. "You're going down, Steele. Today will be your last."

"Like hell." She kicked at his knees. He pivoted and she missed. She reached for the gun again.

He rolled back and his hand came down on top of hers.

She batted it off with her free hand. But she couldn't get to the gun. Instead, she fisted her other hand, jabbed hard at the weapon's handle, and pushed the Luger off the carpet and into the corner.

"Hah," he cried in fury. Enraged, he stood.

"Hijah." He was so quick, before she could block him, he jerked her up by her arm as if she weighed nothing and shoved her hard toward the opposite wall.

Shock flooding her, she flew backward toward the fancy furniture. Her thigh scraped the corner of the marble end table. She felt her flesh rip, along with the fabric of her gown. She felt the blood spill out of the gash as she tumbled back, knocking over an elegant Tiffany floor lamp. She felt the breath gush out of her and the rear of her head slam against the wall.

For a moment, all she could see was blackness.

CHAPTER FORTY-ONE

Parker gazed out through the door of the antechamber at the front of Saint Simon's and scanned the restless, fidgeting crowd. He'd already sent his groomsmen to the vestibule to keep an eye out for the limos, to calm his father, and to hide his own chagrin.

He looked at his watch for the hundredth time. Twenty minutes late.

His heart sank. Miranda was never late. Not even for the special occasions she despised.

She wasn't coming.

Slowly, he exhaled. Might as well admit it. If only he hadn't pushed her so hard. If only he hadn't been so eager to jump at the opportunity she'd given him.

He should have told her they should wait. She was still too raw, too wounded. That tender core of hers, over which she'd built that tough outer shell, was too bruised for her to have any faith in a future together. In a happy, fulfilling relationship that might last more than a few years.

And because he'd been too eager, he might lose her for good now. At the moment, he thought that just might kill him.

He turned to his best man, who'd stayed with him in the antechamber and was looking well turned-out in the dark cutaway jacket, vest and ascot he'd chosen for his groomsmen. "I think it's over, Antonio."

Shock colored his son's otherwise placid face. "What do you mean, Papa?"

"I believe I've been stood up."

"No. Ms. Steele would never do that to you."

He shook his head, about to answer when he felt the cell in his pocket buzz. He took it out and looked at the display. It was Gen. His throat turned to dust. She was calling to tell him the news. Bracing himself, he pressed the button.

"Daddy, are you there?" Her voice was quiet, hoarse.

"Yes, Gen. What is it?"

"Th—there's somebody named Hinsley here."

His whole body went cold. "What did you say?"

"He's broken in. I don't know how. He's got a gun. Miranda's trying to fight him off."

"Where are you?"

"I'm okay. Coco and I are hiding in a closet. We're upstairs with Wendy. Oh, Daddy. I'm so scared. Get here as fast as you can. Bring Erskine. Bring the police."

"Don't come out of the closet. I'll be there as fast as I can." He hung up. "It's Hinsley," he said to Antonio. "He's at the mansion. He's got Miranda. He's got a gun."

"*Mi Dios.*"

With Antonio right behind him, Parker dashed out of the chamber and down the lily-lined aisle.

The crowd gave a collective gasp.

"Erskine," he shouted.

The Lieutenant appeared at the end of the pews. "Parker?"

"Get your men and get to the Parker estate ASAP. It's Dexter Hinsley. He's got Miranda. He's got a weapon and all the ladies are with him."

Erskine nodded and disappeared.

His heart seared with pain, Parker burst out the church door and sprinted down the steps to his Lamborghini. He threw open the door and got in, as Antonio slid into the passenger seat.

"Dear Lord," he pleaded as he jammed his keys into the ignition. "Please don't let us be too late."

CHAPTER FORTY-TWO

Miranda opened her eyes.

Hinsley was standing over her, the Luger in his hand.

"You think you're so smart, Steele. So bad and tough," he sneered, waving the gun at her. "But you're not. You're nothing but another brainless bimbo. You can't beat me. You can't keep me away from my Cora Beth."

Oh yeah?

She glanced at the broken shards of the Tiffany lamp on the floor. Her brain cleared as she squinted at the lamppost that had landed across her lap, its heavy base resting beside her. Perfect.

As fast as she could move, she grabbed the pole, forced herself up on her feet, and swung it like a Kali stick. She hit his forearm and the gun flew out of his hand, this time landing behind the settee.

Incensed, he screamed at her. "Fuck you, you goddamn bitch." He grabbed the lamppost, trying to wrest it away from her.

Fear pounding in her chest, she fought to keep her grip on the pole, but it was slipping. In desperation, she twisted it, turned it, and with one huge effort got his hands loose as she tossed the lamp toward the door. It clanged to the floor and hit a table, knocking down more gifts.

Time to up her game. She lifted her fists over her face, ready for him now. "A little redundant there," she snickered. "And really. 'Bimbo?' 'Bitch?' Can't you come up with anything more creative? Why not 'Gila Monster'? Or 'Bridezilla?'"

Insane rage burned in his eyes. Just the way she wanted it. He'd be off now, his judgment impaired.

"Hai." Like a ferocious bull, he charged her, grabbed the open shoulder of her gown and pushed against her chest with his free hand. He was trying to turn her, get her into a chokehold.

Terror stabbing her, she crossed her wrists in front of her neck and blocked. She swayed, twisted, spun and let out a loud *kiai* as she socked him hard on the jaw with a spinning elbow strike.

Perfect distance. She pulled back and hit him again.

That blow would have felled a lesser opponent. He only stumbled back, wiping his mouth and spitting. But she'd drawn blood again.

They stood, glaring at each other, breathing hard, like two wild panthers ready to pounce.

Her mind raced. Gen would have called the cops by now. She'd be hiding somewhere. If Miranda could just keep Hinsley going until they got here, the others would be safe. But she was almost spent.

Her leg ached from the gash in her thigh. Blood stained her torn gown. Her head throbbed from the bump against the wall. Her arm still bled, and her hair was all over the place. She was a Bridezilla. The way she must look, she could get a part in a horror movie.

Steady, she told herself. Focus. Just a little while longer and Hinsley will be done for.

He raised his fists and danced forward, lashing out with his feet when he got near. She pivoted away. His punches came fast and hard. She ducked, blocked with her arm.

She had to take the lead or he'd just wear her out. She came at him, leapt and positioned her arms for a downward elbow slash against the top of his head. It would have been beautiful.

Except he grabbed her wrist, shoved hard against her clavicle, and slipped his bicep under her armpit. Losing her balance, she fell back against him. As they hit the floor, his arm went around her neck in the dreaded *hadaka-jime*, the naked stranglehold.

God, no. She jammed her hand under his grip just in time. It wasn't enough to break free, but it gave her some leverage.

He began to squeeze. Her heart hammered in her chest.

He hissed in her ear, his foul breath fanning her cheek. "Oh, Steele. Don't you know no woman could ever beat a man? No woman could ever beat me."

She almost had.

Above her now, he held her nearly prone on the floor, the back of her head against his chest. The stench of his body would have made her gag if she'd been capable of it.

"I so wanted to shoot you so your fiancé would find your body bloody and mutilated. I suppose I'll have to do that after you're dead."

He squeezed his arms tighter. He was so much stronger than she thought he was. Her hand slipped. She couldn't hold him back. She felt her windpipe closing. She struggled hard, but it wasn't enough. Terror sliced through her.

There'd be no tapping out this time. No mercy.

Her heart pounded in her chest in sheer panic. Find an escape. There had to be one. Had to be. She couldn't find it. The lights were getting dim.

Fight. Think.

But the room started to spin, and all she could think of was that she'd never see Parker again.

That'd she'd never feel his touch against her skin again, never again bask in his magnificent kisses. She'd go to her death without him ever knowing how much she loved him. She'd left him standing at the altar after she'd sworn she wouldn't. She could have had a wonderful life with him, but she'd thrown it all away.

She wouldn't do that now. He was the best thing that ever happened to her. And by God, if she lived, if Hinsley didn't kill her, she was going to have a life with him. She'd make it work somehow. She'd fight for it as hard as she was fighting for her life right now.

Something sounded from far away. Sirens. Cops? Could she make it? Could she hold on until they got here? Just a little longer. Or was she hallucinating? Imagining that sound? No. The cops would be here soon. Coco had heard Hinsley's confession and so had Gen. That would put the bastard away.

She might not be able to save herself, but she'd saved her friends.

She spread her fingers under Hinsley's grip, straining with all she had. Somehow, she managed to turn her head and loosen the unbearable pressure enough to take a breath.

And then she saw it. The glint of the Luger right there on the floor under the settee. Could she reach it with her free hand? Before Hinsley stopped her?

She rocked a little, hoping he'd think she was still attempting to free herself.

"Don't struggle. It will be over soon." His voice was almost gentle now.

She had one chance. Only one. If she was quick enough, it just might work. With all her strength, she rolled, extended her arm. Her hand touched the weapon's handle. She had it.

Immediately, Hinsley saw what she was doing. "No, you don't." His grip around her neck grew tighter as he leaned over.

His fingers slid over her hand, his sweaty palm over her knuckles. She strained, trying to keep the gun away from him, but he was too strong. She gasped. She could hardly breathe.

She felt him slip his forefinger over her hand and through the trigger. Slowly, she watched the barrel turn toward her face. He steadied it, realizing the awkwardness of his position, deciding what to do.

The pressure around her neck made the room whirl again.

Then he made his move. He released her neck, grabbed her by the hair.

She tried to dig her head into his stomach, but he was too quick, and she was too weak from lack of oxygen.

He jerked her forward. She felt the barrel against the back of her skull. He'd won. Hinsley had won. As soon as he pulled the trigger, she was dead.

There was a crash behind her, a thousand times louder than the most violent thunderclap she'd ever heard.

She was dead. He'd killed her.

But her body jerked and she heard him fall back. She looked down and saw the Luger in his limp hand slide to the floor. She dared to turn around.

Hinsley lay on the carpet behind her, a gaping bullet hole in the side of his head. From the angle, it must have gone through, hit the settee and wedged into the wall somewhere.

She raised her chin and saw Parker in the doorway of the sitting room, his Glock in his hand.

"I didn't know you were such an accurate shot," she wheezed out.

Then dropped to the floor in a dead faint.

CHAPTER FORTY-THREE

"I could have stopped him, if I had just gotten to that Luger."

"Of course, you could have, my darling." Parker kissed her nose. "Try not to think about it."

Miranda sat on the back of the ambulance that was parked along the curb in front of the mansion, one EMT binding up her arm, another working on her thigh. Her wedding gown was shredded and bloody. Her feet were bare. Who knew where her veil was. She didn't care.

She wagged a finger at Parker. "I was right about Hinsley.

"Spot on. I'll have to start paying closer attention to your instincts." She could tell by his tone that he meant it.

"She has a concussion, of course." Dr. Jackson Taggart, who was dressed in a tux as one of Parker's groomsmen, examined the back of her head. "To say nothing of the contusions all over her body."

Or the nice set around her neck. "It was a hard fight." Miranda tried to turn and raise a brow at the doctor, but it hurt too much.

"She'll need rest."

"I'll see that she gets it, Jackson." Parker assured him.

Miranda opened her mouth to protest, then she spotted Erskine on the lawn, also clad in a groomsman tux.

He gestured to Parker. "A word with you?"

"Certainly, Hosea." The EMT moved back and Parker kissed her on the forehead. "I'll be right back." He wasn't going to leave her for long.

Dr. Taggart patted her shoulder gently. "I'll get you a prescription."

"I don't want—"

But he disappeared around the side of the vehicle.

Gen had been leaning against the hood of Parker's car, watching the scene. She took this moment to come over to her. Still in her lavender gown, she stood quietly a moment, as if she were gathering her thoughts. Miranda had never seen an expression quite like the one on her face right now. She couldn't place it until Gen started to speak.

"Miranda, I—I want to apologize for the things I said to you before—" she waved a hand in the air, "all that happened with that madman."

"Wait." Miranda held up a hand and stared at her. That gunshot must have damaged her hearing. "Don't tell me you didn't mean what you said." That she didn't want Parker to marry her? That she thought the marriage wouldn't last? She couldn't buy that one.

Gen shook her head. "No, I won't say that. I did mean it at the time. But I don't anymore." She crossed her arms in front of her, as if to bolster her nerve. "My father was right. I never gave you a chance." Her voice started to break. "I never knew what you were like. I never knew you had such strength, such courage. You—you saved my life, Miranda Steele." She put her arms around her in an awkward hug. "Thank you." She broke into tears.

At a loss for words, Miranda stroked her shoulder. "You're welcome, Gen." She didn't know if this mood would last, but she'd take it for now. Then she took her by the arms. "I couldn't let anything happen to you. You're family."

They stared at each other, neither of them knowing what else to say.

Miranda was relieved when Wendy came streaming across the yard, Fanuzzi right behind her. When she reached the ambulance Gen stepped back, and the girl threw her arms around her. "Oh, Miranda. You're okay. You're really okay."

"And you are, too. Man, am ever I glad to see you." Tears filled her eyes as she stroked the girl's thick, dark hair.

Wendy lifted her head, her eyes vibrant. "Gen ran upstairs after you threw the wedding gift at that horrible man. She told Coco and me to hide in the closet. Then she called Mr. Parker."

"Pretty smart of her."

One of Erskine's men appeared at the curb. He lifted a finger. "Miss Parker?"

Gen nodded and turned to go off with him.

Fanuzzi was holding a cold pack to her head, but she put a hand on Wendy's shoulder in a protective gesture. "Good thing this kid had that stain on her dress. Coco couldn't get it out, and she refused to leave the room."

"That's why Coco came downstairs?"

Fanuzzi nodded. "She was looking for you and Gen."

Miranda smirked. "She found us, all right. How is Coco?"

"Pretty shaken up. She's with Estavez in the back of Parker's car. He's trying to calm her down."

Miranda glanced at the car but couldn't see anything through the dark windshield. "She's upset about Hinsley." She wondered if Coco would ever forgive Parker.

"Only for hurting you. She told me you were right all along, and she should have listened to you about him."

Miranda smiled sadly at that news, feeling both gratified and pained. Coco had heard Hinsley's confession of the murders. That had to be hard to take.

"And there I was out like a light on the kitchen floor." Fanuzzi looked like she could chew nails. "I let that—" she glanced down at Wendy, "—that you-know-what get the best of me."

"I could have used your help. We could have taken him together."

Wendy hugged her again. "Miranda can take care of herself."

Not this time, she thought, as she watched Parker stroll back to the ambulance. Her heartbeat kicked up at the sight of him. He looked so good in that tux. Tall, strong, outrageously handsome. And all hers.

He gave Wendy's hair a tussle. "It's good to see you, Miss Van Aarle." He took Fanuzzi's hand and shook it. "And you, Joan. I'm happy you're both in one piece. As is your husband." Becker was inside, helping the police take stock of the scene.

"Thanks to you," Fanuzzi grinned.

"Good to have a man around the house with a weapon in his hand," Miranda laughed. She never thought she'd ever utter words like that.

Nodding at Parker, Fanuzzi winked at her. "Especially one who can shoot like this guy. C'mon, Wendy. Let's let these two have some space."

"Don't go too far. I need to talk to you all in a bit," Miranda called out to them, an idea forming in her brain.

An EMT handed her a cup of water and a pill. "This is from Dr. Taggart, Ms. Steele. It will help ease the pain."

She shook her head.

Parker gave her his stern, no-backtalk look. "You should take it, Miranda. It will be a few hours to finish the statements."

She watched the van from the county pull up for Hinsley's body.

"When the police are finished, we can go inside and you can get some rest."

She looked at Parker and cocked her head. "Inside?"

His face went deadpan. "How thoughtless of me. We'll go to my penthouse tonight. We can decide what to do about the house later."

Grimacing, she lifted the arm that wasn't wounded and put a hand on her hip. "What about my wedding?"

Parker studied the woman he adored, sitting there in her torn and bloodied dress. It took all his strength not to hit his knees, sobbing and thanking God that she was alive. That he'd gotten here in time. He would cherish her forever. He would never push her too hard or make her uncomfortable again.

He took a strand of her tangled hair in his hand and kissed it. "I told you I'd live with you without vows, Miranda, and I meant it."

Miranda watched the emotion on Parker's face, her heart flooding with feeling. "You don't get it, do you?"

His brows drew together. "Get it?"

"You of all people ought to know how coming close to death can...well, change your mind about things."

"What are you talking about?"

"When Hinsley had me in that chokehold, I had sort of ...I don't know. An epiphany."

He stared at her, as if he didn't dare believe what she was saying. "Go on."

"And I realized how important you are to me. And I knew."

"Knew?"

"I knew that I would fight to stay together. That I wanted to make it last between us. That I really do love you. That I really do want to marry you, Wade Parker. I want to be Mrs. Parker. Your wife."

He stood a long moment without saying anything.

At last, she whispered. "I want my wedding...Wade. Today."

His eyes glistening, he laughed with joy. It was the first time she'd called him by his first name. "Then, my dear Miranda, you shall have it."

After Erskine and his men took their statements, Gen got the bouquets and they all trekked down to Saint Simon's.

The guests were gone and the reception hall had been canceled, but Parker got hold of Reverend Quigley and found him free. He might have been prepared to part with half his fortune to get the minister back to the church.

The setting sun cast a dreamy glow through the stained glass windows as Parker, his groomsmen and her bridesmaids arranged themselves in front of the altar.

Everyone hummed "Here Comes the Bride" while Miranda hobbled down the aisle on Mr. P's arm. Her dress was torn, her body sore, but her heart was soaring.

Eagerly, she repeated the vows as Reverend Quigley uttered them. "I, Miranda Lynne Steele, take you Wade Russell Parker the Third, to be my husband..." Her jaw ached from smiling as she gazed in sheer awe at Parker. Her Southern gentleman, her knight in shining armor.

"...from this day forward, for better or for worse. To love and to cherish..."

Softly, Coco began to sing "*Nuestro amor*" and everyone joined in.

Miranda was so happy, she thought her heart might explode like a Fourth of July firecracker. She squeezed Parker's hands tightly and spoke the words loud and clear, not caring if they echoed to the rafters.

"From this day forward until death do us part." She had a feeling that wouldn't happen for a long, long time.

THE END

ABOUT THE AUTHOR

Writing fiction for over fifteen years, Linsey Lanier has authored more than two dozen novels and short stories, including the popular Miranda's Rights Mystery series. She writes romantic suspense, mysteries, and thrillers with a dash of sass.

She is a member of Romance Writers of America, the Kiss of Death chapter, Private Eye Writers of America, and International Thriller Writers. Her books have been nominated in several RWA-sponsored contests.

In her spare time, Linsey enjoys watching crime shows with her husband of over two decades and trying to figure out "who-dun-it." But her favorite activity is writing and creating entertaining new stories for her readers.

She's always working on a new book, currently books in the new Miranda and Parker Mystery series (a continuation of the Miranda's Rights Mystery series).

For alerts on her latest releases join Linsey's mailing list at linseylanier.com.

For more of Linsey's books, visit her website at **www.linseylanier.com**

Edited by
Donna Rich

Editing for You

Gilly Wright
www.gillywright.com

Made in the USA
Columbia, SC
20 May 2022

60688627R00117